DR GLASS

BOOK I

GLASS MINDS SERIES

Louise Worthington

Copyright

First published in 2021 by Louise Worthington.

A CIP catalogue record of this book is available from the British Library.

Also by *Louise Worthington*

Rachel's Garden

The Entrepreneur

Willow Weeps

Distorted Days

Rosie Shadow

Flash Fiction and Short Stories

Stained Glass Lives

CONTENT GUIDANCE

THIS NOVEL CONTAINS ACTS OF SELF-HARM AND SUICIDE.

‘To love at all is to be vulnerable.’

C. S. Lewis

Contents

Prologue 1

Chapter 1 4

Chapter 2 15

Chapter 3 27

Chapter 4 41

Chapter 5 59

Chapter 6 69

Chapter 7 75

Chapter 8 88

Chapter 9 105

Chapter 10 120

Chapter 11 135

Chapter 12 156

Chapter 13 168

Chapter 14 189

Chapter 15 211

Chapter 16 225

Chapter 17 234

Chapter 18 246

Chapter 19 254

Chapter 20 264
Chapter 21 267
Chapter 22 283
Chapter 23 295
Chapter 24 312
Chapter 25 320
Chapter 26 334
Chapter 27 347
Chapter 28 356
Chapter 29 365
Chapter 30 380
Chapter 31 394
Epilogue 413

Prologue

A meal prepared with love, seasoned and softened, slides out of the oven. Time has made it tender, tastier. It is hastily moved onto a ceramic dish to keep it hot. The stove walls drip with condensation, steam hovers and the kitchen window sweats. The table is laid with a tablecloth as white as a lullaby, sharp knives and a spoon shaped like a cupped hand. This meal isn't finger food: forks rather than an ink pen to write the words of love. Love is written in letters in the steam on the window, in the vapours in the air. It is in the calligraphy of the meat and vegetables, then the fruit dessert of blackberries, which gleam like glass.

The butter is at a perfect room temperature. It submits to the knife, lingering on cutlery like yellow wax from a burnt candle. A thimbleful of salt and pepper to season – a merest suggestion, a hint, like a batting of an eyelash. There is love in the home-made pastry; flakes linger on the rolling pin. There is love in the harmony of flavours in the sauce of wild mushrooms to go with the beef en croûte, and on the glossy wetness of the green leaks. Love is even in the water jug, in those floating slices of lemons and in the tinkling of ice cubes, which bump against each other like flirtatious dodgems. It's in the mint peas, the thickness of the sauce and the delicacy of the beef, which falls noiselessly and dissolves like sleeping pills in a wine glass of claret. This food of longing belongs on pink, hungry tongues, between teeth, in the dark of the digestive system.

Not just one mouth, two lips, one tongue with its beaded taste buds, but several, feeding and tasting to the sound of scraping forks and knives, to the slurping and sipping of civilised wolves. Is this a form of savagery masquerading as appetite? An aperitif to satiating a desire – an urge – to eat, then fuck?

Let's be civilised about it. Let's eat first, then dab each corner of the mouth with a white linen napkin.

Then, and only then, talk dirty with your hands and your tongue. Indulge rapacious taste buds then squeeze the life out of a hungry groin, like those lemons. Ask the wolves what gives them pleasure and they'll say feeding. Is feeding better than touch?

Love me. The food speaks quieter now, for the plate is almost empty. Is anyone listening, or are the ripping incisors too loud to hear it? We take all the best recipes to the grave, wearing an expression like a waistband that's too tight.

Chapter 1

The Farmhouse at Cleave, on the outskirts of Shrewsbury, is owned by Drew Rogers. It is a sturdy, sandstone building with a yard, several outbuildings and half an acre of garden. At the point of sale, the land and large sheds were sold to a neighbouring owner. Drew, a savvy property developer, had moved himself, his wife and son, James, into the property, knowing it would make a wonderful family home – and a packet when he sold it, developed to its full potential.

Like most farmhouses untouched by developers, it has retained its character in many of its features, like the dark wooden beams in the kitchen and the chunky chimney, which climbs up from the roof to enjoy a view of the Shropshire and Welsh hills.

It is such a waste for Drew's labourers, Pete and AJ, to work indoors on a fine summer day, but they do it to keep the boss happy, especially as he has given them a steady stream of work on his various rental properties, and now on the farmhouse. Today it's painting and decorating and a spot of clearing.

AJ looks at his workmate, astonished to see a skip half full of what looks like women's clothes and accessories in Drew's yard. Pink towels and chunky plastic jewellery, feminine bed linen and underwear; it's all on show. There's also a full-length mirror, dressing table and stool and a rocking horse, plus other bits and pieces worth a bob or two.

Pete has an uncanny habit of raising one eyebrow in such situations, which AJ reads as mirroring his thoughts about selling the contents. As Drew is rarely at home between nine and five and hasn't, for the last few days, swerved by in his Range Rover Sport to check up on them, AJ doesn't feel the need to be so discreet about nosing in Drew's discarded belongings and making an easy few quid.

'There's some decent stuff in here,' AJ says, as he climbs inside the skip. His workman's boots make a satisfying thud when he lands inside. He hitches up his jeans so he can bend over without them sliding down any further and exposing his crack.

'What do you think it's worth?' Pete asks, as he scratches his two-day stubble.

'Must be a few hundred quid here, at least for the rocking horse and those leather bar stools. We'd be doing Drew a favour by making more room in the skip. I'll ask Hannah to eBay it. Split sixty-forty with you.'

'Sounds fair to me.' AJ passes Pete the objects to load into his van.

'How is Hannah?'

'Good. Set up qualifying as an accountant, which suits me!'

'I bet,' Pete says, chuckling. Labouring isn't a bad job, but the physical nature of the work has a limited life expectancy; not like bean counting, which you can do into your seventies if you have to.

Half an hour later, with the contents of the skip safely stored in the back of his van, AJ carries the step ladders into the farmhouse and up to the second floor. He and Pete are tasked with painting the walls and ceiling of the master bedroom, which Drew has vacated. Refurbishment to the farmhouse is restricted to a certain number of rooms which Drew isn't using for the time being, as he continues to live in parts of the property. The place doesn't exactly feel lived in, now that Drew's wife, Evie, and son aren't living there.

'Has Drew said when he plans to put this place on the market?' Pete asks.

'Not to me. I haven't seen or heard from him much except for a text to say what to get on with.'

Pete washes down the walls of the master bedroom before giving them a fresh lick of paint while AJ looks inside the other bedrooms, of which there are four, to find out where his boss sleeps these days. He shouldn't, but AJ can't help himself. Drew Rogers, a successful property developer with a letting business, is a decent bloke in the main to work for, but it is clear from the farmhouse in which he is living that life is getting on top of him. No wonder, really.

AJ opens the door with an ornate sign on it saying 'James'. It surprises him to feel a fleeting sense of pity for Drew for sleeping in his absent son's bedroom. A multi-millionaire, choosing to kip on a bottom bunk bed in a farmhouse with four other bedrooms. Who'd have guessed that? Sleeping in the same room as all those glass-eyed teddies and pieces of Lego still strewn on the floor would give him the creeps. He closes one of the wardrobe doors, which is ajar, before joining Pete in the master bedroom. They simultaneously turn their heads to the windows at the sound of a sports car grumbling into the yard. Sunlight bounces off the windscreen and catches the red hair of the driver, like a match to paper.

‘Kat,’ AJ says with a sigh, immediately recognising the owner of the red car and the red hair within it. ‘Again.’

Pete tuts when he sees the battered red MX-5 make a wide circle in the courtyard before disappearing from view.

‘She doesn’t give up easily, does she?’ Pete says. ‘Wasn’t she here yesterday?’

AJ nods. ‘And the day before that. Drew’s given her the brush off.’

Apart from that raspy, sexy voice of hers and her tight little ass, AJ can’t understand what Drew ever saw in her when he had Evie, who was gorgeous and adored him. Having worked for Drew for the last few years, he had had the pleasure of sharing the odd brew with Evie when she’d turned up at one of Drew’s rental properties they were doing up. He appreciated it. Some wives with money are stuck-up and don’t show workmen like him the time of day. Not Evie.

He looks out of the window as Kat pulls out of the yard. It must have been convenience that took Drew to her bed, perhaps, as Kat is a tenant of his. Still is, as far as AJ knows. One thing he does know is that you don't mix business with pleasure if you want a good night's sleep and a quiet life.

'Do you think we should say something to Drew about her coming here all the time?' Pete asks. 'She should have taken the hint by now, if he's not talking to her.'

AJ opens a window in the master bedroom now that the car is out of sight. 'You can if you want, but I won't. Drew might think we're meddling in his business.'

Pete makes a start on painting the walls magnolia. 'You're probably right. He'll shoot the messenger, I guess. What's he hoping to get for this place anyway?'

'Drew reckons he's already got a buyer. Six or seven hundred thousand.' Pete whistles at the sum of money.

'It could be worth a lot more if he developed the outbuildings like he was going to.'

'True enough. Plans change. What do you think he'll buy next? He could buy three or four at auction, maybe more if they need serious work. That's what I would do if I were Drew.'

'Yeah, me too. The bloke doesn't know how lucky he is,' AJ says, then hesitates. He was about to share his concern with Pete that they could be out of a job if Drew is selling all his properties, as he suspects he is. It's fragments of information he's pieced together. Perhaps wrongly, because AJ knows himself well enough to accept he isn't a bright bloke. He knew that before his teachers had told him so. He is not good with numbers or facts, unlike his girlfriend, Hannah, but he's usually pretty good with people. 'I do know he wants Evie's darkroom cleared of furniture and her photography equipment and the summer house taken down before the end of the day. We'd better get a move on with the first coat in here.'

'I'll crack on here, mate, if you want to see to that other stuff,' Pete says amicably. 'Then we might be in for an early finish. Day like today, I fancy a pint in the garden.'

Up until yesterday the farmhouse landing and hall had looked like a gallery, with one framed photograph after another, all taken by Evie, who divided her time between raising their son and her passion for photography. The memory of the pictures is in the grubby marks on the wall, which AJ follows downstairs to the darkroom like a map.

Inside, he flicks on the single red bulb and the light is weak, like watercolour. The room has retained her scent, an expensive perfume. The familiar floral aroma is also in the wardrobe in the master bedroom. Judging by the number of unwashed mugs and wine glasses on the desk, she had spent a fair bit of time inside the room until recently. The desk is almost entirely covered with photographs, mostly monochrome shots of landscapes, plus a few portraits. He shivers, and nervously looks over his shoulder. It's as though Evie is in the room with him following his every move with wide-open eyes. All those photographs left disordered on the desk make AJ feel angry. Why hasn't Drew put them away safely?

He shakes his head. It's none of his business what Drew wants to do with his wife's photographs but, if it were him, he'd keep them in an album, a smart leather-bound one. There are a few shots on the desk of their son, James, and her. *She was a good-looking woman*, he muses, while taking a closer look into her eyes. That blonde hair, and the fancy engagement ring on her finger. A rock of a gem. Money, it buys beauty all right. He sniffs the photograph, as if expecting that to smell of money. The instruction from Drew is to bin the lot, but AJ puts them in a black box with a lid on. The bloke might change his mind one day and thank him. When the plyboard comes off the window the space immediately feels less oppressive, and the sun is still shining outside.

'Pete!' he shouts up the stairs, over the sound of Radio One, 'I'm going to make a start on the summer house while it's still dry.' AJ loves being outside, especially in pleasant weather, and away from the shadows and corners of the farmhouse. Being a builder during the summer, getting a tan while you work is a real perk of the job. He rolls his sleeves up, exposing hairy arms, both tattooed in dark-green Maori-style shapes.

'Alright, mate!' Pete replies cheerfully over the tones of Oasis.

The summer house is only a few months old. AJ knows this because he and Pete had erected it for James on his third birthday. Drew had said to chop it down for firewood, but he thinks it's too good for that. Way too good. Another young family could get joy from it, so he dismantles it piece by piece and loads it into his van with all the other stuff.

Drew needn't know. He just wants it out of sight. Hannah is a dab hand at selling stuff on eBay. They need the money more than Drew does. He's loaded, while they're skint.

Chapter 2

Pity the person whose mother abandoned them, whose father disowned them and then died, leaving her an orphan. A contract is made with her face to keep the snake of secrets firmly in her mouth. The expression shows no emotion; it's a smooth road recently laid, perfectly made, without flaw or lump. Whatever jealousy or fury she may have felt at one time, her polite, clay face doesn't betray her.

Except no one does pity Kat Stiles. Just like Mary Lennox from *The Secret Garden* – only Kat is a twisted, nasty little version with a pert pair of tits and a pierced tongue. Not even Kat pities herself. Why would she? A young, confident woman who fears nothing and no one. Someone who knows herself and her sex drive, and the weapon of her sexual allure, better than anyone.

Without a family to take care of Kat, and men like Drew coming in and out of her life, she had made her own family. Stan, her python, is like a little brother to her. Luckily, there are always men around for company or entertainment. Some she plays like a puppet on a string, moving their randy arms and legs this way and that, a nod of their head, a jiggle of their body. Sex is a play in a travelling theatre. Sweet, hungry Kat with red, fiery hair, a living devil, breathing and moving with all the other blackened souls. Drew loved her for these things. For a time, at least. He'd turned out to be just like all the rest.

Today, Kat presents as a quietly menacing figure who is humming as she strolls along Welsh Bridge into Shrewsbury town centre. There is a smell of coffee on her breath after she sips some in a vegan café on her way to the last of the pawnbrokers, D & R. Before coffee, for fun, she had shopped for fruit and veg, organic only, saying 'please' and 'thank you' to the staff before paying the bill, presenting as a charming woman enjoying a simple pleasure, knowing full well she will return home to feed Stan live hamsters, mice and rats, squirming and squeaking in her hand, which she breeds herself.

A smile is etched on her face because she can walk among shoppers without heads turning in horror while holding the darkest of secrets in her handbag. Inside is a valuable engagement ring. Not hers.

D & R is tucked away down a narrow street, next to a charity shop. A bell above the door jingles as she opens it and steps inside. The shop is smaller than it looks on the outside, with an impressive window of stock under glistening white lights. Two soft chairs covered in a garish print add some bling to an otherwise functional space, and framed posters on the walls specify all manner of clauses and codes of conduct, which no one ever reads, but are a good piece of arse-covering by the pawnbroker. The man has made a mint in the most upmarket of the pawnshops in the vicinity by not asking too many questions. Kat feels her presence is acknowledged before he speaks, so she corrects her posture and paints on a warm smile.

'How can I help you, madam?' the pawnbroker asks from behind the leather-topped antique desk, well-practised at not overtly looking customers up and down before seeing their goods, having been in the job for fifteen years and two recessions. He has probably seen all sorts in his time.

As the pawnbroker adjusts his tortoise-shell spectacles, a wider smile creeps across Kat's lips as she delves into her handbag and opens the ring box. It's a slow-moving smile, a slither, revealing teeth so white they could have been cleaned with Ajax. She shows him the precious item in the palm of her hand.

'Feast your eyes on that!'

It's a sapphire and diamond ring, which should be on someone's engagement finger right now, only the owner doesn't need it anymore.

The pawnbroker raises his eyebrows and looks at the ring, then fleetingly at her clay face. His eyes are misty. Is he waiting for Kat to come out with a story which might explain how she is in possession of an exquisite and valuable ring? It's bound to be one of the finest engagement rings seen in his career.

'May I?' he asks, and when she nods he carefully places it on the desk.

He takes a closer look at a tiny inscription on the band, only visible with a magnifying glass. Kat does not attempt to conjure a tale; she just looks at it with her head to one side, like a mother doting on a newborn.

'Well?' she asks.

He hears her impatience and so gives Kat an encouraging smile. It's a wonder the bloke isn't rubbing his hands together right now. 'Lovely,' he mutters.

In a steely tone, she says, 'I want the cash, not a loan.'

'I see.' He places the ring on his scales. 'Well, it's a good weight,' he confirms. That eagerness of his suggests to her he has never seen such a large sapphire before. 'And in good condition, for an antique ring.'

'Excellent condition,' she corrects.

He places the loupe in his left eye to take a closer look and is silent for several minutes, before putting the ring and the loupe back on the counter. Between approving murmurs, Dominic looks directly at her. 'Blue sapphire is said to be a stone of truth, wisdom and…'

'Strength. Yes, I know. I've called in at a couple of other pawnshops. I like to do my research first.'

'Right,' he says, trying to hide his disappointment that she isn't as ignorant as he would like her to be by taking a second look at the ring. 'Well, the clarity of the diamonds is excellent.'

'Flawless. I know. The diamonds are three carats.'

'Do you have identification or certification with you? Only, we have certain protocols.'

'What's it worth to you?' Kat snaps.

'I can't—'

'Look, I'm not stupid, and neither are you. That ring there is worth a lot of money. Make me an offer,' she says impatiently, putting one hand on a skinny hip.

'As you want cash today, I'll give you £5,000 for it.'

Kat laughs, tossing her head back, her mouth wide. 'Pass it over. It's all of my divorce settlement, that is. Let's not waste any more of each other's time,' she says, her voice like flint.

'Settlement, you say? May I at least take a name?'

'Kat Jones.'

'Alright,' he says a little breathlessly, clearly wanting the ring to be his and not questioning the authenticity of her surname. One which couldn't be more common, but it's the best she could do on the spot.

'It's worth around £30,000, possibly more.'

'It's incredible. £10,000.' He sees a flicker of interest in her eyes before they close and she puts her hand out for the ring to be returned. '£12,000, and that's my final and best offer. That's all the cash I have available.'

'I know it's at least worth double that, so I want the money in cash, now, no questions. Then we have a deal.'

'Sign here.'

A version of pleasure changes the expression of her face a little: a softening around the hard edges of her eyes and mouth which makes him half-smile back. Her hands grab the cash the way a cat claws at a warm blanket for a night off the streets, remembering the feel of its mother's teats.

They both stare at the shop window at the same time, hearing a noise on the street outside: two males laughing and chatting. The speech of one of them is slurred and loud, a nonsense trail of language about a 'bloke who had it coming'. It's a vernacular familiar to her, having grown up on the rough side of Shrewsbury. She knows the sounds to avoid, the way a wild animal knows when one of its own kind is injured and dying.

Once it's quiet outside, Kat puts the paperwork in her handbag and pushes the bag up high on her shoulder. 'Good doing business with you,' she says. The bell jingles and she closes the door behind her. To earn that amount of money from washing and valeting cars would take her till retirement age.

It's a sunlit June afternoon as she pauses by the window of a shop selling stationery. Kat looks up at the sky in such a way, anyone would think the hairline cracks in the sky had been mended while she was in the pawnbrokers. The shop, called 'Adore', sells cards and sentimental tat, like fluffy keyrings and teddy bears with 'Happy birthday' or 'I love you' stitched across a belly hanging as low as a hen's stuffed crop. Seeing the emotional drivel, she strides away to the butchers, then the pet shop for a few extra special treats for Stan and then the Co-op for a bottle of cheap fizz to celebrate the windfall.

Kat takes a shortcut across the college's football pitch onto Dawson's Rough and then the route winds into Hartlepool Estate, where her terraced house nestles at the end of the road. It's a far cry from a farmhouse, but it's her home.

After showering with a rose-scented soap, she dresses in clean clothes and applies mascara and eyeshadow. In the full-length mirror on the door of the single wardrobe, she appraises herself and toasts her reflection with the glass of sparkling wine. The blue jeans fit well, and the T-shirt is suitably tight to show off her ample bosom. She runs her hand through strands of long, red hair and lies down on the double bed. Dirty clothes and several pairs of shoes are strewn on the floor. The sheets haven't been changed for months. There's no need to these days, without Drew staying by.

Above the bed there is a framed print of a nude woman with a colossal snake coiled around her peach flesh, its head resting in her palm next to her head. Her long, fiery red hair drapes down her back like a waterfall. Kat likes to gaze up at it, imagine herself in the picture. Beneath it there is another print on a similar theme, of a nude snake charmer. She calls him Drew.

Opposite the bed is a terrarium for Stan, right where she can see him and he can see her. A lot of people take issue with having a pet snake in the bedroom, but Drew didn't. He liked the way he and Kat seemed to communicate by protruding their tongues in synchronised movement. He would have readily had Stan in bed with them if she'd let him, only Kat wouldn't want Stan to get squashed when one of them rolled over, as they liked to do, taking it in turns to be on top. When Stan was just a few years old, he liked to curl up around her naked body at night and move around her, slowly sizing her up. It was a sensual time when they bonded, until Stan started to fast in readiness for a big meal. Kat.

Stan is happy enough and well fed in his enclosure. Only the two of them know that inside his long thin belly is a gold wedding ring. Lucky its owner was washing up at the time Kat made an uninvited visit to the farmhouse. The citrus smell of washing-up liquid had never smelt so good. Kat takes a slurp of fizzy wine and burps. That fat gold band of a wedding ring. It’s her pension, stored in the safest, most loyal customer-focused bank she knows. Stan. A secret, illicit marriage of sorts, between flesh and snakeskin. The best kind. Perfect.

Chapter 3

Dr Emma-Jane Glass's caseload is demanding in a different way than it has been in previous months. She was treating two clients who loathed members of their family: one young man, a twenty-five-year-old journalist, claimed his mother had been cruel to him as a child, while the other client, Melanie, had unresolved anger around her sister's sexually provocative nature. She no longer feels the need to see Dr Glass.

Her job doesn't rewrite the past for people, but it can improve their daily lives. Unfortunately, when she challenged Melanie about her thoughts and feelings at a point Emma-Jane felt she could cope with, Melanie kicked off, stormed out of the office and hasn't returned since. Emma-Jane believes in the principle of respect for the dignity, rights and choices of others, and therefore hasn't chased Melanie to return. That decision is

Melanie's to make. If a client doesn't have trust in her as a psychologist, she isn't of use to them. Trust and honesty are fundamental to progress.

It is a Saturday morning when she has undisturbed time to reflect on these things. Emma-Jane checks her emails on her laptop at the kitchen table. An email from the British Psychological Society reminds her to undertake a training course – an update on online therapy – before the end of August, and a short course on exercise and nature for stress and anxiety management. Some of her colleagues offer an online service to clients, which is popular, but so far she has resisted, while others meet with clients in the great outdoors, believing in the remedial benefits of nature. There is also an email from her respected clinical supervisor and old friend, Dr Celia Domes, asking if they can rearrange their appointment on Tuesday as she has an abscess requiring a dentist's urgent attention. Emma-Jane replies to Celia with a sympathetic message and alternative times.

The motivations behind maternal filicide – the act of a mother killing her child or children – had interested Emma-Jane during her year of clinical training at the local NHS hospital. The emotive topic was now back in the news, following the recent tragedy of Angela Lamb taking her young son's life. Emma-Jane had delved into Angela's and her family's past, only to find Angela hadn't wanted her second child, Teddy, who displayed hyperaggressive behaviour towards her and his sister. The oversimplification of the tragedy in the news had inspired her to write and publish an article in the journal *The Clinical Psychology and Counselling Review*, which has a wide readership of professionals and students in the UK. The title was 'Altruistic Violence in Maternal Filicide', which was controversial in itself before even getting to the meat of the article. Her supervisor, Celia, had warned her about publishing the article by pointing out the sympathetic position towards the mother, fearing it might have invited strong criticism and potentially damaged Emma-Jane's professional reputation.

Emma-Jane hadn't listened because she felt the Angela Lambs of this world needed a voice. The article was criticised for a lack of theory and the underplay of Angela's poor mental health. In the article, she presented the tragedy in the context of a woman coping with depression (but not insanity) and raising an unwanted child who was causing considerable distress to herself and her beloved daughter. She concluded Angela's motive was altruistic and stemmed from having an unwanted child, as opposed to the 'inhumane and barbaric mother-monster' portrayed so over-simplistically in the media, which Emma-Jane took offence to. The outrage she felt was in part because of her work: she understands no suicide or murder is caused by a single motive, but a combination of complex and interwoven factors.

Instead of lying low for a time, she had opted to defend her position on Shropshire Radio, confidently asserting that professionals underestimated the prevalence of thoughts mothers have of harming their children. *It needed to be said*, she'd thought. That, and how tragic the deaths were.

The interview had been broadcast four weeks ago and, so far, she has received no feedback or reaction from colleagues in the profession which, she concedes to herself, speaks volumes. *Let them take a step back from associating with me*, she thinks. *If that's what they want to do. It can't seriously harm my career.*

Can it?

In her bright, modern kitchen, she makes herself a coffee in what she calls 'Lucy's mug'. Lucy is her best friend and colleague. It is one of Lucy's favourites, with a chunky handle and a picture of Hadrian's Wall on the side. The Roman wall is dear to Lucy as she grew up nearby, in Carlisle, and her elderly parents remain there. After two slurps she fancies something with her coffee, so she takes a packet of chocolate Hobnobs from the cupboard and barely notices she's eaten most of them by the time her hot drink is finished. *Unconscious eating.*

With half a biscuit left, she places it on the table and looks at it. *I'm not hungry. Why am I stuffing my face?*

Four months ago, she had readily offered Lucy an office at her new premises in town, rent-free for the first three months, while Lucy got on her feet as a self-employed nutritionist. Having a friend and a professional in the same building is a great boost, worth the financial loss for a short period of time. They share a kitchen, an entrance and, more importantly, all the ups and downs of working for oneself.

The marketing messages about the practice promote holistic health, with Emma-Jane taking care of the mental, emotional and social side of clients' needs as a qualified clinical psychologist and Lucy covering their physical well-being as a nutritionist. So far it's been a mutually beneficial partnership, and one Emma-Jane is enjoying immensely.

It has been hard for Lucy to adapt to self-employment and a move to Shrewsbury in one go. Lucy is a true friend, who knows she mustn't nag Emma-Jane about her weight or binge-eating habits. That's one of several topics of conversation which are off-limits, as well as her undivided devotion to work at the expense of a love life. Emma-Jane's steadfast choice to remain single and devoted to her work is unwavering. Lucy has other ideas, and seems increasingly desperate for a man in her life. She wonders if Lucy has a date tonight.

The post lands on the hall mat after the letter box closes with a firm click. On Saturdays it usually arrives around ten o'clock but it's early today, so she makes herself another coffee to enjoy while reading it. The first item is a flier from a local shop, which holds no interest, but there is also an envelope which has a more personal quality, with a stamp and small address label in an informal font.

Emma-Jane opens the white envelope and stares at the letter in her hand, which seemingly gets heavier with every second.

She hasn't received hate mail before. To hold the letter in her hands makes it feel like the hateful person is in her house, intruding on this moment in the kitchen, on the weekend, a person uninvited and unwelcome. Spiteful. She looks over her shoulder. Her next impulse is to scrunch the letter up and put it in the bin, but she has enough self-possession to put the letter down and catch her breath before doing anything too hasty. Her heart is racing. Who would do such a thing?

Dr Glass.

Or bitch. Dr Bitch…

The writer has gone to the trouble of finding out her personal address, presumably so the letter has more of a knife-edge when opened in the comfort and privacy of her home, rather than the office. Judging by the quality of the paper, no expense has been spared. *How nice of them.*

She reads the letter right through, and again for a second time, forensically, as she was trained to do. As a psychologist, having been in training for six years before getting her doctorate and then undertaking clinical practice, she is a scientist, and it's important in these moments to think like one.

The writer is reasonably well educated, judging by the technical accuracy of the content, and careful enough to type both the letter and address label. There's no postmark on the envelope. Was it hand-delivered? If so, why the stamp? Knowing it's probably pointless, she runs to the kitchen window looking out onto the drive to see if anyone is there. Now she thinks about it, it's strange that she didn't hear the crunch of gravel underfoot when the post was delivered. Or did she?

Is the front door locked? She runs to check, then settles down at the kitchen table.

Think like a scientist.

The nasty letter isn't personal after all. The writer doesn't use her Christian name, though they know her personal address. It's most likely from an unhappy client, which is a professional matter. Everyone is entitled to their own opinion and reaction. Not everyone can engage in open discussion. If anything, she concludes, it's weak, a kind of bullying.

Or is the hate letter related to her published article about Angela Lamb and maternal filicide? Perhaps Celia is right about there being some kind of backlash. What motivates a person to take time out of their day to write a hate letter? To travel here, with one express purpose: to frighten her. How strange to think they are out there, somewhere, now, perhaps walking, or driving, sitting on a bus, mixing with people like they are just getting on with their business.

Pleased with the way she has coped so far with the stress of receiving the letter, she reads it through a third time.

Dr Glass.

Or bitch. Dr Bitch…

Have you started looking over your shoulder yet? See that bloke at the bus stop, that kid in a hoody sitting on a swing, that woman pushing a pram down the street outside your office. Think of me. Who am I? Which one?

Your business is my business now.

How many more are going to die before you stop meddling? One, two, ten, Dr Death?

I hope you're listening. Can you hear glass smashing? Those sharp little pieces will be your only legacy. No family. Just shards of glass.

For all her reasoning using the rational power of an erudite brain, her hands shake. She swiftly gets up from the kitchen table, checks the back door is locked and, as she walks back towards the kitchen table, she has an impulse to look over her shoulder again.

'Damn you!'

Flopping back onto the chair, she takes the letter, and it quivers in her hand.

'Whoever you are, you are not well. Not mentally well *at all*. You're angry. You're hurting, and you think that by targeting me, and perhaps other people, it will alleviate your pain. But it won't. It will only make it worse in the long run. You don't know that, though. You're impulsive. Irrational. I'm not. I'm not impulsive or irrational.'

Should I call Celia, or report it to the police? If she keeps the letter, then the option to report it to the police at a later date remains open; if she receives more letters, or feels harassed, truly frightened, that will be the time to report it. Or are they watching her now?

Do nothing. Forget it.

Emma-Jane gets up to turn the radio on and then pours herself a glass of water. Her hand is still shaking when she brings the glass to her lips. Sunlight bounces off the glass. A door bangs upstairs. She accidentally drops the glass, and it smashes on the floor. She kneels to collect the largest fragments, hating the mess and the adrenaline surging through her. A shard cuts her middle finger, so she sucks the blood and swallows it. The copper taste in her mouth is vile.

The sunlight is still streaming through the kitchen window, and the clock reminds her she has the entire weekend ahead of her in her lovely home, where she is free. Her dry cleaning can wait, and she can always read the newspaper online to save a trip to the newsagents. Stay inside. Stay safe.

Safe, she thinks, staring at the hate letter clutched in her trembling hand. In the lounge, the bookcase is almost full of fiction and non-fiction, arranged alphabetically. Most of the books are about psychology or counselling, and a few are on specialist topics she has taken an interest in over the years, such as grief and loss. The spines of her many travel books are colourful and eye-catching, in among the serious fonts and hues. Not that she has travelled any further than Europe, but one day, when the time is right, she would like to travel to Egypt and swim in the Red Sea.

She slides the hate letter between a book about emotional intelligence and another on personality disorders.

Early on Monday morning, the hateful letter will be removed from the privacy of her home to reside in her office, where the doctor works.

Chapter 4

Without Emma-Jane's financial and emotional support Lucy wouldn't have had the confidence to set up a business as a nutritionist; not with the limited experience she has. Self-confidence has never been her strong point, but by having an office directly opposite her friend, and meeting her most days after work to debrief, Lucy is slowly able to believe her business will succeed. There's a fine line to walk between supporting one another and protecting the confidentiality of clients, particularly in Emma-Jane's line of work, which is governed by the strict ethics of the British Psychological Society. Lucy respects that and tries to support her friend as best she can, when it's clear some clients take it out of her friend more than others.

Lately, a young woman called Vanessa has really got Emma-Jane down. Lucy knows Vanessa's daughter died very suddenly. Grief is debilitating. She knows that, having lost her boyfriend in a car accident. But that's in the past now.

This business is the here and now, and her future. The office is situated in Shrewsbury, off the main high street on Byar Lane; a convenient and discreet location for clients. Shrewsbury is a great place to live and work, with the Shropshire hills close by.

There isn't any free parking but there are plenty of car parks in town within walking distance, so clients aren't put off. Their rented premises is a single-storey building, which a passer-by might not notice if it weren't for the gold plate to the right of the front door stating Dr Glass's long line of qualifications. One day, Lucy's name will be added, but it's too soon for that, perhaps, for the extra cost. It's a thought she has most mornings when she arrives for work. Lucy had had a temporary plastic sign made for the other side of the door in a functional font. It still gives her pleasure to see her name there.

In the kitchen, Lucy fills up the biscuit tin with chocolate digestives and opens a new packet of tea bags. The kitchen is only just big enough for the two of them to stand and sip their tea or coffee but it has everything they need, including a small fridge and a microwave to make lunch and, sometimes, dinner in, for those evening appointments offered to clients who work long hours themselves. She wipes down the surfaces and closes the door behind her. Emma-Jane likes things to be clean and orderly.

Lucy's two o'clock appointment arrives punctually – a new client who had made the appointment online, detailing her need to put on weight quickly. When Lucy welcomes Miss Jennifer Steed, a sales assistant for a phone company, she isn't what Lucy had been expecting. After taking in Jennifer's luscious long blonde hair, her overwhelming impression is of a big, beautiful woman. Everything about her is ample, from her hair to her size, to her large brown eyes and jangling green and red beads.

Lucy immediately questions the accuracy of her memory. Perhaps she's thinking of another application?

'I hope I'm not late,' she says breathlessly. 'I didn't have the right change for pay-and-display, and so I had to nip to Boots to buy something to *get* some change, and there was a queue, as you'd expect. It's always the way, isn't it, when you're running late. If I'd had tons of time, I would have had all the change I needed.'

'Don't worry; you're not late. Make yourself comfortable. I'm Lucy. Thanks for completing the online form. Would you like a drink? Tea, coffee or water?'

'Water, thanks.' She knocks back a glass in one go, so Lucy refills it from the water jug. Lucy gives her a few moments to compose herself and catch her breath. She notices how small and delicate Jennifer's feet are in gold pumps beneath the tent of her colourful maxi dress.

As Jennifer drinks a second glass of water, she takes a good look around Lucy's office. It is decorated in pale blue, with large, framed posters on each wall illustrating a healthy meal and a balanced diet. Lucy had taken great care to balance useful information with feel-good measures displayed in bright fonts. BE THE PERSON YOU WANT TO BE. EAT TO BE WELL. LOVE YOUR BODY.

'I like your posters.'

'Thanks.' Lucy is both relieved and anxious when she skim-reads Jennifer's application form. Her memory was correct. 'Alright, so I can see from the information provided you'd like to gain weight quickly. You are thirty-five and take infrequent exercise. What I like to do in the initial session is get to know you a bit better and work out a bespoke plan that's realistic for you to achieve your goal on. Do you have at least an hour available?'

Jennifer nods and arranges her long, patterned dress so it billows out around her, having been trapped underneath her thighs. She reminds Lucy of a queen on a throne. Only a hint of her bountiful cleavage is on view, but her bosom jiggles with each slight movement she makes to flick her hair or adjust the dress. 'Yes, that all sounds good to me. I've been trying to gain more weight for about four months now, but I seem to have reached a plateau. I eat at least three thousand calories a day, more when I'm with Ross, so it doesn't add up.'

'Ross?'

'My boyfriend. He's lush,' she says and tosses a tendril of hair behind her back, which curls around her waist like a Burmese python. 'We've been together six months.' She says it like they're married. 'He keeps a close eye on me.'

'Is Ross a doctor?'

She laughs and tosses her long hair over her shoulder again creating a jiggling movement, which Lucy is quickly made familiar with. 'He's a baker. Well, more than that. A business owner, too. He has a bakery in Malpas – "Pie in the Sky". It took him ages to decide on a name. It was a toss-up between "The Sweet Spot", "The Muffin Man" and "Sticky Buns".'

‘I think he made an excellent choice with “Pie in the Sky”.’

‘Me too. At one time Ross told me it was going to be called “Squashing Delights” and I hit the roof; squashings are what he likes me to do in the bedroom – you know, for me to sit on him and wriggle around a bit – and that’s fine, but not on a shop sign! It could put some customers off their pastries!’

Lucy keeps a straight face as she switches the scales on. ‘Do you want to hop on the scales so we can get a benchmark weight? Just remove your shoes, please.’

Jennifer uses the arms of the chair to stand up and climbs onto the scales without her ballet shoes.

‘So, at the moment your weight is eighty-two kilograms.’

‘Oh God, is it? I’ve lost two pounds,’ she says miserably.

'Let's take a height measurement, if you'd like to stand here. Thanks. You are 168cm. That's great. If you'd like to put your shoes back on and have a seat.'

'Ross took me out for a curry at the weekend, and it didn't agree with me. Prawn balti. I should have stuck with chicken biriani as I normally do, but he said to try something new – so me being me, I did.'

'Your body mass index, or BMI, for your age and height is thirty-two, which suggests you are obese. Your ideal weight for your build and age is between nine and eleven stone or fifty-seven to seventy kilograms, so you see, you are over what's thought to be a healthy weight.'

Jennifer waves an arm in the air, dismissing Lucy's information in one imperious gesture. Her bracelets jangle in discord.

'Being obese has several health risks, such as type 2 diabetes.'

‘I’m not here to be healthy,’ Jennifer says bluntly. ‘I thought you said this first session was about getting to know me, so you know how to help?’

‘I apologise; BMI is a useful starting point to go from. Over to you.’

‘Right. In a nutshell, I want to put on another two stone. There’s nothing complicated about that, only my body has stopped gaining. I think three stone will make it difficult to get around and I need to work. Ross likes big women, you see, and I like Ross. Simple as. He likes to watch me stuff myself. It turns him on. Should I tell you more about our sex life?’

This time Lucy puts her hand up and shifts uncomfortably in her seat. ‘You already told me about squashings. It isn’t usually necessary to give a blow-by-blow account.’

‘Well, Ross likes… certain things, and the bigger I am, the better. A few extra stone have made all the difference, but it’s not enough.’

'Why is there an urgency to gain weight?' Lucy senses Jennifer's annoyance. 'Slow and steady is best where weight loss or gain is needed. The body maintains a healthy weight, which is gained or lost gradually. You will have heard of people going on crash diets with dramatic results, only to put all the weight back on – and more – once the diet ends.'

'Yeah, I know all that. And Ross and I know that big is beautiful.'

'I see. Does the overeating turn you on too?'

'I like food,' she says simply, 'and he loves a wobbly belly. It's his favourite bit of me,' she says, looking down at it with the expression an adoring mother wears when gazing at her child's head. 'And mine.' Lucy expects her to stroke the folds of flesh, but her hand caresses the slim arm of the chair instead.

'Eating ripe fruit in front of a partner can be very erotic. Pears, peaches, plums, strawberries… Take your pick, depending on the season. Grapes. Oranges; they have a citrus tang, and they are good for you and your skin, hair, nails. That way, it's a win-win.'

'I see where you're going with this, but Ross and I are incorrigible carnivores and sugar-junkies – and don't say fruit has sugar in it because it's just not the same, and you know it. Don't you enjoy the sweetmeat of happiness? Don't tell me; you only eat salad.'

Lucy laughs. 'I don't, of course. I love meat, but—'

'Health is so important. You said. Only Ross is hungry for me, and I am hungry for him.' She flicks her ballet shoes off and bends and flicks her toes; the toenails are painted a fierce shade of pink. It reminds Lucy of summer cocktails. The unselfconsciousness of her client is refreshing but concerns about the requests are buzzing around her brain.

'I know what I want,' says Jennifer.

Lucy looks back at the application form, feeling defeated. Her advice is falling on deaf ears. 'Are you troubled by the discomforts of over-fullness? I mean, does your body send you signs of physical distress because it can't handle the quantity? I have to ask these questions, as a nutritionist.'

'Look, thanks for your concerns and all that, but I'm paying for this, and I want to put on two stone as quickly as possible. Yeah?'

'Let's move on. I see from your diet sheet you eat a lot of fast food. It's high in fat, but it can make you lethargic. It's possible to gain weight from foods which are healthier. I can't condone eating fried and fatty foods to meet your goal.'

Jennifer shrugs.

'A diet high in good fats like avocado and nuts is an option, and smoothies high in protein, such as caramel apple shakes, and foods high in starch such as rice and potato. Within a couple of days I'll have a diet sheet for you, and I suggest you try it for a week and let me know how it goes. Return this time next week if you can, and I'll retake your weight. How does that sound?'

‘Anything else I can eat? While I think of it, Ross and I are going away for a couple of days. He’s treating me to a spa weekend, dinners included, and afternoon tea. It’s that prominent place in Chester, by the racecourse.’

‘I don’t know Chester that well.’

‘Anyways, I’ll eat what he wants me to eat then, and more.’

‘Why would you do that?’

‘That’s what we do. Ross usually chooses really well. And the most calorific, of course. He can eat what he likes and never gains a pound. Highly strung. Always on the go.’

‘You could purchase a protein supplement if you wish, to add to cereals and drinks. To keep healthy, eat a variety of foods – fruit and veg – keep up the fluids – water – and take some gentle exercise, such as using the stairs rather than the lift or an escalator. Yes?’

'Sex is exercise,' she says darkly, 'but *he* won't be getting any if this doesn't work.' Jennifer rises from the chair and flicks her long hair over her shoulder. Lucy sees her ankles and feet are swollen and, by the amount of water she'd drank, there was quite a thirst to quench; an early warning sign of type 2 diabetes. 'I hope it works. Ross is paying for your time.'

'Why don't you bring Ross with you next week? I have an offer on for couples at the moment.'

'I'll ask him, thanks, but I don't think so.'

'Or, if you refer a friend, you get one session free. Anyway, I hope you enjoy your weekend away. See you next week, Jennifer. Take care of yourself.'

There's no offer on for couples or referrals. Still, it is all Lucy can think of to respond to her growing unease about Jennifer's abuse of her body to sustain a relationship with Ross and the lack of business coming through her door. That, and her decision to treat Jennifer.

She is not her first client with a request to gain weight for sexual pleasure but this one worries her, because a previous client had enjoyed her fatness and overeating. It was a desire born out of self-love and gluttony. She isn't so convinced that's the case with Jennifer. In her mind, she has a duty of care to, at the very least, provide information about the risks associated with obesity, overeating, let alone his risk of asphyxiation from squashing. With an excess of eleven stone sitting on top of his head, wriggling and gyrating, how long can a man live on the air in his lungs before it runs out and the block of darkness, the cement of unconsciousness, pulls him down as if to the bottom of the sea? If nothing else, meeting Ross would satisfy her curiosity about what he looks like and what Jennifer sees in him. Perhaps Ross will be more open to her advice? The thought alleviates some of the unease she feels in the pit of her stomach – but not all of it.

Lucy waits a few minutes and then approaches Emma-Jane's office but, when she hears her friend talking and laughing and a man's voice, she makes a U-turn back to her office. The man's voice sounds like Drew Rogers; a hunk of a client. The sound of Emma-Jane's laughter is a surprise.

The office feels very still and quiet after Jennifer has gone. Lucy doesn't have another appointment until the following morning and, while she has admin and diet plans to work on, her mood isn't in the right place to settle and work. Pity she doesn't have someone to get out with for a quick drink, or a run along the river. Looking on the bright side, she does have a date the night after next. Perhaps he's the one.

In Carlisle, Lucy had had a few brief flings: one was more sex than anything, the other fizzled out after a few months of dining out and titillation. So, since returning to Shrewsbury, she'd signed up with a dating agency. She figures if she keeps an open mind and expects nothing to come of it, she won't be disappointed. Meeting people is difficult, with working long hours and then using her free time for training or trips to Carlisle to see her elderly parents. Her online profile specifies older men, those aged forty to fifty, because she thinks an older man is more likely to understand some of her foibles.

She stares at the wall, the messages in focus then blurring to a smudge. BE THE PERSON YOU WANT TO BE. EAT TO BE WELL. LOVE YOUR BODY.

As Lucy stares at a colourful poster on the office wall illustrating the idea of a colourful plate, part of her envies Jennifer and Ross's passionate relationship, even though their sexual habits based on his love of her wobbling flesh sat on top of him aren't to her taste. She can understand some of the pleasure of watching a person you love eat something delicious, but not a four-course meal! Perhaps once Jennifer gains just a few more pounds of flesh Ross will be satisfied and they will stop fixating on food. As it is, it seems like there isn't a cauldron big enough for her appetite for him, which makes her meals for one seem like gruel served up in minuscule wooden bowls, her kitchen a sterile shell of a place and her body a silent temple.

Someone will come along, that's what her mother says. *One day. Just when you are least expecting it. Just at the right time.*

Chapter 5

Next door to Lucy's office, Emma-Jane makes her last client of the day as comfortable as she can. It is 7.30pm, a late appointment, which is Vanessa's choice. After losing her young daughter to an asthma attack, Vanessa is struggling with grief and depression. Avril, her daughter, had just turned ten, and was Vanessa's world. The young woman had brought her up as a single mum after Avril's dad made it clear he wasn't father material.

'Good to see you.' Emma-Jane is pleased to see Vanessa looking unusually fresh-faced, with a suffusion of colour in her cheeks. Instead of her usual black clothes she's wearing a bright top and ripped jeans. Her head is lifted, and she makes eye contact straight away. 'Come on in. Take a seat.' All these little signs give Emma-Jane hope that Vanessa is starting to deal with Avril's death, after a very difficult depressive time. After the usual preamble about confidentiality and ethics, which has to start every session, Emma-Jane smiles warmly at Vanessa. ‘How are you today?’

‘Oh, I had such a great sleep last night! Let me tell you about my dream first, before I forget. Okay?’

‘Yes, go ahead.’

‘I dreamt I grew dandelions in the earth, and they cast a spell. A gust of wind shakes just one dandelion, and I see Avril’s face in it, in the white head of it. Then, it disintegrates into tiny pieces, and Avril is travelling in the air, floating.’ Vanessa raises one hand in the air as she describes the image. ‘Then, I run to different windows – I don’t know whose house I’m in – and I see her travelling by, carried on the air. I think I’m awake and I look at my alarm clock, then put the light on. On my pillow, there’s all these white fluffy dandelion heads, all in little pieces.’ Vanessa smiles an innocent smile, almost childlike, her head on one side. She looks young and innocent. 'Perhaps it's a sign of hope, of coming to terms with Avril's death.'

'I see. What a lovely dream!' Emma-Jane smiles and nods, sensing that Vanessa desperately wants her to agree, but she does not want to read something into a dream which may or may not be there. There's progress evident in her appearance and the lucid description of her dream. 'And you look well, well rested. It makes such a difference, doesn't it, to outlook, everything, when you feel refreshed? And of course, with time, the intense grief you feel will fade. It will, with time.'

'Days like today I can believe that. Others, not so much.'

'That's normal. Are you ready to try hypnotherapy again today?'

Vanessa nods and climbs onto the couch and soon she begins speaking through her hypnosis.

* * *

I am in my bedroom changing the sheets when I hear Avril banging on the window. 'Stop that! For heaven's sake! What has gotten into you?'

Avril is gasping for air as she stands by the window in the lounge. It looks like the pain is in her chest and the back of her throat and by the wideness of her eyes, the tightness quickly worsens. Avril looks scared. She is moving away from the window to the sofa. Her feet move like she's been dragged backwards, like she didn't choose to go that way; pedalling backwards, pedalling air.

More chest pain, like daggers now. Her chest rises with each tortured intake of air.

Eyelids flutter in an anguished face.

'Get… my… inhaler!' Avril bleats between coughs and wheezes, a voice like her insides are blocked, like her windpipe is tacky and clogged. 'Quick… ly.'

I feel frightened. I know the signs. It's a severe attack.

Fuck! It's not in the kitchen drawer. I am an organised mum. Why isn't it in the drawer, where it should be? I am running, turning, twisting, looking high and low, and Avril is wheezing.

I had seen the blue inhaler recently. I am sure of it. So how can this be happening? I look around the lounge and kitchen, looking but not seeing. Panic. Unable to take in what is happening and what will happen if I don't lay my hands on the inhaler any minute, any second, and time is ticking. Make it stop. Stop the clock!

On the bureau there's a pile of old magazines, a few schoolbooks and one of Avril's soft baby blankets, which she refuses to part with. Perhaps it's under that pile. I look, rummage, toss it all to the floor. But no inhaler. I toss the cushions off the sofa and root under the seats and chair.

Be calm. You'll find it. Think, I keep telling myself, but it isn't working.

'Mum!' she begs. 'Hel–' There's a look of terror on Avril's face as she falls to her knees, then onto all fours. An animal now. Primitive. Survival. Her head hangs as if staring at the carpet, then rises with each attempt at breathing. Her breathing is rattling now. There are no other sounds in the house, except the crumbling and sickness of Avril's lungs, like a hot wind trapped inside a small space, and my urgent footsteps running from one room to the next, from one cupboard to another, emptying drawers and ticking, ticking…

'Christ! Where it is?'

'Hel…'

I run to the bathroom to look for a spare inhaler in the cabinet. Relief comes when I see the blue and white box on the top shelf beside the Rennie, talc and Head and Shoulders.

I grab it. 'Christ. It's empty.'

A flash of inspiration comes. My handbag. I upturn it on the lounge carpet. Nothing. I run back into her bedroom, where I keep another leather handbag for smart occasions, and I look in there, just in case. Nothing.

I am desperate now. Once or twice before Avril has blown into a paper bag to regulate her breathing, so I rummage in the bin for the MacDonald's bag I threw in there yesterday. The bag has got wet stains of food on it, but it is good enough. Avril's eyes are bulging, and her chest is heaving.

'Take this! Blow! Blow. You can do this.'

Only she can't. She can't catch her breath. The panic owns her. I hold her head despite knowing it's futile. Avril can't blow into that bag any more than wipe her own nose. There's only the faintest recognition in Avril's eyes that I am there. The terror has gone. Now, it's still water. Stagnant.

'Don't die! Pleeeease!'

The crackling and rasping are poison in her system. Her body is closing down. I know it, feel it. 'Oh God, Avril!' I grab the phone and call 999. Her face is blue.

They tell me to put my ear to her mouth. 'She's not breathing!' I listen for a heartbeat in her chest and feel for a pulse in her neck, her wrist. Nothing. Nothing. Nothing.

It's all my fault, because I couldn't find the inhaler. I wonder if I didn't dust properly yesterday, or whether the temperature is too hot or too cold in the apartment, whether it's the new carpet, the weather, whether someone at school has been horrible to her, whether…

I open her mouth and blow. Nothing happens. I try again and again.

'Oh my God. Oh my God. My baby!'

I lovingly stroke the fine hairs on her cheeks, still rocking her, just like I did when she was a baby. I rocked her to sleep, or sometimes I rocked her because I was so full of love for her. 'I couldn't save you!' I am wailing, I can't stop.

I carry her into my bedroom and wrap her in my duvet, then I carry her downstairs to my car as though the warmth and movement and tenderness might resuscitate her. I put a seat belt on Avril. I don't know why. It's difficult to drive because of the tears and snot and it's hard to concentrate, but I pull up outside A&E and I don't know why I'm here, but it's all I can think of to do.

Inside there are too many people around, talking, watching, sitting, and there are too many bright fluorescent strip lights and lots of signs shouting one thing after another, which might as well be in a foreign language to me right now. My arms are heavy from carrying Avril. She's heavy and limp. I keep walking, not really sure where I am going or what I am doing. Everything is slow and weird and people are whispering, until a nurse gently puts a hand on my shoulder and smiles kindly, with her head to one side. The nurse leads me to a chair and gently takes Avril out of my arms. I realise I only have one shoe on. I fall onto the floor and bang my head.

***

By the time nine o'clock comes, Emma-Jane is exhausted and ready for home. Vanessa had left a while ago, but her recollection of Avril's death lingers in the four corners of the office. Some days are more emotionally draining than others. Both Vanessa and her other regular client, Drew Rogers, take a lot out of her because of their intense emotions of grief and loss and her need to maintain her distance. It's hard not to get emotionally involved.

Chapter 6

One week later, there's a light tap at Emma-Jane's office door. 'Come in!'

Lucy's smiling face appears around the side of the door. 'Was that the very handsome, very gorgeous Drew Rogers I saw leaving?'

Emma-Jane nods.

'You don't look too happy about it.'

'Poor bloke. He was almost in tears again. You know he's recently divorced? I can't say too much, but he is devastated.' She arches her back to stretch it out after spending nine hours in a chair. 'Anyway, how did your date go? I'm gathering from your continued interest in Drew Rogers, not that well.'

Lucy shrugs. 'Not really. The bloke talked at me the whole time, and I could hardly get a word in edgeways.

I couldn't wait to finish my drink and get the hell out of there. Next time I'll order a half.'

'At least it wasn't a three-course meal.'

'God, no way. A drink and a packet of crisps took long enough. I've got another date on Saturday night. We've emailed and spoken on the phone. He enjoys running and has a dog. Two big ticks from me.'

'There you go then. I have a good feeling about this one. What's his name?'

'Martin.'

'How do you feel about that?' she asks, because Lucy's ex-boyfriend, and love of her life who had died in a car accident, was called Martin.

'It's okay. He's probably got a middle name I can use, like Herbert or Dick.'

'Does he smoke?'

Lucy shakes her head.

'Good.'

'I won't date smokers.'

'I'm clearing my desk then heading home. You?'

'Sainsbury's shop, then home to watch *Lewis*. See you tomorrow.'

Emma-Jane sweeps her black hair behind one ear. 'You might bump into Drew! He was on his way there. You'll probably find him at the deli counter: he's a foodie.'

'He gets better!' Lucy laughs. 'By the way, did you get that letter I left on your desk? It appeared under my door earlier.'

'No! My desk is a tip.' She lifts a box file to find the letter underneath. Her heart sinks. It's more hate mail. 'Thanks,' she says, as neutrally as she can muster to disguise her unease. How quickly her heart rate has increased just at the sight of the envelope, let alone its contents.

'You okay?' Lucy asks, sensing something.

'Yeah, too much paperwork! See you tomorrow.'

Emma-Jane watches Lucy go, relieved to be alone to open the letter in private. Lucy has enough on her plate with a new business, and she senses the loneliness her friend feels, and the frustration at not meeting someone she can share her life with. Ever since Martin's death and then sleeping with a couple of men on the rebound, Lucy has had her flings and romances, but they never last long. She admires Lucy for still trying to find love. It takes time, courage and perseverance. And hope. For Emma-Jane, her work, the business, is her only love. *At all costs*, she thinks, glancing at the letter with narrowed eyes. When she listens to Drew's morose outpourings she feels glad her heart is locked safely away, and her selfishness and guard keeps it there, unbreakable.

The envelope seems to shout at her to open it, so she gets on with it before locking up for the night. The sound of tearing paper is loud in the silent office. At least the sender is invading her workspace, not her home, this time. So, they know where she lives and works.

Who do you see in the mirror on the wall? Does that face of yours fail to remind you of how fragile you are, how easily you can break? You are misguided to think you are bulletproof when you are just made of glass, like the rest of us.

A glass woman living in a glass house. How many stones shall I throw to send you picking up the pieces?

I shan't handle you with care.

She stuffs the letter back in the envelope and inserts it between two files on her desk. It crouches there, with the other letter she'd removed from her house, so it is out of sight. In her line of work, unstable minds are her bread and butter. Like with the last letter, there's a stamp on the envelope but it's been hand-delivered. That's the bit which unnerves her – they have been to her home and now her office, in person.

Outside, the sky is murky. It isn't far to walk to her car, but it feels like she's speed-walked ten miles by the time she is inside her Golf with the doors locked. She immediately switches on the interior light and checks no one is on the back seat before turning the ignition and driving home. Her blood rushes. The evening is all hers. A blank sheet of paper.

Chapter 7

Jennifer's bloated, beaming face confirms to Lucy that her diet plan is working. She doesn't know how to feel – is it a success, or a failure? Now, Jennifer is back after two weeks and, with the practice being so busy, it has slipped her mind to speak to Emma-Jane about her concerns and the ethics of treating her.

'Good to see you. Take a seat.'

'Thank you!' Jennifer says breezily, giving Lucy a wide smile, which reaches her brown eyes. 'It is working!' She stands in front of Lucy with her arms outstretched. 'Five pounds – in one week! Ross is so happy. Me too! My boobs are bigger! Honestly, you should have seen his face when'

'That's great!' Lucy interrupts, putting one hand up, quite unsure of where the conversation was going but not wanting to take the risk. ‘I’m pleased you’re happy; and Ross, too.’

‘Ross is on his way here. He should be here in a minute.’

‘Excellent.’

‘So, on to stage two. What’s next?’ Jennifer asks, collapsing into the chair. She dumps her handbag, an orange and black suede tote bag, to one side. She certainly knows how to make herself comfortable.

‘Have you experienced any uncomfortable side effects from the diet plan?’

‘Wind.’ She laughs. ‘And I’ve been weeing a lot. More than usual, I should say.’

Lucy leans forward in her chair. ‘More than normal?’

‘Don’t look so worried! I feel fine!’

'I mentioned the risk of type 2 diabetes last time we met. Urinating often can be a symptom. Perhaps you'd like to be tested, just to be on the safe side?'

'Honestly, Ross keeps an eye on me, like I said last time I was here. I'm fine.'

'Any other side effects?' Lucy asks, using her notes to keep the consultation on track, which is harder with some clients than others. Jennifer leans forward towards Lucy and sticks her tongue out. 'Black tongue,' Lucy says.

'It wasn't like that before.'

'No?'

'No! It tastes a bit metallic. Have I got bad breath?'

'Have you tried scraping it with your toothbrush?'

'Not really.'

'It's most likely a disorder commonly called "black hairy tongue" if it's not a birthmark. Excessive protein or poor diet could be the cause, or more oral hygiene is perhaps needed, which should help with bad breath.'

'I don't want dog breath for the weekend. Ross would hate that! What do I do?'

'Start with scraping the tongue with your toothbrush.'

'Blow me. I was feeling terrific about myself before you told me my breath stank!'

'I didn't say that.'

Jennifer is listening now. 'Ross has made me all these lovely meat pies with your protein supplement.'

'Health is so important, and perhaps your tongue is telling you to stop gaining weight.'

Jennifer rolls her eyes, like a child bored by her teacher's admonishing.

'I'll be adding more fruit and vegetables to your diet plan this week – owing to that tongue of yours. As before, plenty of water. Less of the protein supplement, but choose red meat over white.'

'Alright then. Sorry for getting a bit arsy; only I love Ross, sex, all that, you know.'

'No problem at all.'

'Do you have an appetite?' Jennifer asks, raising her eyebrows.

Lucy lets the question hang in the air between them for a moment, in which she could choose to ignore it, to maintain the professional distance between them, or answer, and so halve it. This big, beautiful woman is getting under her skin. Why? Jennifer defies the culture of size six and asks questions her own mother doesn't; nor Emma-Jane, for that matter. Jennifer is thriving on life, on sex, on food, and what does Lucy have?

'If you invited me for dinner, what would you cook?' Jennifer continues. 'I know! If I guess correctly, I get a free session and diet plan. Deal?'

Amused, and slightly self-conscious, Lucy nods in agreement and begins to laugh.

'I'm thinking… If you were letting your hair down, so to speak, surf and turf. Food after sex, um, I know I'm digressing, but I'd say toad in the hole! A weekday meal, okay, with me: lentils, lots of other pulses and mushrooms, seeds and stuff, bits that get stuck in your teeth. Spinach! A side salad with rocket. Maybe fish… Tuna. The sort of meal where you never feel full. How am I doing?'

'That certainly sounds like a healthy meal, a balanced plate.'

'Was I right?'

'Weekdays I eat a healthy diet, but weekends I'm not so strict on, especially when I'm exercising. If I was cooking for you I'd probably make us a chicken Caesar salad, with fruit salad and natural yoghurt to follow.'

'Yeah, I could get that down,' Jennifer says, smiling, 'but I'd still be hungry.'

Lucy hears footsteps, and then there's a knock at the door.

'That'll be Ross.'

Jennifer wriggles in her seat, preparing to stand up, but Lucy beats her to it and opens the door.

'Ross?' He nods. 'I'm Lucy. Come in.'

He ducks as he walks under the door frame; all six-foot-two of him, even though there are a few inches spare to clear his head. Lucy thinks he probably weighs less than sixty-three kilograms soaking wet.

'These are for you,' he says, proffering a tray of cakes. 'Chocolate and orange cupcakes, white chocolate éclair, a raspberry jam doughnut and a coconut slice. All freshly baked this morning. All very unhealthy and delicious.'

'Oh, lovely! Don't tell anyone I'm a cake fiend! And so's my colleague next door, Dr Glass.' She puts the cakes on the table and Ross has his hand outstretched to shake. The handshake is soaking wet.

'Jennifer hasn't stopped talking about you since she came to see you and she's so happy about gaining weight.' He crosses his long limbs, his feet in distressed leather cowboy boots.

Lucy arranges her notes in her lap to give herself a moment to compose her thoughts. They say opposites attract. Ross is as thin as a beanpole. She was hoping for the complete opposite, given the risks of asphyxiation from squashing. Jennifer and Ross smile at each other, he takes her hand in his and holds it in his lap, in case it might move away. Jennifer eyes up the cakes.

'I have tried recipes for healthier cakes for my customers at the bakery, with less sugar and butter, but the taste isn't good at all. We've had some success with healthier toppings, like yoghurt and apple. To be honest, I do that much baking at work that when I get home I love cooking meat for Jennifer – fried, battered, roasted. We do it every which way, don't we?'

Jennifer grins.

Lucy tries to discreetly wipe her hand on her trousers. ‘They look delicious, thank you. I’m just pleased Jennifer is happy with her progress, but I wanted to talk to you both about the risks of obesity. Some nasty side effects are showing.’

He turns to look at Jennifer quizzically. Suddenly, Jennifer sticks her tongue out, then back in again.

‘Let me have another look,’ Lucy says, leaning forwards. ‘Obviously I didn’t see your tongue before you gained weight, but when a person puts on weight, the tongue can get fatter. The human tongue has a high percentage of fat. Does it feel bigger?’

Jennifer shrugs.

‘Has your sleep been affected?’

‘Not really.’

‘Hop on the scales.’ The room feels hotter, smaller, as Lucy thinks about how to get Ross and Jennifer to listen to her, to stop playing their games with weight and squashings in bed. ‘I think you have gained enough weight now and need to stop. It is my duty to repeat my concerns. It wouldn't be professional of me to help you gain more weight. With your swollen black tongue and the other ailments we discussed previously, my advice is to stabilise your weight. Or, better still, gradually lose a few pounds.' She looks for a reaction but doesn't get one from either of them. 'I think we should leave it here,' Lucy says.

Jennifer gives a moody shrug when Lucy doesn't show signs of bending. 'I'll go somewhere else then, to someone who'll help me. Money normally sorts out an overactive conscience.'

'Not when it comes to health.'

'That's crap. If you've got enough money, you can get what you want.' She crosses her legs, putting a barrier between them. It seems Jennifer is used to getting her own way.

Lucy doesn't want to argue the toss with a client who's getting increasingly agitated.

'I want to eat out tonight,' Jennifer says to Ross, sounding like a petulant child. 'Beef burger and lots of chips.'

'We can do that. As soon as I finish work, I'll take you. Where do you want to eat?'

She shrugs and her bosoms wobble. Staring straight at Lucy, she says, 'Burger King.'

He kisses Jennifer's hand and keeps hold of it in his lap. Lucy thinks he'd probably lick her face right now if it made her happy. It's Ross who needs Lucy's help to gain weight and to look at treatment for his dripping wet hands.

'Perhaps you'd like to see me on your own, Ross? Here's my card,' she says, passing it to him while avoiding touching his soggy hand.

'Not me. You know, life's too short to be miserable. See you.'

As soon as they leave Lucy pushes a whole cupcake into her mouth. Cream and chocolate squirt onto her chin but she keeps biting and chewing, not enjoying it, but needing to fill the hole of being single when it seems almost everybody else is in a relationship, in love, in bed having great, fun sex or popping out children. Not only that, she doesn't feel in control of her decisions as a professional. Perhaps more experience is really needed before working for herself. Her parents had said as much. It's not just the technical knowledge (which she has), it's the skills to get people to listen and see sense. To trust her judgement.

Before she's swallowed all of the sickly-sweet cake, Emma-Jane knocks on the door. 'Lucy? You there?'

Lucy opens the door and immediately her friend bursts into laughter at the sight of hamster cheeks and a gooey face. Crumbs have collected at the sides of her mouth and down her top.

'Have I just stepped into a child's birthday party?' Emma-Jane asks, laughing, then she takes a cupcake and copies her friend. The icing is pink, encrusted with tiny marshmallows and hundreds and thousands of sprinkles.

In the centre of the cupcake, soft caramel squirts into her mouth. ‘Mmm, delicious.’

Between chewing and giggles, and watching her friend stuff her face, Lucy feels better. Four cakes down, they sip water, and the giggling eventually stops.

‘I feel better for that,’ Lucy says, patting her stomach. ‘Not the cakes; two is too many one after the other, but for the laugh.’

‘Me too. I feel gross, but it was worth it. I haven’t laughed like that in a long time. We should do this more often!’

Chapter 8

This month Lucy has to pay rent for her office on top of her flat so she avoids spending lots of money at the delicatessen, but, at the sight of Drew, a basket full of attractive-looking food hanging from one hand, and his charming tan brogues, she is lured there.

Emma-Jane is the consummate professional who keeps details about her clients in confidence but, with having an office directly opposite from her, Lucy does occasionally bump into her clients. Some are friendlier than others. Drew is an exception. Friendly and handsome, not to mention well dressed, and the owner of a farmhouse. More than once she's imagined him sitting on an enormous sofa covered in throws and soft cushions in front of the fireplace, an open fire roaring in the hearth and his toes wiggling in the warmth.

‘Fancy meeting you here!’ she says, hoping the cliché will be read as that. She smiles, self-conscious under the bright, fluorescent strip lights and the hovering assistant.

‘Yes!’ Drew looks startled from a reverie; he was obviously immersed in the choice of delicious cheeses, meats and salads. She watches his face change expressions, a shape remoulding as he tries to figure out where he’s met her before. She puts him out of his misery as a mother and a child squeeze past with a laden trolley.

‘It’s Lucy. I have an office in town, in the same building as Emma-Jane – Dr Glass.’

‘Of course! The nutritionist!’ he says, and she’s surprised by the sudden light in his hazel eyes. ‘How could I forget?’ He takes her hand and kisses it. Lucy blushes and relaxes her shoulders, relieved he knows who she is. The kiss is a romantic gesture which is all at odds in the supermarket. ‘I’m shopping for dinner. One day at a time. I’m rubbish at planning my meals ahead.’

He turns back to look at the contents inside the deli counter. 'The olives here are excellent, and the salami.'

Lucy raises her basket to show him the contents for her supper. 'I like the bargains close to their sell-by date.' Her basket holds broccoli, carrots and asparagus.

'Are you vegetarian?' he asks, bending down a little to look, allowing her to check out his head of hair and the attractive silver threads in his sideburns which give him a look of a young George Clooney.

'No, I eat meat and fish. "All things in moderation" is my motto.' The memory of Ross and Jennifer flashes before her.

'Quite right too,' Drew says, though she can't tell whether or not he's sincere. He has three bottles of red plonk in his basket of goodies. 'I could cook for you – tonight, I mean. There's more than enough for two here; then you can see how the property developer fares against the nutritionist. Purely platonic, of course. What do you say?'

A little shocked, but flattered, she replies without delay. What was it Ross had said? *Life's too short to be miserable.* 'I say, why not?'

'Where are you from, Lucy? Does your home town have a signature dish?'

'Good question. I'm from Carlisle, Cumbria. My parents still live there. It's a village near the Lake District. So, Cumberland sausage and Cumberland tattie pie.'

'What's in that?'

'Oh, it's delicious. Lamb, black pudding and potatoes. Stodgy, hearty food; great after a long walk.'

'That sounds tasty for a winter dish. What's your number? I'll text you my address. See you there around seven?'

Moments later Lucy has his phone number, his address and a date. Her heart is thudding with excitement. The need for shampoo and tea bags had evaporated from her mind when she was in the supermarket and only returned moments later, when she was climbing into her car to race home for a quick shower and change. *What do I wear?*

His farmhouse lifestyle builds in her mind as she applies a touch of eyeshadow and mascara: a farmhouse table and chairs, perhaps a Labrador who sleeps beside the Aga, and a free-standing cream bathtub with lion's feet. She imagines waking up in the morning to the birdsong behind linen curtains or Venetian blinds.

She adds a layer of lip balm. *Get a grip. You're getting carried away.*

With a boyfriend in love with her, Lucy thinks, she could go to the weddings and christenings she's invited to but regularly declines with excuses. She'd stop screaming into a pillow after a disastrous date when the loneliness makes her feel uncomfortable in her own skin but the longing for male company is still there, like a constant shadow.

She tries to look like she hasn't made too much of an effort, which is difficult to achieve when she has. All the way to Drew's house, she tells herself: *It's just dinner. Don't expect too much; not a thunderbolt.* Perhaps she should call Emma-Jane to tell her where she's going for dinner, but what if she disapproves because he's a client? *She won't mind*, Lucy reassures herself, while resolving to tell Emma-Jane all about it after the event. Lucy isn't his therapist, or nutritionist for that matter.

Lucy parks beside a Range Rover and knocks on a chunky oak front door. When he opens it, she catches the scent of aftershave and shaving lotion. Not the zesty smell Martin used to wear. This is muskier, and not subtle. Before leaving her house, she sprayed perfume in the air and walked through it twice, only to feel it was too faint and immediately squirted her wrists and neck. Now she's worrying it's too strong.

Drew's lips didn't quite form a smile when he opened the door, but almost. Enough to give the impression of one, and perhaps the promise of a real one later. 'I wondered if you were coming!' he exclaims, and steps back to let Lucy into the house.

'Sorry, I got a bit lost. Your drive is quite hard to find in the dark. It's not a road I've driven along before.'

'You're here now,' he says, giving her a chaste kiss on the cheek as a tepid welcome to the farmhouse she'd so been looking forward to seeing after imagining it so vividly.

Lucy had predicted that it might be on the cooler side (unlike her little modern place, which is cheap to heat), so the brushed cotton top and trousers she'd chosen, with a suede jacket, feel like the right choice given the temperature inside. Drew is wearing a smart, open-neck shirt – no tie, unlike when she saw him in the supermarket.

'Come on in. We're eating in the kitchen; hope you don't mind. Let me get you a drink. Red wine?'

‘Please. Just the one, and a small one at that. I’m driving.’ She follows him into the kitchen, trying not to stare at the house or him too much. There’s evidence of work going on with the dust sheet at one end of the hall and picture hooks left bare. In the kitchen there is an opened bottle of wine and peelings from vegetables.

‘I hope you’re hungry!’ he says, pouring her a glass of wine, and topping up his. He gestures to a chair. ‘Make yourself at home.’

Drew turns his attention to cooking the steak. He adds butter, rosemary and garlic to the skillet and, with a practised movement, tilts the pan from one side to the next to baste the steak with the butter. Lucy takes in the mismatch of old and new furnishings and the photograph of a little boy positioned centrally on the window shelf, smiling behind the glass in a chunky wooden frame.

‘Do you like cooking?’ Drew asks.

'I probably should, given my job, but when it's just me to cook for I tend to go for the quickest and easiest option.'

'Why should you? It sounds to me like you're hard on yourself.' He looks her in the eye. 'Only do things you enjoy!'

She takes a sip of wine as he serves up the meal. *I keep hearing that lately.* 'This is a good wine,' she comments, and reads the label: Châteauneuf-du-Pape. 'Perfect with steak.'

'I think so. Plenty of body.'

The farmhouse kitchen table is simply laid. A large plate of meat and a dome of green in a salad bowl catches her eye. 'That looks very professional. Thank you.'

'Presentation is important, don't you think?' he says, looking straight at Lucy and then back to his quickly devoured meal.

She feels herself blush, so takes a sip of water to hide her face. 'I think it all depends on the dish and the occasion. At home, I eat a lot of salad with meat, with roughly chopped-up veg or fruit – depending on what needs eating – and it's delicious, but looks like a dog's dinner!'

'Dining for one. It's not always fun, is it?'

Lucy smiles as she tucks into the meal. 'It can feel a bit solitary if you're used to the company, that's true.'

'It's a pleasant change to share dinner with a woman who enjoys her food. My ex-wife, Evie, she would make all the right simpering noises when the food was being prepared but, as soon as she sat down to eat it, she'd play with it, move her fork around – it used to drive me mad. On rare occasions, she did well; she'd excuse herself before the end of the dessert to make herself sick.'

'Sick? Oh dear, was she bulimic?'

'I suppose so. Do you like crème caramel? It gives me an excuse to use my brûlée torch!'

'That is delicious, but I am getting full, thank you.'

She looks around the kitchen. The age of the place is evident in the thickness of the walls. She admires the stable door, the window ledge of chunky oak and the red tiled floor. 'It's a great house. As a property developer, have you done up a lot of houses?'

'Oh, yes. In the last ten years, I'd say more than ten. I buy smaller properties to do up and rent out, but I always have one large property to live in while it's being developed. I avoid capital gains tax that way.'

One wall is being replastered. 'Are you doing much work to the house?'

'It's all going to look different. A facelift of sorts. New carpets. It'll be decorated throughout.'

'Sounds more like reconstructive plastic surgery to me, and it looks nice as it is… but I understand why you want to change it.'

'Buyers at this end of the market have certain expectations. I'm not sentimental about it. It's a business, and it needs a facelift, anyway. Where do you live?'

'Renting a flat in Shrewsbury. Before I look to buy I need to see how my business goes. It's very early days.'

'You should sound more confident than that. Believe in yourself. If you don't, customers won't. Think of yourself as your shop window. I mean, you look very trim and healthy, but it's more than that – a positive, can-do attitude.'

Lucy looks away to hide her jaded expression.

'Sorry, I'm lecturing you. I'm passionate about business.'

'My father tells me off when I'm negative about myself. He says there are plenty of enemies out there who will do that.'

'That's true. He's a wise man.'

'Ex-police.'

Once they have both finished the meal and while Drew puts the dirty plates in the dishwasher, she takes a closer look at the photograph which had caught her eye. 'Is that your son?' she asks, gesturing to the image, hoping it will be a talking point to get Drew to open up a bit about his private life.

'James. It was taken last August on his third birthday. Evie, my ex-wife, was good with the camera.'

'I see that, and he's a sweet-looking boy. Curly blond hair.'

'He didn't get that from me as you can see, but he had my dark eyes.' Drew has his back to her so she can't read his expression. The silence feels thick.

'So, it's his birthday soon?' she asks, hovering by the table.

'Yes, the twelfth.'

'Have you been divorced long?'

'Long enough! How do you like your coffee?'

‘White, one sugar. Thanks.’

He fills up the cafetière and carries it over to the table on a tray with cups and saucers. ‘So, how well do you know Dr Glass?’

‘Oh, I know Emma-Jane really well. I’ve known her a long time. Now it’s great to be working alongside her.’

‘Quite a history then?’

‘You could say that!’ she says, forcing out a laugh to release some tension. ‘We are very different but get on so well.’

‘Different in what way?’ he asks, pouring the coffee and adding milk and sugar to hers.

‘She’s confident, self-assured and terrifically studious. Her work is… well, everything. If it wasn’t for her support and encouragement, I wouldn’t be working for myself, or in Shropshire. I’d be living with my parents in Carlisle, bumbling along.’

‘It sounds like you respect her a lot.’

'Yes, I do.' Lucy takes a sip of coffee. 'Do you mind if I use your bathroom?'

'Ah, the downstairs loo is being updated. Up the stairs, take a left. The door has a brass handle.'

The stairs are wonderfully uneven and the bannister is old wood and beautifully imperfect, but the light bulb in the landing light has blown, so it's a semi-dark and slightly gloomy space. Lucy doesn't allow herself to linger too long over the three framed photographs of James at different ages, positioned at even strategic intervals. The second to top stair creaks loudly, making her smile and remember stories of old of children sneaking out at night and being caught out by the very same thing. When she opens the door to the bathroom she gazes around for a few seconds with her mouth open at the contemporary bathroom suite and décor, the massive wall mirror and the wall-to-wall tiles. Even the floor is tiled in the same neutral shade of beige. The character of the place has been eradicated, replaced with bling.

On her way back down, Drew must hear the stair creak. 'In here!' he calls from a room off the hall, sounding slightly drunk.

Lucy follows the sound of his voice to the living room. 'Wow! I love an open fireplace. What a room to relax in.'

'Not furnished any longer, or lit, but perhaps another time we could eat in the dining room – if you have enjoyed my company this evening, that is. That has an open fire too.' She sees his eyes are softer now, after the wine and the first course, and perhaps he is more at ease in her company. As much as she would like to stay and drink a second glass of wine, she has to drive home. That's her way on dates. Keep control. Seeing his slight inebriation makes her feel a little less vulnerable than she did when she arrived at the large, imposing farmhouse.

'I should get going. Work tomorrow. It's been a lovely evening. Thank you.'

He kisses her goodbye and she feels his flat hand against the small of her back. The pressure is just firm enough for her to want more.

Chapter 9

Emma-Jane looks at her watch for the second time. Unusually for him, Drew Rogers is late. If he doesn't arrive in the next five minutes, she will ring him on his mobile. Even though it's in her terms and conditions, which all her clients sign, billing a client for an hour they didn't actually attend feels most unsatisfying. The policy is there to protect her from potential clients who jib out at the last minute, or completely change their mind but fail to tell her. Time is money. It is a business, even though she's in the business of people's minds and their health. Of all the people she's worked with recently, Drew knows time is money. It isn't like him at all to be late for an appointment.

It isn't good for her to worry about her clients needlessly, but she cares about them. Poor Drew, so depressed after his wife left him and took their child with her. She is about to bring up his details to ring him when the front door bangs and footsteps announce his arrival. A firm knock on the door confirms it.

'Come in!' Emma-Jane calls, keen to sound friendly and not even slightly annoyed at being kept waiting. There's bound to be a good reason.

Drew makes himself comfortable in his usual chair, opposite Dr Glass. 'I called in at The White Lemon for my usual products, then the butchers for a ribeye steak and cured bacon and soon regretted that, I can tell you. The queue didn't move for ten minutes. People dither, have you noticed? I've made my mind up about what I want to buy before I go in, but others… Simpering, umming and arhhing. Bloody annoying.' He sits stiffly with his arms on his lap, reminiscent of an army officer. 'I guess some people haven't got something better to be doing.'

'Well, you are here now.' Emma-Jane sees he's wearing a new, expensive-looking watch and his chequered shirt complements his olive skin tone. 'How have you been since I last saw you?'

'Much the same. Sleeping better with a bit of help. Pills, a decent glass of whisky after a meal. Nothing too heavy, but it helps. I've been sorting through my wife's things. The farmhouse is…'

Dr Glass doesn't move or speak. She lets the silence do the work.

'Too big for me. It's a funny thing, I hadn't noticed it before, the size of it, even though it feels like… Evie is still there.' Unlike some of her clients, he's comfortable making eye contact with his hazel, shrewd eyes except when his ex-wife, Evie, is mentioned. He takes a deep breath. 'I shan't be developing the outbuildings. My plan was for us to live in the farmhouse, develop the rest and sell it off. Not anymore.'

'Good that you're sleeping better, and it's understandable to find the house bigger now it's just you living there. Has sleeping better helped you cope with running your business and making those decisions?'

'It would seem so. I am decisive of late. I have a team of two who look after the maintenance and minor building projects. I trust them to get on with that side of things, so I manage my own time. Yesterday there were a couple of houses of interest at auction at Birmingham Auction House but, when I got there, I changed my mind. I realised I don't want more houses, more tenants, more tax, so I spent the day in the Birmingham Art Gallery, something I've never done before.'

'That sounds good. A change. Why there?'

'Evie was a photographer and, at one time, we had dozens of her work on the walls in the farmhouse. I went there out of curiosity, really, to see what the appeal of art is. The pre-Raphaelite drawings and paintings held my interest, especially of Medea. Do you know about Medea?'

Emma-Jane shakes her head.

'She was a sorceress and wife. When her husband deserted her for another woman, Medea poisoned both her rival and her two children.'

'Was the exhibition themed? I think in the past I've seen advertisements for themes or styles.'

'There were different exhibitions on different floors. It's a huge place. You should go. I was very taken with a sketch in chalk. So simple, in black and white, depicting a mother with her child feeding from her breast. It was called *Infant's Repast*. Exquisite. Do you have children, Dr Glass?'

It isn't unusual for clients to ask her personal questions, so she isn't shocked by the impromptu probing. 'No, I don't.'

His face suddenly brightens, flashing a half-smile. 'I expect you have more female clients than male.'

'Why would you think that?'

'No reason.' He straightens an imaginary crease in his trousers. 'I'm thinking of dating again. Evie was vivacious, stunning. I shall do well to find someone as attractive. She had blonde hair. Your hair is very dark. Is it natural?'

A little surprised by the personal nature of the question and the rapid changes in subject matter, she doesn't respond immediately. Lucy recently told her about their meal together. *Is he referring to his date with Lucy?* 'Yes, it's natural. To think about dating again is positive,' she says, nodding encouragingly, happy to be on professional territory again.

'I've had the master bedroom and en suite redecorated to my taste, changed the mood. Previously, I never paid much attention to what went on inside the house; that was Evie's domain. She had everything she wanted. Jewellery, clothes, plus expensive engagement and wedding rings. My mother used to make the remains of a roast on a Sunday last the best part of a week and was buried wearing her wedding ring. You'd think Evie would wear her wedding ring like it meant something. Goodness knows where her rings are now!'

'It's good you're making it your own space, with your stamp on it. It's therapeutic to clear away things you don't need and to change the look and feel of a space.'

'Don't patronise me,' he snaps. 'Don't!'

'I wasn't.' She pauses, and waits for the sharpness in the air to dispel. 'I'm sorry if it came across that way.'

'I'm finding it increasingly difficult to come here and open up. It's an unnatural thing for me to do. Do you understand?'

'Yes, I do. That's why I suggested hypnotherapy previously, which you didn't like the sound of. How can it be made easier for you?'

'You give nothing of yourself while I am expected to unstitch my insides and let it all fall out right here, on this carpet.' He gestures to the floor. It's a surprise to see his hands move from his lap. He looks down, as if blood and guts are there.

'It's your decision. You choose what you talk about and how much of a chosen subject. It's in your hands.

You are in control of what we talk about, what you think about. I am only here to listen and to help you find a place in your mind where you are comfortable with past events and comfortable in your skin.'

He places his hand back on his lap. 'I know I'm a successful property developer. I own five properties. Four are rented out at the moment and, when the fifth is ready, that'll get me a decent income, though it's not centrally in town like two of my other properties. I pay more tax than I should. The money in my account and my assets confirm my success, but *you*? How do *you* know you're doing anyone any good?'

'That's a good question, and you're not the first client to ask it. Psychology is a science, but of course, human beings are complex. My aim, in simple terms, is to promote change in a mental or emotional state.'

'Change?' he asks, quizzically.

'In your case, that means alleviating some depressive symptoms to increase your sense of well-being and to help you deal with stress.'

'Then you're not helping me. It's not working.'

'I am confident in my diagnosis, Drew, and we are pinpointing the causes.' A sudden grin surprises her. 'Depressive symptoms, like a prolonged low mood, disrupted sleeping patterns, anger and irritability are prevalent. Now is a good time to set a realistic goal for the future.'

'Claptrap.'

'Depression isn't something anyone can easily snap out of. Am I right in thinking you are angry with me because I ask you to talk about Evie? I understand it's painful for you.'

'Ah, her. She's in this very room.' He looks up to the ceiling. 'You know she wore her camera like a picture frame. I should have looked at her photos more closely, and then I would have seen it coming. I could have done something, or prepared myself at least. It was the shock. The devastating shock of it. Visceral.' Drew's dark eyes look angry, but his expression is unchanged.

Dr Glass waits and lets the silence do the work.

'Have you ever had an electric shock? Like voltage charging through your body. The pain and the lingering of pain through every vein and fibre in your body, which keeps on jarring because you're too stupefied to let go of the wire. There should be a law which punishes people for causing such pain to others.'

'Evie has caused you pain, and you sound angry about that. The sense of loss is perhaps greater because you don't understand why she left you. Added to that, it came as a total surprise.'

'That's a succinct recap. Thank you. I see you are listening. Ten out of ten.' He smiles a sarcastic smile. 'I used to love watching the two of them in our house; a glass in my hand, or a mug of coffee, depending on the time of day. You know, when my son was born, it was like a miracle. I still haven't forgotten the first time I held him. Tiny hands. Small breaths, so integral to my own within seconds. And fingers, long and thin, curious about life and not afraid to touch. Evie said over and over how small they were. Helpless. That moment eclipsed everything in my life before.'

Drew turns his head and looks through the window, as if to turn his gaze away from the silence between them.

Sensing he doesn't want to say anything else, she responds, 'It is a lot to cope with when you were clearly in love with Evie and adored your son. You said they live abroad with her new partner?'

'I used to think I saw tenderness in her eyes, or a subtle smile on her lips that was just for me. Love. Evie said she loved me all the time, and she took photographs of the word "LOVE" made from sticks or stones, all kinds of things, which took time to arrange, to photograph and develop. It was a labour of love, I thought. Romantic. Silly, perhaps, but I thought there was truth in the clicks of her camera, but no woman would take herself and her child away knowing and feeling love.'

'You are hard on yourself. You weren't foolish to believe Evie loved you.'

'I was,' he retorts. 'It's arrogance. I had affairs and expected her to love me despite them. They meant nothing; just sex, entertainment, some ego-stroking because young, nubile women wanted me. I fancied them. Nothing more.'

Emma-Jane senses his mood swing, so remains silent. That face still looks relaxed, but the eyes and the tone of voice tell the truth. 'Go on.'

'That last time, I saw… The panicked look she cast over the clock. An excuse about an appointment or other. She whipped James into her arms. A hasty chaste goodbye, like she couldn't get away fast enough. She'd been crying. I kissed her goodbye, and her mouth had shrunken to a bee sting. I said goodbye, and that was it.

I thought they were coming back. If I'd known that would be the last time I—'

'What would you have done?'

'Begged her to stay.'

'Drew, have you given any thought to the suggestion I made last time we met?'

'What was that? My memory isn't what it was.'

'I'm not here to tell you what to do, of course, only you are a man of means, and perhaps you have already explored this route. A team of professionals could help you find your wife and son and legally secure access arrangements for you.'

His jaw tightens. 'It's out of the question.' He stops talking, perhaps unable to speak for a moment. His brown eyes shine with emotion, hurt cleaving through him. 'James was busy playing with his toy tractor when she walked out of the house, carrying him in her arms. I didn't even kiss him goodbye. It's too painful to talk about James anymore. He was my only son. My boy,' he says with emotion. 'I'm done talking. You are done listening.'

'Hypnotherapy might help you focus and then relax. It's something I can offer you. Do reconsider. It's quite a common treatment for depression or long-term conditions like breaking bad habits and treating PTSD.'

Drew sighs profoundly, and his eyes darken. 'No.'

The sternness in his tone catches her by surprise. 'Would talking about your affairs in more detail be helpful?'

'What more is there to say about them? Kat was the last, and I have no interest in her now. The woman had delusions of grandeur, and she meant nothing to me. Not then, not now. I'm a virile man of means. Women like me.'

'Do you regret your affairs?'

'Why should I?'

'How did Evie feel about them?'

‘She knew about them, if that’s what you mean.’ Drew clears his throat. ‘That’s all for today, doctor.’

‘We have fifteen minutes left.’

Drew rises suddenly from his chair. He looks at the two uneaten cakes on the coffee table. ‘Pity you haven’t eaten those. They might sweeten you up.’

‘If you feel you want to return, you know how to contact me. Goodbye.’

As soon as the door is closed, Emma-Jane flops onto her sofa and shoves the first cake into her mouth in one go, then immediately eats the second one. Feeling full and thirsty, fat and out of control, she closes her eyes. After the first three sessions, in which Drew was tearful and restless, she had noticed his hands rarely move from his lap. He’s a model of self-composure and control, a mirror image to her in many respects, as she has learned to keep still to encourage the client to speak. If anyone is in control right now, it’s him.

Chapter 10

'Candles! They look lovely in here with the red walls – oh! and your antique furniture! I love that large chest with gold handles.' Lucy blushes with pleasure as she catches Drew's eye and walks around the dining room in his farmhouse.

The lit candles are a romantic touch she appreciates, on top of the enticing aromas coming from the kitchen and Drew looking handsome in a navy stripped shirt and tan chinos. It's such a treat to have dinner cooked for her by this handsome, successful man. Ever since the last date Lucy has felt lighter, hopeful.

Above them, the central light directly over the dining table is a rustic iron chandelier with six candelabra bulbs. It casts an additional warm, honey light. Drew toasts her glass before they sit at the table and then leans forward and kisses her softly on the mouth. The kiss is long and gentle. She closes her eyes and luxuriates in the dark sensuality of it. Everything else moves out of her consciousness; there's just him and his lips.

'Wine and kissing go so well, perfect in fact; like smoked salmon and scrambled eggs,' Drew says.

'Or tuna and pasta! Carbs and protein!'

'So true.' She notices him looking at her again, and each time her tummy does a forward roll. 'Candlelight is flattering, isn't it, and atmospheric, especially in an old place like this. I'm not as young as you and need it!'

Lucy is surprised by his self-deprecating comment. 'Don't be daft! You're what? Forty? I'm not far behind.' She can't read his expression to see if his modesty is genuine or if his ego is being sufficiently stroked, so Lucy decides to change the subject to a neutral topic of conversation. 'How's your week been with the sale?' she asks. 'You mentioned this place is going on the market.'

'Yes, it is. A private buyer has approached me about this place and, provided we reach a mutual agreement, I will save myself about £6,000 in estate agent fees. God only knows how they justify their rates. I upset the director of Morris Estate Agents, William, who I said as much to. I've bought and sold properties through them for years, and had them manage the recruitment of tenants.'

'That is a lot of money, just for selling a house. Most get found and sold on Rightmove, anyway.'

'Precisely. How about your week at work?'

'I took your advice. I've taken the bull by the horns and spent double my usual budget on advertising, and I've sent tweets at the same time each day, around eleven, like you said, when people are thinking about a coffee break and gearing up for lunchtime.'

'Has it had the desired effect yet?'

'I took two bookings this week from the advertisement and I've got around twenty new followers.

Plus, several new enquiries. I'm definitely going to keep it up.'

'Excellent. You will come out of the shadow of Dr Glass's business then, and you'll be flying with new clients and confidence in yourself.'

'Oh, I don't see it like that at all. We complement and support one another, but I recognise I need to do more of my own business generation. With the summer coming up, people will think about getting in shape for bikinis and shorts.'

'That's a good point. See, having a confident mindset works wonders.'

Lucy raises her glass. 'To confidence.' As tempting as it is to glug back the wine, Lucy takes a modest sip, thinking of the drive home and work tomorrow. She can hardly lecture her clients about sticking to less than fourteen units of alcohol a week when she's knocking it back. 'If the business keeps growing I shall look to buy a property early next year. Rent is dead money, after all,' she says with a smile. 'Perhaps you've got some tips for me on where to look? What are your rental properties like?'

'For rental properties I follow a few simple rules. Terraced or semi-detached houses. The newer the better, I'd say, unless you've got DIY skills or know good people. I'm lucky: I have two labourers, AJ and Pete, who take care of the maintenance and building side of the business. Anything old and you could face a nasty surprise like rising damp, or worse, subsidence, which can be expensive to put right and, for someone needing to purchase with a mortgage, almost impossible to buy in the first place – and then difficult to sell.'

'Are those all your rules?'

'I buy close to decent shops, like a Spar or Co-op. In this area, it tends to be Co-op. Many of my tenants don't own a car and so they need to be able to walk to a local shop for their groceries. It's a selling point.'

'So which areas of Shrewsbury do you buy in?'

'My rule of thumb is generally only a three-mile radius from the town centre, and the closer to the centre, the more rent I can charge. My strategy has been to hang on to the properties for as long as I can afford to, or until they are on the cusp of needing work. Some of my tenants have been there for over ten years and think of the house as their own. I have two properties which are empty at the moment. A previous tenant ransacked one of them. I can't tell you what a mess they made of the place.'

'That's rough. What did they do, exactly?'

'About five grand's worth of damage, that's what. It's not habitable as it is.'

'That's awful! Do you know why the tenants made such a mess of it?'

'Why do some people do what most animals don't do? I have no idea, nor do I have time to dwell on people who are a waste of space as far as I'm concerned. If they've got issues, or something to say, then speak, seek help, communicate, but to wilfully destroy the interior of a house… That I cannot grasp or respect an iota.'

'No. I understand that.'

He shakes his head. 'If I didn't have a business head, it would feel almost personal.'

'Apart from my parents' house, I can't say I have any attachment to a building because I've moved around so much. I lived in halls while I studied at university, which was fine, but not exactly home-away-from-home. Mum and Dad's place is the closest to a home so far. I think that while you're renting you're always half on the move, even when you're not aware of it. I suppose once you've got your own place you buy more and more stuff so it becomes a big thing to move, whereas for me it's a few bags, a suitcase, a duvet. Not much more.'

'It's a healthy thing to live like that rather than being burdened with possessions and expense. I've realised that since I've confined myself to a few rooms here at the farmhouse while it's having a facelift. It surprises me how little I really need here.' He pauses, and she is about to speak when he continues, 'The kitchen, a bed, a sofa. At one time, we lived in all the rooms.'

'Well, it's a lovely place. Did your wife take these photographs?' Lucy asks, getting up from the table and peering at the framed shots on one wall of the dining room.

He nods.

'They're excellent. Not that I'm an expert, but I'd like one of an atmospheric landscape on my wall. Like this one. Where was it taken?'

The focus of the shot is an old sycamore tree, set in a dip in the landscape, like the land has bowed down to worship the beautiful tree situated in a barren spot. There is light and dark between the branches and beneath the tree's canopy is a dainty cross.

'Local. Must be. We've always lived in Shropshire. It'll be Nesscliffe. I've kept those shots because my son,

James, loved trees. This one especially. He said it was Robin Hood's Tree. He had a terrific imagination.'

Lucy looks askance at Drew's handsome face. She doesn't know him well enough to read his impassive expression or mood to judge whether to correct him or not about the location of the sycamore tree. Drew is a private man and might not want to talk about it for reasons she can only guess at. Now that she looks at it closely, it's almost certainly Sycamore Gap, near Hadrian's Wall, at Hexham.

Sycamore Gap, or the Robin Hood Tree – as she called it as a child, like James did – is a popular spot for photographers, but in Evie's version the wooden cross at the base of the trunk is distinctive. It's a little creepy seeing the cross there, knowing that James loved the tree. The monochrome shot makes it look sad, haunted even. A strange choice, given James's fondness of it.

Drew tops up a large crystal wine glass with red wine. She hears the glugging sound as her mind works over something: the familiarity of the photograph scratches at something in her mind, like she's seen the composition of tree and cross before. But where? Unless Evie's photography was published in newspapers or magazines, it's unlikely Lucy would have come across it.

'Has the photo been printed or displayed anywhere else?' she asks.

Drew laughs a hollow laugh. 'Evie was an amateur. A good one, but I very much doubt you've seen her work before.' He tilts his head back and takes a swig of wine.

Lucy dismisses the uneasy thought and tries to think about the evening meal she is about to enjoy. How can she have seen the photograph before? She knows how the mind can play tricks. As she looks more closely at the photographs on each side of the Sycamore Gap, she realises Evie had taken close-up shots of the foliage and from underneath the canopy. The tree must have been special to them both.

'I'll bring the main course in. Won't be long.'

'Alright. Shout if I can help.' She scooches over to the other side of the large dining room, where there's a dark wooden chest. Its surface is bare, except for a bowl ladened with a rainbow of fruit. It catches her eye; the fleshy plums and dark cherries especially. On closer inspection, she sees that the fruit is spoiling. Fur clings to the flesh of the plums and one has imploded to reveal its guts, like a weeping vagina.

'I hope you like salmon and prawns. It's tagliatelle.'

Lucy backs away from the bowl and joins him at the table, hiding her distaste with a fake smile. 'Looks delicious. You're an excellent cook. Martin, my ex-boyfriend, was a whizz with the BBQ, but not so keen on using the oven.'

'You're not together any longer?'

'No. He was killed in a car accident. We'd just got to the stage, after three happy years together when, well, we were ready for a more serious commitment, when I lost him. It was a while ago now, but he was very special to me.'

'I'm sorry.'

'Better to have loved and lost than never to have loved at all.'

'You think so?' he asks, doubtfully.

'Ask Emma-Jane! She's the expert!'

'Oh, is she in a happy relationship?'

Lucy laughs. 'With her job, yes.'

'Does she know you're here this evening?'

Surprised by the question, Lucy shrugs. 'Of course.'

'What do you miss the most, now you live alone?'

She is taken aback by the personal nature of his query.

'The sound of someone disappearing from your life forever is ear-splitting. I have the radio, TV, the lights… Even the stupid fan in the kitchen, just for background noise to substitute the noises another person makes.' Surprised by the sudden personal admission, Lucy thinks before she speaks, but Drew continues before she has chance to. 'I find the sounds of cooking replace some old sounds; her shoes on the tiled floor, for example. But nothing can replace the joy of a child's laughter or their running along the landing. James walked nowhere.'

'It gets easier. After loss, I mean. At first, it seemed like there should be a hole in the pillow beside me. I had long periods when I didn't think about Martin. Since moving back to Shrewsbury, that's not been so easy.'

'Love is sadistic. It unskins. Vampires, bloodsuckers, the horror available to watch on TV – all that slashing, hacking and sucking – it's nothing compared to lost love.'

Lucy isn't sure whether he's joking. He looks thoughtful – or is it acting?

'I think a lot about the shape and feel of loss. I even visit art galleries in pursuit of seeing it artistically presented, without success so far. I read, of course, but I'd still like to see something visual and interpreted. Of course, you can see loss everywhere, as Dr Glass has shown me, if you let the greyness of loss colour perception. That's not what I mean. In my darkest of moods, I did, yes – not so much now I'm pleased to say, ever since I started planning my future.'

'She's very good at her job.'

'And you are her number one fan!'

'I'd love to see the rest of the farmhouse after the meal.' Her stomach grumbles. The aromas from the kitchen smell delicious and, because she has normally eaten by that time, every minute feels like two. Her hunger is like a third person at the table.

He puts his glass down. 'Unfortunately, that isn't possible.' He pauses for a moment and half-smiles, perhaps recognising he was blunt. 'There's still a lot of work going on in many of the rooms. Perhaps another time. I hope you will not rush off now!' He leans forward and his shadow is cast over her and the table. The kiss is gentle and searching, almost as satisfying as a full tummy.

Chapter 11

Emma-Jane doesn't need to ask Lucy how her most recent date with Drew went because she can tell; by the serene expression on her face and the quick way she giggles at the smallest thing. It's lovely to see her friend happy, but it worries her that the romance seems to be moving very quickly, with them seeing each other every other night. Not that it's any of Emma-Jane's business, but it seems like Lucy is well and truly head over heels for someone she barely knows.

In her office, she watches Lucy flick through pages on her iPad while sipping a mug of tea, humming all the while. Emma-Jane puts her head to one side as she tries to isolate her feelings of concern. It isn't jealously at seeing her friend happy, is it? Is it protectiveness? But why, she isn't sure. Although Drew has his issues, she can understand what Lucy sees in him. He is a client; perhaps that's what it is.

She leans over to take a closer look at Lucy's screen and sees images of a sycamore tree, one after the other: sometimes in colour, sometimes in monochrome.

'Are you planning a hike somewhere? Looks remote, wherever it is.'

Lucy doesn't look up. She scrolls to another image, more of the same. 'No, just surfing.'

'What are you looking for?'

'Nothing much.' She suddenly gets up from the chair and stretches. 'I'm going home. Do you want me to lock up?'

'No, I've got a late one with Vanessa.'

Lucy gives her a supportive smile before leaving the office. They are always tough sessions. 'See you tomorrow then. Night.'

Emma-Jane offers a few sessions in the evening to accommodate clients, like Vanessa, who don't want to bump into people they might know and feel compelled to speak to on the way in or out of the door. On their last session she had suggested Vanessa keep a dream diary to bring with her but, when she arrives an hour later, she is empty-handed.

'Make yourself comfortable, Vanessa,' she says, after the usual preamble to the start of a session. 'Have you been out anywhere since I saw you last?' Emma-Jane asks, disappointed to see the colour that was in her cheeks paled to an alabaster hue.

'Only the cemetery; to the shop for food but I bought nothing in the end; to put the bin out…' Vanessa wrings her hands. 'I started walking to her primary school at three o'clock, because that's what I used to do, to collect her. I forgot she—' Her voice breaks. The crack is as loud as crockery smashing on the floor.

'Three o'clock must be a difficult hour. Your mind has gotten used to a particular routine at that time. We get trained, conditioned, to do things at a certain time. Is there a new routine which could occupy that time? A new habit to replace the old, perhaps?'

Vanessa shakes her head. She looks thinner and tired, growing more waif-like with every visit. That glow in her aura following the dandelion dream has long gone. This Vanessa is a ghost of that self.

'I had another empty apology from a neighbour. More empty words. Sounds. They might mean something to them, but not to me. Meaningless. I wish they wouldn't say anything to me… What do they know about emptiness? Why are they sorry? How dare they speak Avril's name to me?'

'Go on.'

'I felt angry, and so I dropped some litter over the hedge when they'd gone. Silly, but I felt better for a while.'

Emma-Jane stays still, waiting for Vanessa to continue.

'Someone else, last week, told me to keep my chin up. Not a friend; someone with a nice face I used to chat to now and then. He said, "funny how life goes."' Her eyes widen. 'Funny?'

'You felt angry, and that's a normal, healthy reaction to grief. Dropping litter was a small liberation. When you experience loss, you will go through stages: denial, anger, bargaining, depression, acceptance. Some days you will feel all of them at once—'

'You've told me that before, Dr Glass. I know you want me to move on with my life, but I want to hang on to the old, good times. The special ones. I can't do anything else. Why would I replace my love for Avril with something else? I wouldn't be me then. Because she is no longer with us, it is right I am incomplete.' She sighs loudly. 'It's only right.'

'You are brave. There was no warning to prepare you for Avril's sudden death. You were happy and well. Then suddenly, everything changes. Your life looks and feels completely different. No one expects you to keep going like everything is as it was before. Be gentle with yourself, and maybe allow yourself some pleasure. A meal out, a trip somewhere in the fresh air, perhaps?'

'I don't want to. It's pointless. Might as well play a video game. How does buying a hot sausage roll from a café or a gastro pub or an expensive hair product make it any better?' Suddenly she looks up at the ceiling, like she's heard a gunshot and a bird is about to drop into her lap. 'I don't think you understand.'

'Help me to. Talk to me. All I know is the worst has already happened to you.'

Vanessa looks at her like she's shouted swear words. Her pale, heart-shaped face bobs above her tiny shoulders like a balloon. 'My friend, Edith, said I should have another child. I laughed when she said it. Imagined myself walking down the high street, with my purse in my handbag, nipping into a few shops to browse the babies. Hold them in my arms like I'm trying one for size. Edith's never had kids. Just dogs. She thinks it's like getting a new dog when the old one dies. I hadn't realised how much I don't like her till then.'

A lorry thunders by outside. Speeding, Emma-Jane thinks. She shows she is listening by sitting forward a little. 'I am not here to tell you to move on, or to put it behind you, to go on holiday, or buy a dog, or take up gardening or cooking, for that matter. Your friend, Edith, means well by encouraging you to get pregnant again, thinking that if you have another child you will feel like your old self. You may never feel like your old self again. Space and time, quiet, is perhaps what you need most, to allow you to know your loss and your grief.'

'When will I cry my last tears?' She looks down at herself, her narrow legs, the bony hands in her lap twisting a cotton handkerchief. It looks like it was her father's handkerchief, or a man's at least. The amount of cotton on that little lap catches Emma-Jane's eye. A dainty hanky wouldn't absorb the river of tears. She needs a man-sized one. A giant, for an elf of a person. 'There's nothing left of me except grief for her. To come here, to get out of bed and start a new day, it takes all my energy, like my heart doesn't work properly.'

'Are you eating well?' She already knows the answer. Vanessa's faded jeans look baggy. The thinness of those legs makes her tan, leather boots look like they belong to someone much taller. 'Even just a bit and often is a good start. Things you fancy. Do you like soup? It's easy to eat and digest, and fresh soup can be very nutritious.'

'I was going to eat before I came here, but then the post came. Something for Avril. I opened it. One Christmas, she wanted to adopt a donkey. They sent her a photograph and a thank-you note for the donation. I can't bring myself to cancel the subscription, to tell them she's gone. Her post is piled neatly at one end of the kitchen table.'

'Could you set yourself one goal? Perhaps to put the post in a drawer, or somewhere less prominent? It would be a step forward, when you're ready, to coming to terms with your loss.'

Vanessa shakes her head. ‘I dreamt about Avril last night but, as soon as I woke up, I couldn’t remember a single detail. I laid there with my eyes closed, hoping some recollection might come. It’s like she is robbed from me all over again. Missing. When will I accept I won’t find her again, and stop looking?’

‘Is there a way you can say a goodbye to Avril? A goodbye isn’t stopping you from loving her. You can give yourself permission to say goodbye and still love her. Love yourself, too. Be kind to yourself.’

‘I love myself. I do. I want to set myself free.’ She sobs.

Emma-Jane hides her disquiet as Vanessa cries.

‘Do you think I’ll know when I’ll give up waiting for that light at the end of the tunnel?’ She sighs. ‘I’m sick of looking down the tunnel. It’s dark, so dark, and long.’

'No one is expecting you to do anything except be and feel. If you want to cry, then cry. Take each day at a time. Can you picture Avril smiling and laughing?'

'I picture her a lot. I picture her on the other end of an imaginary phone, like you told me to. I wish she could answer.'

'Did you give writing your feelings any more thought?'

'Yes, I've made a start.'

'That's excellent! A new purpose can be a good thing. Well done! Perhaps bring a piece in if you'd like to. I would love to read it.'

'I'm rewriting some of Avril's favourite movies. Cinderella, Snow White, they all end happily. Avril loved those stories. I am rewriting them, just for adults, with a realistic ending,' she says, wiping her eyes.

'You are right. Life isn't a fairy tale. Sometimes it's convenient to forget that.'

'Forget? I can't go to so many places. The park, the local shop… She's in my head and my heart, and I don't want to get her out anyway, so there is nowhere else to go.'

Emma-Jane feels hollow after the hour with Vanessa. She emails Celia, her clinical supervisor, for an appointment to talk about her cases to offload and evaluate how she is handling Vanessa and Drew. It seems like there is no garment to fit Vanessa's grief. Drew is grieving too, in a different way. She finds the quietness of Vanessa's sad smile moving, and she respects the way she wears her pain like glass: transparent, fragile. So brave, to not wear a brave face; to wear a real, feeling one.

She glances at the time on her laptop to find it is almost nine o'clock. Lucy had left two hours ago. It would be sensible to lock the front door at this hour, but she doesn't plan to stay in the office for long. No wonder her head is pounding, because she can't remember when she last had a drink of water or something to eat.

Breakfast, she thinks, apart from biscuits and cake. The pain starts on one side of her head, then works its way around the circumference of her skull.

While the session is clear in her mind, she writes her notes detailing what they covered, whether her diagnosis still stands, and signs of progress or concern. She also monitors her own response to her client, in terms of transference. It's usual for her to type quickly and to push the keys firmly so it drowns any other sounds out.

The sharp beep of an alarm stops the typing and makes her jump. She glances behind her at the window and glimpses flashing red from a nearby building, a solicitor's. The alarm has gone off, as it has once before, and that had been a false alarm. She struggles to keep her focus.

Emma-Jane reads the notes she has made, pushing through the tiredness and headache to get the job done so she can get home, take a bath and relax.

Relevant issues: Vanessa is rewriting fairy tales. Revisiting Avril's childhood and changing the ending of the tales to 'realistic'. Lack of hope. Battling depression and lack of empathy with friend, Edith. Does she want to move on? Suicidal thoughts. Looks thinner. Talked about not looking for a light at the end of the tunnel. Not sure she wants to live in the present.

The door handle to her office turns. She watches the metal handle move forty-five degrees as a frown spreads over her forehead. It's probably Vanessa. Not more to deal with. The day gets longer. The handle keeps turning.

'Vanessa?'

Alarmed by the lack of response, Emma-Jane stands up from her desk, bile rising in her throat. With her eyes screwed up, she peers through the gap into the darkness.

'Is that you?'

She pushes the office chair behind her, surprised by the sound of fear in her voice and the tightness growing in her chest like a tumour. A scent, not entirely unfamiliar, catches her nose, tickling her memory. The wheels turn and slide as the chair skids behind her and then there is an agonising pause as the door is ajar.

'Hello?'

Her eyes narrow to focus on the black gap slowly appearing, darkness spilling into her office like black blood. The door was closed. Someone is there, waiting, standing behind the door, watching. Playing. Her hand lunges for the key in the lock just as the door flies open and she freezes like a deer. Her stomach twists in fright and then her expression is mystified and perplexed when she recognises the tall figure standing motionless in the doorway. The man associated with that scent is Drew Rogers.

'Dre—'

Relief washes over her for a second. Emma-Jane is about to speak his name but, before she can do anything else, Drew grabs her roughly round the neck, as if she were a stray, vicious dog. She thrashes in his firm grip, one which is resolute and cruel. Panicking, her legs kick out at the door and the desk, in desperation to be free.

'No!' Her tone is indignant, shocked. 'No!' she screams. Has her client suddenly lost his mind? Is this happening to me, right now, by him? 'Get off!'

Strands of hair catch in her mouth and, with her arms held tightly behind her back, they remain on her tongue until the chloroformed rag is placed firmly over her open mouth. The vile odour brings on another wave of thrashing, sending a pile of papers flying off the desk and onto the floor. The most recent hate letter from Drew tumbles to the carpet, landing face up. It was him. Then limpness, a loss of focus, like the office is moving away from her. His arms and fingers still tight, and the gag fat inside her mouth. Is he going to rape me? Her eyelids flutter like trapped butterflies: she can't scream. Powerless.

A final stab of fear jitters up her spine and then numbness pulls her down, as if under the seas, as the drug takes full effect. Moaning and becoming limp in his grip, she stops trying to fight back and lets her rag doll arms fall to her sides.

***

He lays her down on the carpet, a shape of entwined limbs and hair, and rearranges her so she is lying neatly, face up. He kicks her leather chair out of the way to make more room for her legs, which splay out. Drew switches the light off in the office and a ghostly glow from the computer is an echo in the room.

It is good that she fought. He wouldn't want a pushover to convert to his way of thinking. A feisty, intelligent woman. Looking at her now, she is attractive, in a dark-haired way – not his usual type. It's her learned mind which interests him. The pliable nature of it. The synapses and the neural pathways have been corrupted. He needs to change that. Make Dr Glass see clearly.

The alarm continues to sound down the street and the light flashes on and off through the blind, lighting the room in a scarlet hue, like the red-light district. There is no alarm to sound in this office building, except the internal wail and siren of Emma-Jane's frightened heartbeat. Drew smiles with triumph when her head lolls to one side, like she's been lobotomised. The red light flashes on and off over her face and body, across the desk, up the walls. It's almost erotic, he thinks, and lets the moment linger, savouring it, before the next stage. This is the last time he will see this office. Not that he'll miss it; especially that chair. There's another waiting for Dr Glass to sit in at his property. Not a comfortable one – the chair isn't about relaxation; it's about surrendering and listening. Concentrating.

Dr Glass had talked confidently on local radio about that woman, Angela Lamb, who killed herself and her son, Teddy. She defended the monster. Sympathised. The thought puts a bitter taste in his mouth. He spits on her. The glob of saliva lands on her neck.

'Good.'

But, knowing she won't be unconscious for long, he focuses on what he needs to do to eliminate her records of him: his address, phone number. Drew wriggles the mouse to her computer, bringing it back to life. He puts his name in the search box, wanting to delete his contact details. Time is precious; he has to get her into the car and to the house before she comes round. Abruptly, he yanks the filing cabinet drawers open and rifles through the papers, but he finds nothing with his name on it.

'Fuck.' He scratches his head. Then, an idea comes to him. He clicks on email and sends a brief message to Lucy. He smiles, thinking trusting, gullible Lucy will believe it. The woman has her uses.

Late night yet again. Taking a few days off from work. Need a holiday.

Would she sign it 'love'? Probably. Her number one fan.

Love, Emma-Jane x

The floor is covered in papers that had toppled from her desk, which he collects into a neat pile. He returns the upturned pot of pens and pencils knocked over by the tussle to its proper position. Lastly, he puts the two hate letters he sent her into his back pocket. Looking down at the slack features on her face, her arms and legs akimbo, he thinks, Dr Glass isn't so respectable now. A grin spreads across his face. He's got a few things he wants to teach her.

His letters were a little tasty starter before the main meal, which she will enjoy from a location of his choosing. The letters took time, care, and there was an element of risk with hand-delivering them, especially to her house. All that glass – how perfect that Dr Glass should live in a glass box. You'd think she'd have a clearer perspective on life, but no.

It's taken several months of planning to get this far, and several pointless hours with her, in this very room, talking, talking, talking. Did she listen? Soon, she will spend hour after hour on a chair. One she will be tied to, and cuffed to for good measure, to be sure he has her full attention. He deserves nothing less.

He bends down and strokes her thick, black hair like she's a pet cat. Drew notices her nails are painted a dark purple hue and the thumb nail is chipped. A small imperfection. Did the fall do that? This time next week they will look different again.

'Ready for your little holiday, are we?'

Not taking any chances, he handcuffs her wrist to the heavy wooden desk before he moves his Range Rover. Mud has conveniently smeared the number plates. Ten minutes later, he pulls up as close to the office building as possible. The streets are quiet now, and the stuttering street light lends him a helping hand to move in the shadows.

He dresses Emma-Jane in his dark overcoat and pulls a cap over her head. If someone were to see him heave her into his Range Rover they might be forgiven for thinking the person is worse for wear, and Drew is doing a good turn in helping them get home. A smart car, and smart dress. It helps.

'There we go,' he says loudly over the sound of the alarm, in case anyone is watching. 'Soon get you home to bed. No more whiskies for you!'

In the leather passenger seat, he fixes her seat belt before turning on the radio to Classic FM. The empty house is only a few miles away, bur far enough to enjoy Beethoven's 'Symphony No. 5', followed by Vivaldi's 'Four Seasons'. The smell of chloroform in his recently valeted car is a bit annoying, but needs must.

He turns up the volume of the radio. His mood is buoyant as he pulls away, the red light and alarm still flashing, still sounding – but no one cares enough to stop or stare.

Chapter 12

The worry of his mobile phone ringing at the late hour reshapes AJ's body into an exclamation mark. Erect from his bed, he travels to the small landing where his phone is, resting like a toad in the dark.

'Who the hell is that?' Hannah asks from the bedroom.

'Drew,' he says, sounding more alert than he feels as he answers the phone. 'No worries. I was awake anyway.'

'Bullshit,' she mumbles and sighs, pulling up the duvet to her chin. Drew talks for several minutes. She thinks, No doubt giving orders, listing instructions. Why doesn't he call Pete? It's always bloody AJ. He's too soft, that's his problem. Too decent.

'Downstairs?' AJ asks. 'Yeah, we'll get on to that tomorrow. Where are you staying then? … No worries … Not a problem. Bye.'

Hannah switches on the sidelight to see AJ's boxers are bunched up under his balls. He scratches them, looking perplexed.

'What did he want?' she asks, as he climbs back into bed after readjusting himself.

'I think he's a bit pissed. Didn't realise the time. He wants me and Pete to get the rest of the farmhouse sorted, now he's moved out proper like. Honestly, Hannah, he was slurring, and at one point he hiccupped. I almost laughed.'

'Where's he living now, then?'

'He didn't say. He's only just moved his stuff out. One of his other properties, I expect. There's four or five of them. To be honest with you, I'll be glad to be away from the bloody farmhouse. It gives me the creeps, all those empty rooms and outbuildings.'

'It's not like you to be creeped out by something like that. What's with you, AJ?'

'I just don't much like the old farmhouse, to be honest. I prefer to work outside, and Kat – that young woman I told you about – she keeps pestering me and Pete about where Drew is living, his new phone number... She's sniffing around the place asking questions, like a bloody sniffer dog on heat.'

'Tell her to get lost!'

'Drew's my boss. His personal life is his own business, and he's pretty stressed out at the minute anyway, but his shit stinks as far as I'm concerned, and I'm getting caught in it.' AJ drops his head on the pillow like it weighs a ton.

'Have you told Drew about her pestering you?' she says with an accusing gaze. 'He needs to know if she's coming round all the time. Honestly, AJ, I think Drew would want to know.'

'No, I haven't said, because the bloke isn't my best friend or anything. If she doesn't take the hint soon I might, in case it gets out of hand. He's obviously dumped her, and she doesn't like it. Pete thinks she comes around at night, because the barriers were moved, but I don't know about that.'

'Really? She could go to prison for stalking Drew. I read about that in my weekly mag. For her to be calling round after what's happened sounds wrong to me. Insensitive, at the very least. I mean… After. Anyway, this bloke—'

'Are you hungry? I fancy toast, or something? I'll make it.'

'It's one o'clock in the morning. I've got work tomorrow; so have you, for that matter.'

'Piss off. I fancy jam on toast.' He flings back the duvet and pulls on one of his old T-shirts, with a pint of Guinness on the front. 'Do you want some or not?'

Hannah puts her arms above her head on the pillow and grins. Her boobs peek and bounce above the duvet.

'I'll take that as a yes.'

One bulb in the kitchen has gone, so it's a dim, gloomy light, but enough to switch the grill and the kettle on and butter four pieces of white bread under. It's one of Nigella Lawson's tips for delicious toast – the double buttering, with a touch of salt. As soon as the toast is done, he butters it a second time and races upstairs with a tray.

'You'd better be awake!' AJ calls as he climbs the stairs, the aroma of warm toast making him salivate.

'There's not much chance of getting some kip around here while you're banging around down there! Are you sure you haven't invited Drew over?'

He feeds her a slice of toast. 'You know me better than that!'

She likes to be fed, like a tamed wolf. 'Mmm,' she says, and licks her lips, conjuring images of the moon. 'Delicious.'

Not a howl from a wolf, but a secret shared. A rivulet of butter runs down her chin, which she wipes off with a finger. She licks and nuzzles like a wolf. AJ feels the blood returning to his penis, an ache. He feeds her a second slice, still warm and buttery, the colour and heat of sunshine. 'You do something to me, Hannah.'

Hannah passes him a mug of tea from the tray and takes one herself, which she slurps loudly. The surge of blood in his penis drops like a cold temperature, but the static of her is loud in his brain. He puts his mug and plate on the carpet and reaches for the sidelight to switch it off, wanting to be close to her, to listen to her heartbeat. Hannah puts her mug down too and snuggles up to AJ with her head on his chest.

'I love you, Hannah,' he says. 'I'm going to make you proud one day. I am.'

'Silly!' she says, stroking his chest. 'I already am, and I love you! I couldn't do what you do. You're good with your hands! Not many men can say that, and especially not the men I work with all day long, in suits and ties and manicured nails, who are so fussy about everything.'

'Fussy about what?'

'Parking in the same spot, for instance. Or, having their coffee break at the same time every day. Eating the same bloody type of biscuit, even! I just find them a bit prissy, not real men, like you, who needs a bath at the end of the working day and has muscles from hard graft, not a stupid machine in the back bedroom.'

AJ laughs and cuddles her. 'Do you remember that episode of Only Fools and Horses? The last one, when they became millionaires by chance. God, that would be amazing. You know, to have your luck turn like that after years of scraping and grafting.'

'I love Rodney.'

He laughs, remembering a short story he'd read in one of her weekly magazines. The theme was basically that we are all lovable rogues and insecure monsters, hoping someone will find our quirky or our monstrous side lovable. Even people like Rodney find love and fortune, becoming a Drew Rogers of this world. 'Listen, we gotta keep saving and then buy a place to do up. We would have to put up with the dust and mess, but it'll be worth it when we sell it and buy the next one. I can do brickwork, carpentry, some basic plumbing. You'd do a grand job of the interior design stuff.'

'I'd love that! Curtains, and soft furnishings. Betsy at work buys loads from TK Maxx; you know, designer stuff, but on the cheap. Her house is amazing!'

'What's your dream home?'

Hannah sighs, and he is more aware of her warm breath and body than he cares to be now. A jellyfish beside her. Suddenly, she laughs. 'You know, nothing too fancy. I like cosy. A cottage would be nice for just the two of us. I like beams and fireplaces and uneven floorboards.'

'Sounds like a builder's nightmare!' he says, laughing, hoping she can keep loving a version of himself without edges or weaknesses, like the self he knows and sometime hates, the self he sometimes cuts with a razor in the morning to state his feelings and make himself as imperfect, as he knows he is. 'I can live with that, as long as you're happy.'

'But we're going to go on holiday, aren't we? Somewhere hot. I'd like Greece. The beaches in Corfu look amazing. Just a week of sunshine is enough.'

The corners of AJ's mouth tighten. With it being the middle of the night and feeling uncertain about where future pay cheques will come from, all the summers ahead appear as a desert, with him labouring his way up one sand dune of a thousand feet after another, his workman's boots sinking into the sand with every stride he takes. The image is so vivid he can hear the wind and feel the sweat drying on his back.

The room settles in readiness for slumber as the aromas of toast and butter and pipe dreams fade into the four corners of their rented house. Hannah's breathing becomes slow and deep but sleep is a mirage for AJ, who turns on his side and holds his pillow to his head in the vain hope it will stop whirring. In the morning he will dress, eat a cooked breakfast, mop up the egg with a slice of bread, get into his grimy white van and put in a hard day's work lining Drew Roger's pockets by improving one of his many properties. Then he will come home, knackered and hungry, and watch the television until he finds the energy to make a meal for them both; something quick and cheap, like spaghetti and meatballs.

He rolls onto his other side, away from Hannah, and stares at the red digits on the alarm clock. The feeling in his stomach can't be hunger, not after the evening meal and then the toast they've just eaten. What is it? He sees their regular Thursday night meal – the pale noodle flesh of spaghetti on a plate beside minced meat, smeared in blood-red tomato sauce. What is it that will make him feel better? His belly will not feel full until he's got enough money to not worry about getting sick or losing his job, not earning a month's pay and being sunk under that red line that gets harder and harder to cross every month, like the finishing line for a lad in an egg and spoon race who keeps tripping over his feet and dropping his egg.

Failure. Sometimes he thinks he can smell it on himself.

It's in the corner of his eyelids some nights, when he is too tired to blink, let alone speak to Hannah. There's a weight on his eyelids now, an antique coin which belongs to a billionaire, pushing his lids down. Tiredness. It's there all the time. Even when he wakes up. He's not even thirty yet. What will it be like when he's fifty, sixty, seventy?

School. He's been thinking about it lately. The reports his teachers sent home. If he'd tried harder, would it be different now? All that ink, that paper, those classroom walls and a strange person standing there at the front, like an omen. Is his van, his toolbox and his muscles, his strong, toughened hands, the sum of him?

He strokes his bicep; firm and bulging from labouring, not hours in a gym. Earnt. Not glistening under LED lights in a fancy mirror-clad place beside babes in Lycra with hair in pigtails bouncing like a rabbit's tail left and right. Graft. Hard graft. Where will it get him?

Chapter 13

On her way to work, Lucy distracts herself by checking her emails on her phone. It surprises her to receive Emma-Jane's email telling her she is taking an impromptu holiday, but she has worked some long hours lately. Good for her.

That's not the most pressing thing on her mind, however, having listened to the local news on Shropshire Radio in the car. Lucy fights the tears pricking at her eyes as she strides from the car park to the office and the tragic news begins to sink in. She puts a hand over her mouth to keep the pain inside as she jogs along the pavement and, as soon as she steps inside her office and closes the door, breaks down into floods of tears.

Ross is dead.

Ross, attentive and doting beside Jennifer. She can see them sitting side by side now, holding hands, in these very chairs. She thinks of Jennifer in her chunky red and green beaded necklace. A mere pendant would not have been any kind of statement, not even a full stop. She can hear her jangling and the swaying of her hoop earrings. That, and the bounce of her ample bosom, jostling with the banter of her clothes, the clashing colours, fabrics, patterns, buttons. Is Jennifer dressed in monochrome now? She'd once said she likes to play her accessories loudly, like trumpets. Is the bugle playing 'Taps' now? Is she wearing her signature plum lipstick like a bruise? They were so in love. Poor, poor Ross, and Jennifer.

Lucy doesn't know whether to sit, or to stand, or go for a walk, or do nothing. Hide. Run. Is she to blame, somehow? If only Emma-Jane were here to talk to. It's futile, but she checks Emma-Jane's office is empty, just to be sure. Seeing that it is, next she dials Jennifer's number, and it immediately clicks to voicemail. The first time she hangs up, then she rings again to leave a message of condolence. It's something. What else can she do?

'Jennifer, it's Lucy. I'm so sorry. I've just heard about Ross. It's terrible. I don't know what to say. Please, ring me if you can. Take care. Bye.'

Moments later the mobile rings, showing a number Lucy doesn't recognise, but she answers it on the second ring. Her heart thuds. If it is Jennifer, what can she say? Will Jennifer be angry with her?

'Hello? Lucy speaking.'

'It's Jennifer.' The tone is emotionless, entirely out of character. If she hadn't given her name Lucy would not have recognised the small voice on the other end of the phone. It's almost childlike, like she has magically shrunk.

'Jennifer! Oh God, thank you for ringing me back. I'm so sorry about Ross. I've only just heard. It's—'

'The police interviewed me. They questioned me. The officer spoke to me like I was a fucking cannibal or something. Like it was my fault! I love Ross! I can't believe it!' She sobs and Lucy waits, one hand over her mouth. 'I won't be charged. They know it was an accident, but they made me feel responsible!'

Lucy doesn't know what to say next and is ashamed, in part, by feeling relieved Jennifer isn't angry or blaming her. 'I'm so sorry. Wh—'

'It's my fault,' she wails. 'I suffocated him. One minute we were hugging, and then… squashings… crushed under my… I wish I was dead.' And she hangs up.

Lucy immediately tries to ring her back, but there's no answer. Has squashing killed Ross? Did her weight block his windpipe? Did the air in his lungs run out while she was sat right on top of his face? She puts her head in her hands, hating the image, and hating the anxiety caused by knowing about their sexual preferences and playing a part in them by making Jennifer heavier. Does that make me culpable?

'Oh my God.' She dials Emma-Jane's phone, desperate to talk to her friend. What should she do? The phone clicks to voicemail so she leaves a message asking her to ring back and hangs up.

Ashamed by the selfish thought that she might be culpable, she thinks of Ross and remembers a quotation she'd read, something about eating being touch carried to the bitter end. How true that turns out to be, she thinks sadly. Lucy paces the office. What do I do now? My reputation. My fragile confidence. Ross is dead.

Perhaps she isn't cut out for this work? She should return to Carlisle, live with her parents for a time, while she sorts her head out. Lucy looks again at the chairs Ross and Jennifer had so recently sat in, held hands in, talked excitedly about their future in. Soon he will be in a casket, motionless, in the dark, buried. His heart still intact, but frozen. His hands, cold.

Unable to spend another minute in her office, she throws a few things into her handbag and heads home to pack a bag for a few days away. The further away from Shrewsbury, the better. Half an hour later she points her car north, toward Carlisle and her parents' house. Running, yes, I'm running. But who wouldn't?

On the way she phones her clients and postpones them. It isn't the professional thing to do but she is in no fit state to work. Goodness knows what advice she'd dish out. After Jennifer and Ross she doubts she will have the confidence to open her door again. No wonder Emma-Jane needs a break, she thinks, dealing with death and grief day after day, hour after hour.

The journey to Carlisle is one she knows like the back of her hand. Usually, she phones her mum just as she leaves the A69 because the route from that point to their house is less than thirty minutes. She usually says she is less than an hour away, preferring to arrive in good time so her mum doesn't fret. Since she turned eighty-six she's become a worrier.

Lucy occupies her whirring mind by imagining sitting at the kitchen table with them, tucking into Mum's home-made Victoria sponge cake. Dad slurps his tea, holding forth on some subject or other and then Mum plans the Sunday roast, even though it's only Thursday. The image is comforting. Hopefully, Jennifer will have a family to comfort her in her hour of need.

An hour later, Lucy has a change of heart about immediately going to her parents' house. She decides against ringing them to tell them about her imminent arrival. It can wait for a few hours. She turns right towards Hexham instead, and parks in a familiar lay-by with easy access to the footpath which runs alongside Hadrian's Wall. The sun is shining, and it is a quiet and beautiful place to get some exercise and de-stress.

She changes into walking gear in the lay-by and packs a rucksack with a few supplies and extra layers. Her phone is on the passenger seat. It's been on silent for the journey, and it's been a refreshing change not to be a slave to messages, but she takes it with her, just in case.

The terrain is largely flat at first, and wonderfully serene after the booming in her brain. The events of the day begin to lose their jaggedness after an hour and a half of brisk walking. A buzzard's lonely cry from above announces its orbit before it lands on the wall ahead and remains motionless. Its necklace of feathers is beautiful, she thinks. Perhaps it's looking for its mate for life. Like me. Like Jennifer will.

Lucy likes the freedom of rambling without a fixed route, just to walk one way and then back the same. Keep it simple. Not that she has an OS map with her, anyway. She knows the area fairly well, having walked here with family and friends. During the peak of summer, they tended to avoid popular sections of Hadrian's Wall – like Segedunum, the most Eastern fort on the Wall – because tourists would flock there, changing the atmosphere of the place. Over the years, Lucy has found the least popular sections to walk, where it is possible to not see another soul for miles on end. Bliss.

It's the rugged, remote landscape she likes, and the simple beauty of fields grazed by sheep rolling for miles. Large chunks of the walk are edged by Hadrian's Wall: made from hand-carved stone, weathered by storms and wrapped in moss, almost 2,000 years old. She walks for several hours in the company of the remains of forts, the skulls of sheep who didn't last the winter and distant farms. The solitude and isolation among the crags and stiles, beside the heritage of the Roman wall, is a perfect antidote to a chaotic, stressed mind. It's quieter, but not quiet.

Ross. I can't believe he's dead.

With each footstep, though, Lucy puts distance between herself and poor Ross, and the professional conflict she'd felt all along in treating Jennifer. Now Ross is dead, and there is nothing she can do about that. As Emma-Jane says, there are people through Lucy's door who should go through hers instead, but you can't force them. Perhaps she and Emma-Jane need to intervene, to work together, but it's easier said than done. Lucy decides to text Emma-Jane to let her know where she is but, as soon as she reaches for her phone, she sees the battery is dead.

'Shit. I'm an idiot.'

Annoyed with herself, she stuffs the useless phone in her rucksack and keeps walking, even more briskly than before, because she is annoyed. Gradually, the temperature is falling, which tells her she must soon turn back the way she came, but not just yet. The sun is going down, throwing her shadow in front of her for company. Lucy strides towards a lonely tree, suddenly feeling alone herself now that the light is fading and the landscape is losing its colour.

Even the grey stones of the Roman wall take on an austere, barren face, while the heathers and mosses pale into the semi-dark. The tree looks both beautiful and forlorn in the fading light; its branches extend like arms and the twigs of fingers point to the sky and to the earth, to heaven and hell.

The darkness is coming.

If Lucy hadn't been enjoying her walk so much she wouldn't have walked so far in one direction. Ten miles, or more. That'll be twenty by the time she's back at the car.

'Oh God.'

Panic doesn't set in because of the sound of birds hiding out of sight, and she can just make out the dots of sheep on the skyline. It's wild and beautiful. Nearby, there is a bothy, a stone cottage now dilapidated; shelter for animals, at one time. She moves closer to see it better and feels like she has gone back in time to a gentler way of life.

Then she knows it is the Robin Hood Tree on the horizon; not a nebulous shape but unmistakably Sycamore Gap, and, given that she's walked so far, it would be silly not to see it close up. It rises from the contours of the landscape like a giant, taking her back to the framed photograph in Drew's farmhouse. The one Evie had taken.

Local. That's what Drew had said. Nesscliffe.

James loved trees.

Even before she reaches Sycamore Gap, Lucy remembers where she'd seen Evie's photograph before that day with Drew. It was in the newspaper, and above it was the tragic article about a mother who took her own life and that of her son, James. Evie Rogers. They had died here, at this very spot. A rope, a modern-day hanging. Their throats and lungs had given in. Evie Rogers had hired a 4x4 to drive them as close to Sycamore Gap as possible so that it wasn't far to walk with James and the step ladders. The poor walkers who discovered the dangling corpses found toys at the base of the tree. Dropped teddies, probably fallen from a height, from James's hand, when…

And the cross. Lucy remembers the wooden cross from the photograph.

James loved trees. Drew told her that, but not the rest. Drew's wife. Dead, not divorced, not abroad. Dead and buried.

Lucy puts her hand to her mouth to stifle a sob.

Here.

She shivers now. The tree branches seem to bow down as if in mourning, weighed by terrible sadness and understanding. The little cross Lucy saw in the photograph is gone, but sadness is fixed in place by the roots of the tree and the knowledge Lucy has. Neither will perish.

‘Why didn’t you say something to me, Drew?’ She shakes her head, struggling to process the tragedy. She puts her head in her hands; the horror of understanding, the darkness and the isolation exacerbated by not having a useable phone.

‘Oh God,’ she says, tearful now.

The starry sky is all twinkling silver glass eyes watching, from afar, waiting to see what she will do next.

‘I’m such an idiot.’

The wind through the branches sighs as images of Drew, Ross and Jennifer click through her mind. The low, sad sound of the wind sends her eyes up to the dark network of branches and light-green leaves. Feeling self-pity and desperation, Lucy closes her eyes. Her skin tingles.

The blonde, beautiful wife to a successful businessperson. That was the gist of what she remembers reading. A young mother, and a blond little boy. Found hanging from Sycamore Gap. Her stomach churns. Maternal filicide. Lucy even knows the correct term, from Emma-Jane's published article on the subject in that scientific journal.

Poor Drew.

Why a mother would deliberately kill her own offspring makes no sense to Lucy, though she knows it happens in the wild with almost a third of other mammal species. The bleating sheep on the nearby grassland seem to mourn the human tragedy and echo the sound of sadness in stereo. She sheds a tear for Drew's loss, for the dead mother and child, and for herself, for almost falling for someone who isn't who she thought he was. A widower, someone who didn't let her see all of the rooms in the farmhouse. Was it because, behind closed doors, the memory of what was once loved inside is painful? Drew, a man who kept his past a secret. Why?

Why pretend Evie and James were still alive, knowing all along they were dead and buried? The thoughts unsettle her. She hopes Emma-Jane has helped him deal with the tragedy. All that loss… Not one, but two members of the family. At once. How terrible. To wake up one day and your life will never be the same again. Lucy knows grief after losing Martin. If only Drew had opened up about it, they might have helped each other.

She sits down beneath the tree's canopy to pull out an extra top and a beanie hat from her rucksack and adds them to her layers. She is shivering; from shock, and the temperature has dropped again, more so under the shade of the sycamore, perfect for protection from the elements for animals. Her nose runs from the cold and from crying. It's a disgusting thing to do but, without a tissue or company, she uses her tongue to wipe the snot away; as much of it as she can.

Perhaps Lucy is sitting where Evie and James sat in their final moments? She rests her back against the sturdy trunk, wishing it were a friend, a warm human to lean against, with smooth skin and a sense of safety that comes from companionship. She misses human company as much as the sun in that moment. If only Emma-Jane were here. Even the white phosphorescent face of the moon is blocked by the leafy canopy and network of branches, some as thin as the bones of a skeleton.

She shuffles forwards from under the lone tree. The remnants of clouds are barely perceptible in the sky above. They could almost be a vapour trail from a plane jetting off on holiday, perhaps to a warm climate. Getting away from it all. Are you flying off somewhere nice, Emma-Jane? I wish I were with you. The branches stir, this time vigorously, and a symphony of sighs and moans begins, broken by the sudden sound of a child's voice in her head. Did James plead with his mummy to remove the rope? To take him home to Daddy? Did he beg and wail, Mummy! Mummy! I don't want to play anymore.

James's name is luminous in her overactive mind: it could be written on the wall, on the trunk and in the sky in sparkling white lights. The tree hasn't moved an inch but it feels as though the branches have wrapped themselves around her wrists and ankles like handcuffs. If only her imagination would stop working, stop painting a grizzly picture of a child's corpse dangling from this branch like a Gothic Christmas decoration. The sheep bleat and the sudden forlorn sound in the dark makes her head jerk. Lucy is suddenly sick and keeps on being sick until there's only bile and retching. The stench of Ribena, coffee and the remains of muesli churn her stomach.

Exhausted from the long drive and even longer walk, then the puking, and with a body starved of food and water, Lucy forces herself to take several cautious sips from her water bottle and then wipes her eyes and nose to try to get a grip of herself. The problem is, Lucy is completely drained of all energy. Sapped.

Shivering, she rubs her arms and pulls her coat over her hands. Once she feels better, she'll walk back. It'll take time, but she's fit; she can do it. Twenty miles. It's a distance she's walked before. Her eyelids feel heavy and heavier. She closes her eyes and falls into a deep sleep.

When Lucy wakes, two hours later, her hands and face hurt with the cold from a hard frost. Although her stomach is rumbling from hunger she can barely breathe, let alone eat. The full moon and frost cast the landscape in an auroral light, duping her into thinking it is morning at first, but then she sees the twinkling grass and brittle blades are white and even Hadrian's Wall has a ghostly glow. Low-hanging cobwebs are intricate lace patterns festooned between branches, some as tenuous as kitten's whiskers. Fallen leaves sparkle with frost in a parody of Christmas festivities.

She puts her hands inside her coat to warm them up and blinks to wake herself up properly. The temperature is so low her breath hangs in the air like smoke. Stars pepper the vast sky so far above; Lucy has never felt smaller and more alone in the universe.

'Hello!' she shouts. 'Anybody there?'

A sheep bleats. In that moment, she wishes she could push her face into its wool and wrap her arms around its well-fed padded body to ground herself, to be sure of the world she is living in so she doesn't disappear into the horizon.

'Come on, Lucy,' she says, her breath hanging in the air. 'Get up, get walking, get back to the car.'

Slowly, she stands, her legs stiff from sitting in an awkward position for too long. The remote rural landscape feels hostile now; she longs to see rooftops, traffic lights and flashing neon signs to takeaways and shops. Anything to punctuate, tame and colour the planet. If only she could smell fish and chips, with salt and vinegar and a squirt of ketchup!

Then, Emma-Jane's voice and face pop into her head. They were at the office, when Emma-Jane had said that Drew was divorced. Drew had said 'ex-wife' when they had dinner. Not dead wife.

Lucy stares at the tree. But that's not what happened. He's not divorced. A widower. He's a liar.

Emma-Jane probably doesn't know the truth either. The unease spreads up from her stomach into her throat. Maybe Drew hasn't told his therapist. But why? Her stomach clenches again.

Lucy runs for half an hour under the stars – loaded with history, a past which is following her every step – and then slows to a jog until her legs and lungs are too tired to keep moving at speed. To cover the miles as quickly as she can she walks, then jogs, walks, then jogs, at intervals. The moon is still eerily bright in the sky, lighting the way back to the car. She has no idea how long it will take or what will happen to her next, but she will not stop moving until she knows where Emma-Jane is.

By the time Lucy returns to her car she is crying with exhaustion and worry. The smallest thing is too much to bear. First, she can't find a phone charger, and then she can't get the seat belt on, but she has her car keys and a bottle of water. Think positive. Get back to Shrewsbury. Don't cry. That's as far as she can think right now, so she points the car south and drives, hanging on to one thread of good fortune – which is, her parents aren't worrying about where the hell she has got to.

Chapter 14

When Emma-Jane comes to it's as if she's watching a film made with a handheld camera. The hand that clasps it is shaking too much. Gradually, the film jerks, and then, when she realises it isn't a video, the wind is knocked out of her. She notices the Anaglypta wallpaper in an unhomely lounge stripped of furniture. Cuffed and tied to a chair, this is her cell and, worryingly, the wallpaper is splattered with dried blood, like the scattering of stars in the night sky. Her blood? Looking down at herself she doesn't appear to be bleeding, but those splashes of blood are a portentous constellation she cannot navigate by.

Above her head, the naked light bulb does nothing to alleviate the gloom of the room, which is heightened by the sound of rainfall outside the curtained window – that, and the proximity of her captor in her peripheral vision, asleep on a mattress in one corner of this hateful bare room.

Drew Rogers. A client. A successful man. Before she speaks, Emma-Jane tries to process what has happened to her, the chain of events leading to this abduction. The smell of the room she finds herself in is something new. Besides her own personal body odour and the reek of urine from having had no other option but to pee herself at some point, there is a distinct smell of washing powder from Drew's clothes. Rose, or jasmine or something. She imagines pink packaging. Her hands shake within the handcuffs, but she can recognise the positive potential of having a captor with scrupulous self-maintenance. It hints of self-respect, self-regard, therefore he might be open to discussion about the consequences of abducting her. Perhaps?

Not so long ago there had been the sound of a washing machine, and perhaps a dryer, which had connected her with reality and domesticity. A house, a flat, a home. He is clean. He is clean. It gives her a whiff of hope that Drew hasn't lost his mind entirely and might see sense. There's a cat flap somewhere. It rattles. To see a cat, someone's well-fed cat right now, would be comforting.

If he lost his mind, why has he brought me here? Did Drew send me those hate letters? He must have. But why?

The ceiling is stained a grey colour, presumably from age or cigarette smoke, which might explain why the cover of the smoke alarm has been removed and the wires wriggle naked from the ceiling. The two kitchen chairs in the room are wooden, splattered with flecks of white paint. Her abduction has been planned. This empty property, his packed bag, the sessions they shared leading up to her abduction. Did he court Lucy for information about her habits?

Lucy. A surge of warmth and hope passes through her veins at the thought of her friend, somewhere out there.

Meanwhile, with every passing minute, Emma-Jane stinks. Sweat first, then urine, then shit. Why degrade me this way? Have I wounded him?

As thoughts fire into her brain, she sweats. The combined increase in body heat, her own waste, and the stifling heat in the room make for a potent stench. He must enjoy being in control of her habits: when she is clean and when she is filthy. Like now.

Not wanting to alert her captor that she is awake, she swivels her eyeballs as far right as they will travel. His shoes are tan and clean. Expensive. Definitely leather. The socks are navy, with some kind of logo on the side. This well-dressed man had penned those hateful letters and drugged her. How deceptive appearances can be.

The last thing she remembers is being in her office late at night. Was there an alarm? Bit by bit, she remembers talking to Vanessa and feeling concerned about the deepness of her depression and unwavering grief. Then Emma-Jane remembers typing up her notes on the computer.

Drew came to her office. Must have waited for her to be alone. She sees herself sitting at her desk, typing, looking at the computer. Then she looks at the door handle. It was turning. She sees herself standing up. The door opens.

How long ago was it that she had been in her own office? Drew wakes, sits up on the mattress and rubs his hands over his face. That familiar face, and yet, a stranger's.

'Hello, Dr Glass.'

'Drew,' she says. 'Drew Rogers. Why? Why am I here?'

He laughs and rises slowly from the mattress, straightening out his trousers as he approaches and then settling in a chair directly opposite the one she is strapped to. 'You cut to the chase now. Welcome to your new abode. Shall I call you Dr Glass, or something else?'

'That depends on why I'm here.' She waits for an answer, which doesn't arrive. 'Something makes me think it's not for free therapy, so you may as well call me Emma-Jane.' She studies his face, surprised at how handsome he is, even after a rough night's sleep on a mattress on the floor. A monster of a man would befit the situation and make it easier to accept. 'Are you going to tell me what the hell I am doing here?' She tries to lean forward, only to find her torso is strapped tightly to the chair. There's no wriggle room. Tar of anxiety clogs her veins.

'How does it feel to be in the chair, to be the one required to trust, to be open and honest about your deepest and darkest secrets? Here I am, listening; an interesting twist on our usual situation, wouldn't you say?'

'Is that it? Role reversal? I didn't know drama was your thing.'

He raises an eyebrow.

'Am I to be punished for something I have done, or not done? I have only tried to be a good therapist and help you, Drew.' She stares at the curtains, frustrated she doesn't know what time of day it is, or even what day it is. 'Am I here because I failed you in some way? Or because I am a therapist?'

'There's no rush for you to know. You will see.'

'Is this about control?' she asks, rattling her cuffs. 'I want to know!'

'This is not like your sessions, spent with half an eye on the clock. We have way more than an hour of each other's time, so stop asking questions. I will tell you when I'm good and ready.'

She strains to listen to sounds beyond the living room and yearns to hear a car, a voice, footsteps, something to tether her to a place in space and time instead of floating in a void. Are there people nearby? Someone will notice she is not where she should be. It's only a matter of time before she's discovered. Lucy. Lucy will know something is amiss.

'Where are we?'

'This is one of my many properties. Empty, obviously. Between tenants. I put my team on hold just for you. I can see you're happy about that. Once we're done they'll come in, make the place as good as new for the next owners. I'll sell it. I'm done with my lettings business.'

'Is that part of the plan you spoke about?'

He grins at her. 'Yes, as a matter of fact, it is. So, you do listen. Bravo,' he says, clapping. 'And remember. I'm impressed. It was fun to talk to you, really. You're very patient, and you are better than some, I'm sure. My wife saw therapists, lots of them. They never made the slightest bit of difference. A complete waste of her time and my money. I told her as much.'

The sound of a heavy-goods vehicle in the near distance gives her hope she isn't far from civilisation. Drew notices her twitch of hope. 'Don't get too excited about being discovered any time soon. I took the liberty of using your computer to email Lucy. Told her you're enjoying a holiday, after a lot of stress at work. You've been working late a lot recently.'

So he has been watching her. A creeping chill works its way up to her neck. She fights the urge to sigh heavily, not wanting to give him the satisfaction of knowing he read her thoughts. While moving is out of the question, her mind is performing, and that is all she has to hold on to right now. Her throat is dry from lack of water and anxiety, causing her head to throb from dehydration. The room is hot, airless. 'Can I have a glass of water?' The last thing she needs is to feel dizzy or faint, and have her faculties fizzle out.

He opens a small bottle of water, sips it and then pours it straight into her gaping mouth. She can't swallow quickly enough so the water trickles down her neck, chin and onto her blouse. When the bottle is almost half empty, he stops pouring and sits down again, watching her closely.

'You needed that, didn't you?' he says, smiling.

'Thank you.' She licks her lips to savour every drop of water. 'Why am I here, Drew? Come on.'

His eyes are so dark and unblinking they could be holes. Just like in her office, he doesn't just make eye contact. He holds it. 'Don't you know?'

She flinches when he bends down behind the chair and removes the weights so he can swivel the chair and her around to face the kitchen. Then he drags the chair closer, so she can see the kitchen surfaces, the oven and even the back door. This is a whole new horizon for her. 'Like the view?'

'It's a change.'

'I enjoy baking for relaxation. You can watch how it's done.'

Judging by the vein throbbing on the side of his head, blood is hammering in his system. He cracks an egg on one side of the glass mixing bowl and expertly separates the yolk. After adding the rest of the ingredients, he beats the mixture into submission and dips a finger in to taste. The cake mixture perches on the end of his tongue, taking up one of the three inches available. The sweet taste cracks a smile on his otherwise sour face.

'A little boy has twice as many taste buds as an adult,' he says, 'but there are still several thousand to send signals to the brain; be they salty, sugary, spicy, savoury or sour. A tongue is as unique as a fingerprint.'

Seeing his controlled rage in the rough unscrewing of jars and the deft use of the knife through the butter, she doesn't let her fear show. The surreal nature of the experience is so terrible it is almost laughable. Each movement he makes is sure, precise.

'I made James a cake for Halloween. He loved it! Orange and chocolate cake, decorated with ghosts made from white chocolate.'

Cocoa powder, caster sugar and icing sugar are in view. 'What kind of cake are you making?'

'It's called Blood-Red Velvet Cake. Three layers, cream cheese frosting and blood-red ganache. That's the blood. I use oil-based food colouring for the blood so it stays separate from the white chocolate the cake is smothered in. Of course, the finishing touch is a blood-splattered knife protruding from the middle of the cake, but we'll come to that later.'

Her stomach churns at the mention of a bloody knife; in passing, like a secret ingredient to the recipe in his mind. Is he going to poison me, or kill me with a kitchen knife? For now, at least, it seems the muscle of his tongue will get a workout with eating and swallowing the cake. Perhaps that will satisfy him for a time. The lid on his emotions is screwed on tight between jars he has not shared with her. Yet.

'I love the smell of a cake baking in the oven. It's the smell of families,' Drew says. 'Don't you think?'

He slams the cake mixture into the oven. Then, he unzips a leather holdall, perched on top of the washing machine. At the sight of a small, sharp cutting knife,

Emma-Jane sharply inhales and leans backwards in her chair. The chair lifts on two legs, but something behind her knocks the chair back onto the grotty grey carpet.

Drew rolls up the sleeve of his shirt and she stares at his bare arm in complete shock. He has damp patches under his armpits, large stains on the cool blue of his cotton shirt. Those lacerations to his forearm are the unmistakable signs of self-harming. As his therapist she should have known, but he'd kept the dark habit a secret. The scars and fresh marks send another jolt of fear through her: her diagnosis had been depression, but this habit points to an inability to verbalise emotional pain, sometimes self-loathing, and other issues, to seek release from self and feelings of hurt, anger. A desire to help this poor, suffering man grips her as tightly as he had gripped her neck the night she was abducted. Am I here because Drew needs me?

He looks longingly at the blade and then at her. 'Some people have tattoos. I prefer scars. While the cake is baking, there's work to do.'

He rolls the sleeve up a couple more inches and the old scars, like welts sucked by leeches, stand to attention on his forearm. He stares straight ahead, as if he is stuck at the traffic lights, waiting for it to change from red, to amber, to green. Emma-Jane knows what he's going to do and can do nothing to stop it, but she has to try.

'It's much easier for me to be open with you here.' He removes his shirt and trousers and she gasps. 'Don't worry. I'm not going to touch you.' She gasps again at the ugly patchwork of yet more extensive scars. Cut after cut has been made across his stomach, thighs, torso. Some still fresh, bleeding a little, open like a dribbling mouth. Most are scar tissue; a sad shade of pink that will never disappear.

'Some scars have names like "Christmas", "Halloween", or "Birthday" and "Bramble" and "Talon", for those that are just plain horrible. This new scar will be named after the cake, to mark our first day together.'

'Be kind to yourself, Drew. You're distressed.'

Drew doesn't appear to hear her. She senses his tingling, pulsing skin and yanks at the restraint around her middle as he makes a deep incision in his thigh with the knife. He looks at her angrily, as if she's to blame for his distress. The silence is almost as terrifying as a noise because of the anarchy living inside his head.

'Your pain, Drew, doesn't have to make you do this.'

'It's James's birthday soon. I've been counting down to it with these marks, you see. I like to look at the scars, the grooves of different length and depth, depending on how much pain I'm in. Scars are perfect for someone like me. You see these,' he says, holding up his arm, 'these can't be erased, and nor can the damage that's been done. I cannot undo the reason for them. James, my flesh and blood.'

Her heart is thumping in her chest and perspiration beads trickle down her back. This poor man; she has failed him as his therapist. There's so much pain and distress here, she had no idea. He fingers the blade, and a poppy-red bead of blood sits on the end of his finger. She can almost taste the foul stench of their sweat, caused by the stifling heat in the room. 'Please! Don't, this—'

'Shut up. Watch. Don't speak.'

It's like bloodletting, she thinks, as he reaches for a plastic container to catch the dripping blood. When will it end? She has treated clients who self-harm, mainly females and children or adolescents, but never has she witnessed it in proximity like this. For men there is often a cultural taboo. Perhaps that's why he didn't tell her about the grim habit?

It is impossible to not feel pity for him, knowing that self-harm can be a predicator of death by suicide, and an expression of a deeply troubled mind. It isn't what she expected. Her diagnosis that he was depressed because his wife had left him was wrong and that, almost as much as the loss of her own freedom and dignity, troubles her. Perhaps Drew isn't the man she thought he was? He's not only unstable, he's also an impersonator.

Her own safety and survival take over her thoughts as his face twists and contorts in pain. What if he bleeds to death? Then she might slowly starve to death in this very room. The window provides a possible means of escape, if she can break free from the chair and throw herself, or something, through it. She doesn't have the luxury of knowing where the key to the front door is or the general layout of the house yet. Seemingly, downstairs, there are just the two rooms, with one door.

Drew makes a second incision, even deeper than the first one, and looks pleased when the blood dribbles into the container. 'Whenever James drew or painted me, I had a fat stripy tie on.' He grimaces. 'You know, his outfit was all wrong the last time I saw him, in his mother's arms. It must have been new clothes she bought especially. A going-away outfit for the occasion. Navy blue. Such a grown-up colour. Against his fair hair, it made him look pale.'

A look of dark relief washes over his face as the blade cuts his skin once more and the blood rolls. The expression is of a pleading, begging man, but the pity she had felt is replaced with fear for him and her. His dark glassy eyes frighten her the most, now he is really hurting. Will it be her turn soon? Spots of blood land on the kitchen floor, a cream and brown patterned linoleum which has seen better days. He inserts the knife into the plastic container, then lathers the blade in his blood. She shuts her eyes to the horror and hears him open the oven. The aroma of the delicious cake confuses her senses.

'Open! Open your eyes. Now! I am in charge, and you will only learn if you do what I say! Understand?'

Startled, she nods compliantly. Her eyes jerk open and she stifles a sob in the back of her throat. 'A perfect cake risen to perfection!' Drew clears away the mess while the cake cools. 'Now, for the decoration.'

The red ganache on top of the white icing is horribly realistic. Knowing the knife wedged into the centre of the three layers of dark sponge is smothered in real blood, she wonders if he added other ingredients to the mix without her noticing. Poison?

Her training conflicts with his demands to remain quiet and only watch, to be a passive observer on such human pain. It goes against all that she believes in and has shaped her career around.

'James loved apple crumble and custard. He'd eat it for breakfast, lunch and dinner, given the chance.' He looks up, rambling, perhaps delirious now. The litany 'dear James, my boy' ricochets around the walls of the kitchen. The cake is like a third person in the room. Malignant. She isn't sure if it's the pain and loss of blood or if he's been drinking. Perhaps both.

'Love. I held him in my arms. I felt love; he must have felt it, too.' He holds his hand in the air as if to catch the faint beam of light peeking through the blind, then returns to decorating the cake. 'James was like a dapple of light tingling on the water's surface. James.'

'Drew, please. Stop. Talk to me. I can't sit here and watch or say or do nothing when you are in such pain. Tell me. Help me understand. I am here, listening.'

'Yes,' he says, sniggering. 'You are.'

The hideous cake takes shape. His hand has well and truly come off the tiller, she thinks. She closes her eyes, just for a second, and, when she opens them, the cake is presented on a white plate on her lap. He remains standing right beside her: the knife in his right hand, and his arm still leaking blood.

'You are going to eat some home-made cake, aren't you?'

It's not really a question. She knows that, and, despite the blood and fear, the conflict she feels, her stomach grumbles loudly in protest to the little food and water she's consumed in the last twenty-four hours or so. Soon she'll start to feel weak and her mind won't be as sharp, and that frightens her. Her brain is her ally. Staying on the right side of him, and alert, are her priorities. Block out the rest, she tells herself.

'Yes, of course I am, because that's what you and I both want.'

Drew smiles, pleased with her response, and gets down on his knees. He cuts a slice and feeds it to her, piece by piece. She keeps her eyes closed, pretending she is ignorant to what is entering her mouth, and forces herself to think about the view from Corbet Hill, across the Shropshire and Welsh hills.

'James. Forgive me, James.'

She opens her eyes to see Drew's head bowed in prayer. The words of contrition loop in her head, stirring feelings not of fear now, but sadness. The cake drags down her throat; the bloody icing, too.

'I want to help. I do.' The dark patches under his eyes make him look twice his age. This pitiful, troubled man. He looks so utterly vulnerable now, after appearing handsome only so recently. 'You loved James. Dearly. Let me help you.' The clink of her cuffs is hateful as she attempts to stroke his dark hair, his tear-stained face. He rests in her lap, passively, and closes his eyes. His blood leaks onto her shoe. It is a red pupil staring right back at her.

The space behind the locked front door is another country; she needs a passport to access its vistas. A picture of a beach, a calm, blue sea comes to mind: all those foreign trips she's thought about and never taken. Will she get the chance now?

An image appears, of a mermaid washed up on the shore, drying out, marooned. Doomed, and changing into some other thing. She hates the chair and its anchored position. It skewers her to the spot, like a lump of meat. Her shadow stretches out in front of her, over his head. Thank goodness Drew is asleep, snoring on her lap, his head placed just where the bloody cake had been.

Chapter 15

AJ takes no pleasure in removing the nameplate from what was once James's bedroom door. He remembers having a 'KEEP OUT' sign on his bedroom door as a child: not like this wooden, hand-painted sign, which probably cost a packet. James's is written in black slanted letters, like a signature, and in one corner there is a little boy running with a cat. Will Drew want to keep it?

Unsure of what to do with the sign, he puts it in with the other items he's found and been undecided about. He has a black box with a lid which is in Evie's darkroom. Inside, there's mainly photographs of Drew's son, James, and weird-looking landscapes. Before switching on the bulb in the darkroom he is struck by the luminous finger marks on the walls – a child's hands, finger-painted in fluorescent green and pink, starting at the floor, working their way up the walls and even over the ceiling. Evie and James must have had fun doing that, he thinks, as he switches on the light and places the sign in the bottom of the box.

Back in James's bedroom, on the inside door of the wardrobe, his ever-increasing height has been marked with dates and ages. The marks are in pencil; fine stripes one after the other, marking the passage of time and the rapid growth of a little boy.

AJ had never spoken to the lad, so he doesn't know why it's upsetting him to feel his absent presence and relics of his short life here. He turns the radio up and gets on with pulling the multi-coloured bunting down from above the curtain rail, before making a start on painting the wall. James was perhaps too young to paint or scribble on his bedroom walls like he had done as a kid. The four walls look pretty clean and fresh to AJ, but he'll do what the boss says, to keep him happy.

He finds photographs, still in their frames, in the top drawer of the boy's chest of drawers. The sunshine yellow of James's hair is as bright as an egg yolk. He is sitting on a green stretch of grass. He guesses Evie was behind the camera, taking the picture.

In another framed photograph James is sitting on a ride-on tractor with green wheels and a yellow seat. He straddles it like he's riding the king's horse. The plastic wheels catch on the grit and gravel, so he looks to be pushing hard to get to where he has to go. The wheels are rolling, and Evie is watching James push himself along like it's the most amazing thing she has ever seen. Drew was there for that occasion, behind the lens.

AJ thinks about his own childhood: he had shared a room with his older brother, Jake, who liked to regularly remind him of what a stupid kid he was and what an amazing, clever guy his big bro was. Annoyingly, Jake was right about being clever, as he's made a mint in banking and works for himself, when he can be bothered, as a broker.

The familiar sound of the woman's red sports car parking up on one side of the barrier changes the path of

AJ's rambling thoughts, sending him outside to the front of the farmhouse. He knows who is driving the battered vehicle. Kat shimmies between the barriers like she's in a nightclub and heads straight to AJ.

'Back again!' he says as a welcome. 'You'd think you live here.'

'Wish I did! Is he here?' Kat asks, to which he shakes his head, keeping his response to a minimum. He thinks he can feel Pete staring at them from inside the house. She pouts her red lipsticked lips to show disappointment. Anyone would think a camera was on her, the way she throws her long, red hair over her shoulder. 'When did you see him last?'

He frowns. 'About a week. He's busy,' AJ says, stopping himself from moving away when she approaches him with a confident stride.

'Give him this, will you?' she says, passing him a white envelope addressed to Drew in black, scrawling handwriting.

'I can't promise I'll see him to give it to him,' he says, but takes the letter anyway and stuffs it into his back pocket, where it quickly disappears out of sight. He hitches up his loose jeans.

'Yeah, you will,' she says, with a knowing smile, and, when he doesn't respond, she shrugs and walks away to her car, tossing her hair over her shoulder in one deft movement. For a young woman, she sure has confidence, and bigger balls than some blokes he knows. The car door closes with a slam and she revs the engine more than she needs to, in a pathetic kind of fanfare.

Pete appears, having been stood in the doorway listening in. 'How come you two are all matey?'

'Drew was seeing her, that's how.'

'So?'

'She lives in one of Drew's terraces, on that estate near town.'

'Which one?'

'Hartlepool Estate. I did some work there and got to know her a bit. Needed a new shower fitting.' AJ hitches his jeans up, which are hanging down, revealing black boxer shorts.

'You never mentioned that when she's been here before.'

'No, well, it was a few months back since I saw her last to speak to proper like, that's all, Pete. That was before… before all this.'

'Well, are you going to read the letter? I'd like to if you won't.'

AJ hesitates.

You look guilty as hell. You and her haven't—'

'No! I wouldn't do that to Hannah, or Drew. Jesus! Give me some credit.'

'Come on then. Let's have a butcher's. I'm guessing it's a crawling, gushy kind of letter, wanting him back.

Worth a laugh, eh?' Pete makes a fake lunge for AJ's back pocket.

'Piss off. It's Drew's business, alright? Let's get back to friggin' work,' he snaps. 'The envelope is sealed, anyhow. Drew would know.'

Pete holds his hands in the air in mock surrender and pads off up the stairs. AJ pats his back pocket. The envelope is burning inside, heating his lower body and up his spine, to his neck and ears. He scratches his head and decides to forget about it for the time being and get on with earning a living, while he's got an employer and a pay cheque.

'Bloody hell!' Pete exclaims suddenly as he opens a bedroom window, shouting down to AJ. A car arrives. 'It's like Piccadilly Circus here!'

Pete comes back outside to stand beside AJ. An unfamiliar figure, a scruffy-looking woman, slowly climbs out of her car with heavy legs, like she's been in hospital for a time and is convalescing. It looks like such a huge effort to walk.

'I'll go,' Pete says, and AJ shrugs his answer. Pete tries not to stare too hard at the white-faced woman. 'You alright?' he asks. 'Can I help?'

'Is Drew here? I need to see him,' she says, swaying a little.

'He's not here. This place is being sold. Are you a friend of his?' Pete thinks she is going to break down in tears by the way her face screws up.

'Yes. I'm Lucy. Where can I find him? It's urgent.'

'He owns a lot of property in the area. He'll be staying at one of those. That would be my guess, anyroad. Me and AJ are just labourers for him.'

She nods her understanding, as if talking takes too much effort.

He takes pity on her and a thought pops into his head. 'He owns a place on Hartlepool Estate. He always buys places to rent out near Co-ops. You could try there.'

'Thanks.'

'Mind how you go now.'

***

Later that evening, Hannah glances at the flickering fluorescent light in the entrance to the bar. People are going in the opposite direction to them, which isn't a good sign. The indie band has been on stage for less than ten minutes. Hannah's silver make-up and tight trousers are honey to bees. AJ likes to see her dressed up and attracting a few looks. There are plenty of blokes in there with more money and better looking than he is, and he pushes his chest out, happy she's with him.

'Watch it!' Hannah spits when a pissed-up bloke in a rugby top stumbles in her path. She strides confidently, with AJ in tow looking at her tight ass.

Inside, he scans the room for a table and, finding none, makes a beeline for the bar, where there are free bar stools. There's too much security in the form of burley bouncers to feel at ease, but it's nice to come into the warmth after the damp and drizzly walk there and sink a few pints on a Friday night after a long week at work.

'What are you drinking?' the bartender asks. 'It's happy hour on pints.'

AJ catches a whiff of sweat, Strongbow and Monster. 'Carling, and a snakebite and black, please, mate.' He slides onto the stool beside Hannah and removes his leather jacket. 'As it's happy hour, we might as well have two of each then, hey.' He stifles a burp, but Hannah catches the smell of luncheon meat and spring onion pasty and pulls a face.

The shape of his face changes like plasticine when his phone rings. He stares at the screen for a while before answering it. Hannah knocks back her pint as soon as she knows it's Drew because that usually means a long conversation or some kind of stress. The man calls at all hours and keeps AJ waiting for him on jobs because he forgets to turn up. Lately, he's vanished.

She waits for AJ to hang up before unloading her gaze. 'Now what?'

'He's got a private buyer for the farmhouse and another terraced place he owns.' He runs a hand through his hair. 'He's selling up, Hannah. Wants to cash in all his property, or as much of it as he can at the moment. It's confirmed. I'm gonna be out of a job.'

'That man. He's a fucking tool!' she says, twisting the pendant on the end of her necklace. 'What's his game? One minute it's flat out with refurbs, the next you're bloody out of work.' Hannah frowns as someone barges past.

'I think he's got major personal problems. I can't be out drinking when I'm about to be out of work.' He drinks his pint down in one go and takes a sip of the second one. 'Can we go?'

She lifts the half-drunk glass in the air. ‘I’ve not finished. We’ve only just got here, and I got showered and dressed specially to go out. We hardly go out these days, although the band’s not up to much, I admit.’ She takes a long drink. ‘How much notice has he given you?’

‘He didn’t say precisely. It’s vague, like. Could be a couple of months, or a couple of weeks.’

‘The man has to give you at least a month’s notice. That’s basically the law.’

‘He pays me cash in hand. Drew can do what he likes as I’m just a casual labourer. Moneyed blokes like him don’t give a toss about people like me anyway.’ AJ knocks back his drink and wipes his mouth with the back of his hand. Despite the liquid, he doesn’t look refreshed. He gazes at the optics, like there might be an answer to his work worries there.

‘Why are you so down? You’ll get another job.’

AJ looks away and stares into his empty pint. 'I wish I was born with a silver spoon in my gob; then I wouldn't be working my bollocks off for a few quid.'

'We're doing alright, and at least we've got each other. I wouldn't want to be Drew right now. Not for all the money in the world.'

AJ raises one eyebrow and takes a sip of his second drink.

'Bloody Drew!' Hannah continues, 'Just lately he keeps messing our evenings up.'

'Well, he won't for much longer, that's for sure, because he won't want anything to do with me.'

'So, our plans go up in smoke, just like that?'

'I'm going to speak to Pete about working for him, or working for ourselves, but as a team. We work well together, and he's good on the plumbing side of things, but I can do the carpentry and brick work. He's better at painting and decorating and the admin side. We can get some fliers out in the local paper to drum up some business.'

'When will you speak to Pete?'

'Soon. I promise. We need to get money together so we can buy a place to renovate – two or three bedrooms, walking distance from a shop. That's what Drew's done.'

'The best ideas are often the simplest,' she says, and shrugs. 'Maybe one day you and I will be millionaires, living in our own farmhouse.'

Chapter 16

Drew had once told Kat where the spare key to the front door of the farmhouse was kept; in the single-storey outbuilding, under a terracotta planter on the far right.

The key is small and cold in her hand as she strides towards the oak door to unlock it. Any day now she will be booted out of the house and moving to the other side of the country to stay with her cousin, so one stop at the farmhouse before she leaves is all she wants. There's no sign of AJ or his co-worker, so she seizes the opportunity to look around. It's a place Kat had fantasised about living happily in with Drew. That fantasy had died the same day as Evie and James.

Welcome home, me! As if.

The kitchen is as she remembers, except the Belfast sink is empty and it smells musty, rather than of washing-up liquid. Without the hot water running the window isn't obscured with steam, as it was the day she had been here last.

For all the character and status of the farmhouse she thinks it has a relatively modest kitchen, with a beige Aga, now sleeping and out of date, and an incongruous-looking fridge – an American one, with double doors.

This room had been Evie's domain. Drew had told her Evie was the sort of mother who was so organised she crammed her handbag full of stuff to meet almost any eventuality, so it was terribly heavy to carry around. There were countless lists stuck on the fridge door, as Kat recalls: shopping and such like, reminders and messages – 'ring builder', 'James at dentist'.

The rest of the kitchen has been stripped, with only the dark beams left to give it a homely feel. Kat investigates the space, imagining where the kitchen table and four chairs would go if it were her house. Perhaps she would have a plant, a dresser and a proper oven and microwave instead of a grandma of an Aga.

Her hands are on her hips and her lips are slightly pouting when the cat flap opens to a ghost of a cat.

She lets out a nervous laugh at being frightened by the wind and nothing more. The moment lengthens. She looks down at the red tiles to see a dead mouse on the floor, in the exact spot she had told Evie Drew was leaving her and James for a new life with her.

You say Drew is leaving me and James to be with you? Incredulous Evie had said it more than once. Perhaps three times. You say Drew is abandoning us?

The way she'd said 'abandoning us' had bothered Kat, even then, and it still does now. Posh. Indignant. Shocked. A lullaby pops into her head.

Rock-a-bye, baby, In the treetop. When the wind blows,

The cradle will rock. When the bough breaks,

The cradle will fall, And down will come baby,

Cradle and all.

'Not my fault,' she says to the dead mouse. 'That's dead and buried; so are they.' Kat kicks the mouse to the far right corner.

It's the other rooms she wants to see to satisfy her curiosity before she leaves Shropshire for good. The rooms she's not visited before. Now or never.

In the living room, Kat imagines Drew and herself in wingback chairs, either side of the fireplace, and James playing with a few toys on a rug in front of a lit fire. The hearth has a distinct presence in the room. In the evening, Drew might drink a tumbler of whisky; Kat perhaps a glass of wine, or a gin and tonic with a slice of lemon and two ice cubes to clink against the crystal glass in her right hand, adorned with an expensive engagement and wedding ring. She sees Drew stretching his legs out, his arms behind his head in a pose between smugness and arrogance, relaxing after the heavy strain of the working day and basking in his success.

She had loved him, wanted him all to herself, and had imagined herself here, in his bed, dining at the kitchen table. Silly her for thinking he loved her back and planned to leave all this to be with her.

The French windows at the rear of the lounge, a recent addition not entirely in character with the farmhouse, let very little light into the living room because of the small panes. It chops the natural light into little pieces. The fragmented light is depressing, like prison bars. A soft sound, like a cushion falling off a chair, stops her thoughts in their tracks. The room needs heating, a good airing, that is all, she concedes, before moving down the hall.

The dining room has been stripped of furniture, presumably in readiness for its new owner, except for a few pieces. There is a dark wood chest – a large piece, perhaps antique, with a lid and two drawers with gold, delicate handles. Perhaps it was too heavy to move, or the purchaser took a fancy to that, the grandfather clock which has stopped working and the enormous gilt mirror above the hearth. She lifts the lid of the chest and peers inside, as if it were a coffin.

The day she arrived at the farmhouse to speak to Evie had been a Wednesday; the day after AJ had fired her up and led her to believe her dream was about to come true. She remembers because her first thought that day had been to put the rubbish out for the binmen before it was too late (again). She'd rushed outside in her dressing gown and slippers, only just in time for the dustcart, and got to talking with one of the refuse collectors. He'd taken a shine to her and made some comment about how someone like her should live in a castle, or a listed building. By the time the dustcart had finished emptying the bins on her road she'd made her mind up to speak to Evie.

Red hair. Her mother had said she was impulsive and temperamental. She looks at her reflection in the mirror and takes a strand of her long, red hair in her hand. Even if she cut it all off it wouldn't change her character. Not like Samson. Kat stares in the mirror for so long she senses an intense gaze on the back of her head. She turns, suddenly expecting someone to be in the room, but there is no one. Just her conscience. Guilt.

Looking back into the mirror, Kat pushes her hair away from her face, closes her eyes and shakes her head, enjoying the feeling of her hair waterfalling down her back, touching her spine, her bottom. Drew had liked her long hair and would entwine his hands in it.

She shudders, and assumes her conscience is getting the better of her because there is only her in the room, besides the dark wooden furniture and the mirror. The carpet. The four walls, wallpapered, and the characterful fireplace. Kat takes a deep breath.

She hears a click and then the centre light switches on a harsh glow from a naked bulb. Another click, and the sidelights to the left and right of the hearth illuminate. Kat swallows down the bitter taste in her mouth. Why have the lights come on all of a sudden? It must be old wiring in a place like this.

The grandfather clock suddenly moves its rigid hands to twelve o'clock. The logs that had been left to the side of the grate tumble onto the carpet, leaving splinters of wood, bark and an odour of smoke behind. Or is that her imagination? A solid log rolls further than the others, to within touching distance of her feet.

'For fuck's sake.'

Kat closes the dining room door behind her to explore the rest of the ground floor. Further down the corridor, she opens a door to a small room furnished with a desk. A box sits invitingly on it. The rest of the room is bare. Kat removes the lid from the box and peers inside, fingering each photograph in turn, one after the other. James, Evie, James with Drew, then one miserable black and white landscape after another. No wonder Drew had wanted a bit of life and colour with Kat. Who could blame him? She muses, tossing her hair over one shoulder.

The sound of a door latch lifting tilts her head around the dark room. Upstairs is where the sound is coming from, she thinks. At the bottom of the staircase, Kat imagines making a grand entrance at one of their house parties, dressed to kill. In her mind, she hears the sound of high heels above her head, striding along the catwalk of the landing, then down the stairs, click, click, click like a camera, slowly, so slowly, as Drew's head turns to stare and he grins at Kat, his new wife.

A silly fantasy.

The cold, musky smell of the empty farmhouse brings Kat back to reality. She has seen enough. There's no Drew, no marriage, no happy ever after ending. Not here, anyway.

Chapter 17

Lucy has been to Emma-Jane's house, the office and Drew's farmhouse, but there's no sign of her there. If only she'd answer her phone, then Lucy's mind could rest. Drew doesn't answer his phone or return her calls either. It doesn't feel right.

Clients of Emma-Jane's have left messages on her office landline and pushed notes under the door. Vanessa, a fragile looking woman, had looked desperate when Lucy had to tell her Emma-Jane wasn't available today. Lucy doesn't know whether to contact the other clients or not, to make up a plausible excuse for Emma-Jane's disappearance. But one thing Lucy does know is that something bad has happened, because Emma-Jane wouldn't leave her vulnerable clients in the lurch. No way.

Lucy might as well be standing on a rooftop and watching life go on below. Out there, there are those who look like everybody else, who blend in confidently with each season, while the storm inside them is building, building, taking ugly shape and form, until their traumatised self is reborn into a revengeful, malicious version of the original. These traumatised people sleep deeply, eat well, and each day are a step closer to finding out what they are capable of, the cloaked people they can be. People Emma-Jane tries to help, tries to make happier. Someone has taken her, someone who appears to be someone they're not.

Lucy knows the Hartlepool Estate and is parked up outside 12 Erin Row within the hour. Now she's here, she feels less sure of herself, of what to say, of how to explain her uninvited appearance.

There is a red sports car on the drive to number twelve, next to a 'SOLD' sign. The car has seen better days. The vehicle is a siren on an otherwise quiet street with mainly modest, small cars parked neatly on the front drive or white vans on the kerb. This house is neat. She can see why an astute entrepreneur like Drew would buy the property for his rental business and wonders why he is selling it now.

After taking a deep breath she walks up to the house. The bell doesn't work, so she knocks on the central, frosted glass pane in the door.

A young woman, perhaps nineteen or twenty, with fiery red hair and wearing leather gloves, answers the door. The light bead of her eye and pale face fight for Lucy's attention when the door opens, as the volume of the television in the background is horribly loud. It sounds like a game show, with lots of clapping between talking.

'Sorry!' Lucy says, seeing the woman isn't pleased to have an unexpected visitor. She takes an involuntary step back. 'I'm Lucy. I was actually looking for Drew Rogers.'

The young woman frowns. 'He was my… He's my landlord. Well, he is until I get kicked out when the new owners move in any day!' She aggressively gestures to the 'SOLD' sign. 'This isn't a great time, actually.' She holds her gloved hands up in a way of explanation. There is blood on them; some fresh, some dried. 'I was just feeding my pet between packing up.'

Lucy doesn't know what kind of pet needs to be fed something bloody and presumably alive while wearing gloves, but it isn't at the top of her priorities to ask. The woman's voice is captivating: low and husky. She tries not to stare. 'Does Drew live here?'

'Drew Rogers doesn't live here, no.' She laughs. 'Have you been to the farmhouse?'

Lucy nods.

'I know he's got two houses just out of town.' She looks up as she tries to recall where they are. 'Not far from the Co-op.'

'Which Co-op?'

'I dunno. Who are you, anyway?' A defensive hand slides onto one hip, which looks faintly amusing because of the glove. Conversation doesn't seem to be her strong suit. 'Did someone send you? I've got another week before I'm meant to be out.'

Lucy gives her the warmest smile she can muster under the strained circumstances. 'I need to speak to him about a friend of ours. I haven't heard from them in a while and I'd like to get in contact. I won't bore you with the details.'

'A woman friend?' she asks sharply, with narrowed eyes.

Lucy lies. It's a decision made in a split second, purely on intuition. 'No. Eric Stash. So, you say you're a tenant of his?'

The woman nods, clearly not forthcoming. There's a smell of something unpleasantly tangy emanating from the house.

'Do you have a phone number, by any chance?' Lucy asks, hoping it will be a different one to the number he gave her.

The woman disappears inside and returns with a corner ripped from a notebook. 'Here. Can't say if it's still in use. He's not exactly communicative of late.'

Lucy folds it in half and carefully puts it into her pocket. 'Thanks. What did you say your name was?'

'I didn't.' And she slams the front door. The letter box rattles, a tinny sound. Through the frosted glass she sees the woman's figure move into the back of the house. Lucy is relieved to get away from that front doorstep, from the clasp of elephant grass which has spread uncontrollably in the small patch of front lawn and those bloody gloves.

She drives a short way down the road to pull in at a garage with a Costa Coffee, tittering at the name she'd invented, Eric Stash. Parked up, she tries the phone number the woman had given her, her heart thumping in her chest. She has no idea what she's going to say, but if she thinks about it too long there's a chance she will jib out. The phone rings and then immediately clicks to voicemail. The recording is automated, giving her no reassurance it is Drew's phone. Has she been fobbed off by the woman in gloves? She takes a deep breath and rings the number again, but the same thing happens.

'Bollocks. Now what? There's about ten Co-ops in town, and more on the outskirts.' Lucy sighs. Neither Emma-Jane or Drew return her calls, and the unease she feels keeps growing. If she has to drive round all of the local Co-ops and talk to all the shop assistants, she will. If that's what it takes. The more she learns about Drew, the more worried she feels for her friend.

Lucy parks up beside the Co-op on Angel Street, which is on the outskirts of town near the River Severn. She gets out for a walk with no plan of what to do next, only feeling full of nostalgia and memories of her and Emma-Jane spending time here. There are hundreds of buttercups and crossworts turning the fringes of the roadside into golden bobbing heads, but still, the sky hangs lower and lower above her head.

It will probably rain, Lucy thinks, seeing grey clouds above. She has to keep looking. But where? Who should she speak to? She admonishes herself for not bringing a photograph of Emma-Jane with her. Then she scrolls through the photographs on her phone and finds one. Should she randomly stop people and show them the photo?

The river seems to look back at her in desperation, while willow trees twist their branches like they are wringing out their wetness. There is no order to the undergrowth or the landing places of sticks and branches. The unplanned architecture of nature is all around her, abundantly lacking in symmetry. Unsure of what else to do, Lucy keeps walking.

'Emma-Jane? Dr Glass? Emma-Jane!' The sound of her name flaps in the wind like a torn piece of cloth. Raindrops punctuate the river. Water moves and swills. Feeling the cold, she pulls her jacket around her and turns up the collar. Her forehead and hands sting from the cold. Where the trees overlap too tightly some bend over, twist to the sky, and grow in arches to reach the light, reshaping themselves to survive.

Please let Emma-Jane be alright.

Where are you?

On a trip to the Lake District some years before they graduated Emma-Jane had explained the water cycle to her, detailing several processes, including evaporation and condensation. Lucy glances up at the clouds leaking droplets, perhaps originally from this very river. If water can change state, be carried to a new place, perhaps Emma-Jane has too. But where?

Years ago, they'd loved cycling this way, out into 'the green', as Emma-Jane called it, though Lucy loved the water more than the green space. They'd ride in single file, taking it in turns to lead the way down the paths. Lucy liked to be at the front best, which suited Emma-Jane just fine, as she rode at a slower pace.

Exercise had never been her thing. Even so, as mature students, they'd often walked along the river. She had been such a conscientious student, and always a thoughtful, loyal friend. Without her friendship during university and then after the death of Martin, Lucy wouldn't have managed to keep going. Her friendship has extended to working together, too. Lucy can't fail her now.

The distant hills and the beguiling tinkle of the river fade away. There is nowhere and everywhere else to look. It seems then there should be rows of chairs for people to watch the unfolded drama of two friends pulled apart. One lost. The other, hiding. Lucy and her parents are so proud of Emma-Jane. A doctor! If Lucy's parents knew she was missing they'd travel down and think they were helping, when all they'd really be doing is stressing Lucy out. She can't mention it to them, or anyone, really, as she has no proof there's a problem. Just a hunch.

She wanders back the way she came, wondering why she set off in the first place without a clear plan or route and some vague notion she'd suddenly 'know', like a sixth sense, where Emma-Jane is. Foolish.

Even the sun is like smashed glass, winking menacingly at her, so eventually she returns to her car and drives back to the office to wait for the sound of a key, the latch, something. God, it is so quiet. The unsettled feeling grows in the pit of her stomach, like an ulcer growing on the gastric juices of stress and anxiety.

In Emma-Jane's office, she hunts for Drew's contact details on the computer and in the filing cabinet but finds nothing. She slams the drawer shut, exasperated that they aren't where they should be. Emma-Jane is organised and efficient. It doesn't make sense for there not to be a signed registration form for her client because it's a requirement. With her head in her hands, she waits for her heart rate to fall. The sound of rushing blood is in her ears.

Tomorrow, once she's slept and her head is clear, she'll plan and then continue her search. If Emma-Jane doesn't show up soon, Lucy will have every reason to call the police.

Chapter 18

It is eleven o'clock in the evening and AJ has talked Hannah into snooping around the farmhouse for a bit of a laugh. Hannah stuffs her hands in the pockets of her bomber jacket to keep warm, as it is cold and stale in the house.

'Any furniture or stuff that's left is up for grabs.'

The interior doors to each room had been closed and, as they open the one from the kitchen into the hall, it makes an unwelcome creak. Hannah looks up at the beams in the ceiling; the wood is old and weathered. She stands on tiptoes to touch it but isn't tall enough.

'Serious?'

'Fuck him. Drew's given me notice. I don't owe him nothing. The place is sold.'

'I hope the new owners don't show up!'

‘They won’t.’

‘It smells a bit musty, doesn’t it? I suppose old houses soon get a bit damp when they’re not occupied. Colder than our house, and we don’t have the heating on.’

AJ doesn’t respond. He’s used to working in all temperatures. ‘I reckon Drew doesn’t know what day it is. Anything that’s left in the farmhouse is here because he doesn’t want it or he can’t get it shifted and stored. Come on. What he doesn’t know won’t harm him. The bloke’s loaded, so I don’t know why you’re worrying about a few sticks of furniture.’

‘If you say so.’ Satisfied, Hannah relaxes and kisses him. She tastes of chocolate and old coffee grounds. He watches her move around the dining room with soft rabbit’s eyes, like she’s browsing in a department store, making everything feel lighter. ‘Have you spoken to Pete yet about working together?’

'Not yet,' he says flatly. 'This is nice.' There is a dark chest against one wall, too big for most modern houses.

She admires the fireplace hearth and the mirror above it. 'That mirror's lovely.'

AJ immediately tilts it forwards to take a look at the fixing on the wall and see if it can be removed. 'You'll have to help me take it off the wall. It's awkward, for one.' She moves to get into position to help. 'Not now. Let's have a look round the whole place before we load the van up.'

Hannah giggles with excitement while he looks at himself in the mirror and rapidly frowns. His reflection is impaired by finger marks where his eyes should be, and a handprint right in the centre of his face. A perfect circle of breath forms where his mouth is.

'Gosh! It's perfect for a medieval banquet in here. What's that drink they used to have?' She touches her top lip. 'Mead! That sweet wine stuff. With a big, long, dark wood table and, in the centre, between the candles, an apple stuffed into the mouth of pig's head! You'd sit at one end and me at the other!' She leans over the table.

'What are you doing?'

'Lighting the imaginary candles. Hey! You could have a fab game of real-life Cluedo in here. Was the murder weapon a candlestick or a poker?'

'You've been watching too many films or reading rubbish magazines, if you ask me.' He can tell she's enjoying herself, though, and loves her sideways smile. 'Did I tell you I spoke to Kat the other day? Drew's bit on the side.'

'Oh, yeah. I know. What's she got to say for herself?'

'She looked rough.'

Hannah looks pleased.

'I think she's a bunny boiler. I feel a bit sorry for her to be honest.'

Hannah looks at him with longing. ‘That’s ’cos you’re a good guy, but not everyone is like you.’

AJ moves to the window and looks out into the darkness. ‘There’s no light pollution here at all. No traffic noise, nothing. If we had a place like this we could do it up proper, from top to bottom. Not rush through, like Drew has. A place like this needs time and attention to detail—’ A movement in his peripheral vision shuts him up. He doesn’t move at first, or speak: all his senses are acute and on red alert.

Hannah is gazing at the photographs on the wall. ‘These are nice. Odd that Drew didn’t take them with him. Wasn’t Evie a photographer?’

AJ nods.

‘Shall we take ’em? They might have a value.’

‘Na, look a bit creepy to me,’ he says dismissively. ‘If we keep saving up for a deposit we could buy a tumble-down place and do it up while we live in it. There isn’t much I can’t do myself. Pete’s been doing that on and off for years, living in his van at first, and now he lives on his own in a decent semi with three bedrooms and a conservatory. We gotta get our feet on that first rung of the ladder. I'm sick of renting a shitty little house. It's dead money, month after month.'

'We will get there, 'course we will,' she says and then kisses him. 'I'm sure of it. You and I are going to make our dreams come true! You're really hard-working and soon I'll have passed my first accountancy qualification.' Hannah lifts up the frame and removes the photograph from the picture hook. 'I like this photo of the tree.'

She screams.

Where the picture was there is a hand-drawn sketch of two people hanging from a tree. One adult, one child.

Hangman.

Hannah screams again and drops the frame. The glass smashes. AJ grabs Hannah's hand.

'Come on. Let's get the hell out of here.'

Hannah is crying hysterically and resisting movement. 'Is that them? Oh my God!' her voice trembles and leaks between the fingers over her mouth.

'Hannah!' he shouts, then pulls her out of the dining room and back into the kitchen. Her legs are wobbling and, fearing she is going to collapse, he half carries her outside and into the van. 'Get in!'

He doesn't say anything for a time once they are inside the van. The darkness and the small, familiar space are a welcome cocoon, but Hannah's sobs are too loud to think clearly. Did he see right? A sketch of a hanged adult and child, on the dining room wall? Sick.

The dirty plastic fabric seats offer little in the way of comfort or luxury. His heart rate is slowing down now, alongside Hannah's sobs. AJ takes a deep breath and turns the ignition so the heater will work.

'You okay?' he asks tenderly, which she nods and sobs to.

He looks back at the stocky farmhouse for one last time through the car window. His van is empty, save for a hysterical girlfriend. He isn't good in these situations, when she's upset. The way she continues to rock and wail alarms him. She is beyond being comforted, he thinks, so he drives away.

Hangman.

Perhaps his life isn't so bad after all.

Chapter 19

Emma-Jane's bones feel like rusty hinges from the lack of movement as she climbs the stairs to the bathroom. Once inside she stretches her arms and back, trying to loosen the tightness in her muscles and tendons. It's like corrosion; the sitting, the sedentary hours and days. A tin can left out in the rain. Left for too long she will rust shut, then break. Snap.

There isn't a lock on the bathroom door, but Emma-Jane doubts Drew would come in unannounced. He doesn't threaten her in that way. She runs a bath rather than take a shower in order to make the most of the privacy and the opportunity to cleanse. After four days, she is allowed a bath. His acts of cruelty and kindness are as irrational as he is.

It's a small space, partly covered in dated tiles in a pink and cream decorative pattern that has a faint echo of something Grecian. While the bath fills she goes to the toilet, then brushes her teeth with toothpaste and a finger. Bliss.

To be allowed to spend time in the bathroom is a rare luxury. She makes the most of it by stretching her arms, muscles and neck again and then stripping and bathing. It isn't normal to feel so grateful for basic hygiene, but she does. How quickly simple things she once took for granted become special again, like cleanliness, privacy, the sound of running water and the faint aroma of scented soap. The radiator is scorching hot, like the one in the lounge, but the heat is pleasant on naked skin in here.

Before climbing into the bath she looks down at her body, the soft rise of her tummy and the dip of her belly button. Her thighs are still generous, she thinks. If she were at home, she would shave the crop of dark hair under her armpits and on her legs, which has grown a lot in such a short space of time.

In the bath, she scrubs her skin, hopeful of removing the dead skin, the dirt and the stain of the last four days. How long the days are, she thinks, as she washes her armpits. He's told her it's Monday and she hopes that means Drew will leave the house for appointments. Living so intensely side by side is a curious strain, especially when she is used to living and working alone.

Now she is alone she can think of her captivity as an experiment. During her degree she had read about plenty of psychology experiments and critiqued them. Here she is: a subject. The conditions so far haven't been too bad: loss of freedom, restricted movement and food and water, observing self-harm and the degradation of her own filth to erode her… what? Femininity? He enjoys control, for sure.

Her question is, what's next, and will he let her go? If he does let her go, it will be for a reason she can't grasp. When she's reformed? Broken, like him? That twitch in his eye is getting worse and he drinks wine during the day and evening. Perhaps her death here is inevitable after all.

She submerges her head in the water. Her hair fans out and it is serene, for a short time. Here, she feels like herself, and the pressure of her captivity idles away. In the warm water, the buzzing numbness and humming stiff joints uncoil and relax, after hours sat in the same position as a statue in a deserted museum while buses, trains and bicycles whizzed by outside. Perhaps there are posters shouting ‘MISSING’ above a photograph of her on lamp posts, shop windows and bus stops. She hopes Lucy will start to question things now it’s been four days because Emma-Jane is rarely out of communication for so long, be it ‘on holiday’ or not. She likes to keep in touch with Lucy.

With her head above the water, she makes herself comfortable and moans with pleasure, only to fixate on a cobweb in one corner of the bathroom. A fly is trapped insidc its silver thread. She knows how it feels.

'Clothes are outside the door!' Drew states. She flinches and covers her breasts with her arm.

'Okay, thanks.'

She hears him descend the stairs and relaxes again. Appalled by the colour of the bath water and the soapy scum around the rim, she pulls the plug and rubs herself down with a towel. Embarrassed by her own dirt, she swills the bath clean. There is only one towel; Drew will have used the same one for his showers. The strange intimacy of the situation unsettles her; to be captive and intimate at once. Why doesn't she hate him yet?

She finds grey tracksuit bottoms, a black hoody and a pair of red socks behind the bathroom door. Her breasts move inside the hoody, and her pubic hair brushes against the soft fabric of the tracksuit bottoms. Despite being dressed in baggy clothes she feels vulnerable and self-conscious about her womanly shape. Thank goodness she hasn't got her period, she's thought more than once.

Emma-Jane takes one last look through the bathroom window. The pane of glass is obscured for privacy and there isn't anything to indicate where she is. There is a faint sound of traffic, but no vehicles that she can see. People watching sunsets belong on another planet, which she can only wave to, like a star in the vast sky. To think the oceans are out there, where people walk their dogs along the beach, and children poke at dead jellyfishes, awed by their transparency. If only she could run into the sand dunes and wait for help to come.

The soap was pine scented; the closest she will get to walking beneath pine trees and breathing in their aroma. People out there have washed their sheets and pillowcases and they smell of lavender and jasmine detergent as they flap and wave on washing lines in the fresh, fresh air.

Where am I?

'Are you finished up there?' he shouts, and then his phone rings.

Be strong, she tells herself. Be strong and you'll get through this. He needs me as much as I need him.

She sits on the side of the bath, listening to Drew on the phone. It sounds work-related. Her heartbeat spikes when she thinks he will be called away to work any minute. It's a mixed blessing: there is a fear he won't return and she will die of starvation, or it will grant her a window of opportunity to escape or be rescued. The phone call is finishing up so she makes her way downstairs, feeling self-conscious about her body. If only she had a clean bra and pants.

The washing machine is switched on. Drew is standing in front of the front door, which has a cat flap at the bottom. It sways tantalisingly. 'Bye.' He puts the phone in his pocket. He looks her up and down, like he is seeing her through a new lens while remaining firmly in front of the tantalising exit to freedom.

She misses her home, the bright kitchen especially, and even the empty red biscuit tin on the table and the salt and pepper pots by the cooker. The stainless-steel toaster and the scratched chopping board, with the memory of bread knives embedded in its consciousness. The kitchen clock. The tins of Baxters soup she likes least stored in cupboards she rarely opens and the sharp kitchen scissors dangling from a hook.

'Thanks for the clean clothes,' she says, moving into the lounge, surprised to see several bags and a suitcase in one corner and the mattress made tidy with a sleeping bag. Don't get depressed, she thinks. What a stark, nasty room it is. An image of her light-filled house provokes longing for her home, her routine, with a pointed sadness.

To look at him now, dressed in a clean shirt and pressed trousers, polished brogues on, he looks a respectable, rational citizen. Handsome, with his dark, curious eyes. She knows he's wearing bandages under the clothes, after applying antiseptic cream and gently cleaning the self-inflicted wounds. A secret shared.

She is cleansed, no longer a mess of stinking piss and faeces and sweat. When he moves closer to replace the handcuffs she sees comb marks in his hair, which are strangely touching. In those steady eyes of his she sees something which scares her. What is it?

He isn't bad.

As she looks at his benign expression the stories of his son return as clear images: each one a sharp thorn, a splinter embedding itself deeper into her skin.

He was a good father.

If she were to be trapped here for a year or more, what vestiges of her old self would be left, of that respectable psychologist who wrote the article 'Altruistic Violence in Maternal Filicide', of the hard-working student, the loyal friend to Lucy, the neighbour who keeps herself to herself. Just four days and the situation isn't black and white, but shades of grey. Faces and places are blurred, as though they are travelling in the opposite direction to her. Why doesn't she do something to make them stop?

'Do I have to be tied to the chair? I won't run. I promise.'

He shakes his head but his gaze lingers on her. 'I have to go out for a short while.'

She wishes she could cross her arms to conceal her loose breasts but now she is back in the chair and handcuffed, so she crosses her feet instead and focuses on one corner of the room she hasn't seen before.

'You're nervous,' he states. 'I'm not going to hurt you.'

That's what worries her.

'I know that now.'

Chapter 20

It's seven o'clock in the evening and the sound of traffic and conversation outside has filtered to a thin residue of noise. Lucy finds the door to Emma-Jane's office open when she returns. Her heart quickens and she runs inside, sniffing the air. Is there is a smell of perfume? Coffee? Has she been and gone?

'Emma-Jane!' she says, peering expectantly into the room. The couch is occupied. 'Oh! Can I help you? Is it Vanessa?'

Vanessa nods and sits up a little; her eyes are watery and far away.

Lucy pulls up a chair beside her and softens the tone of her voice. 'I'm Lucy,' she says. 'My office is just opposite. Dr Glass is away at the moment.'

'No, she can't be,' she says, like she is answering someone else's question, and then she closes her eyes.

Lucy stares, unsure of what to do.

'I want her to read my stories.' Vanessa rummages in her handbag and removes a notebook. There is an open bottle of pills in there and a glass bottle. Vanessa clears her throat before reading her story. Lucy catches a whiff of something sour. Her tussled hair partly obscures one eye but she doesn't seem to notice that, or Lucy.

'I will build a new country and make mirrors which heal fragmented reflections in a rainbow spectrum of light; each expression a prism and of perfect wavelength. I will slip through gravity into character.'

The phone rings and clicks to voicemail. Still, Vanessa doesn't seem to hear anything except her own rambling thoughts on the page. Lucy sits forward on the seat, unsure of whether or not to move.

'I'll throw a tapestry over the sun to protect Avril's skin. I will stitch her name into the stars and inscribe her initials in the sand, on rocks, the barks of trees, and I'll make her a necklace of red berries and holly and a dress in deep pink and red hues of a sunset. The hem will catch the clouds and drag them along in the opposite direction to where the wind should take them.

'The pebbles in the river are singing; the blossom and the robin, too. They call me now to be with her. I hear beating wings like clapping, mastering the sky, turning heads, flying close to the sun like Icarus.'

Vanessa wipes her tears and puts the book down. 'I wanted Dr Glass to read them, but she isn't here.'

'Your stories are very moving. I will tell her about them and, when she's back, you could read them to her.'

Vanessa shakes her head, sending a tear down one cheek and into the side of her mouth. 'I don't think I'll be coming back.'

Chapter 21

Emma-Jane jerks awake and, for a moment, she is confused about where she is because she can't hear the idiosyncratic sound of the heating coming on in her own home, or the water in the pipes. She hears a man's voice talking on the phone, footsteps, and then she remembers where she is and who she's with.

Drew Rogers.

She imagines it's a Saturday morning and she is walking to the dry cleaners to drop off her work attire. The post office is next door, and then there is a newsagent, where she used to stop by for a Diet Coke and a magazine or newspaper. It's an ordinary street, with a boarded-up record store, a wine bar and a florist with a yellow door. There's no graffiti, and she likes that other locals are well dressed and walk briskly with a coffee in one hand and a phone or a lead for a small dog in the other. This is where she lives. A professional, a single woman happy to live alone, successful. A simple life suits her. It's work-biased, a life watched through glass, perhaps, but she is doing something good with her time to help others.

Is her disappearance in the local news? Does anyone notice she isn't there? She imagines that street a little differently now: with fewer people, the shops shut. It unsettles her otherwise to think life is carrying on as normal there while she is marooned here, this woman of the community known by shop owners. Isn't she?

Drew looks at her with those intense eyes like he wants something from her. A cure for his pain? Part of her wants those secrets he keeps.

'Why me, Drew? It isn't a random act or a random choice for me to be here, to spend so much time in a chair, here, with you. Is it a power trip? A role-reversal thing? Revenge?' She swallows. 'But revenge for what?'

He takes his time to answer. That's his way. They've had so much time in each other's company that she senses when he is thinking. It seems she can hear it. Then he reaches for her hand, and his touch is warm. 'I'll make you a better therapist,' he says evasively.

'How so?'

He strokes her fingers, one by one, then places his hand against her palm. The skin is soft. 'By spending time in this chair, as a patient, not the therapist who is in control, you'll understand the pain and shame, the anxiety and humiliation. To willingly put yourself in a chair like that takes great courage by the patient. Did you know that?'

'Yes. I see my supervisor regularly.'

'That's different. Two professionals. The dynamics of power are very different between a patient and a therapist; and a therapist and her supervisor.'

'I never minimised how hard it is to take that step. It isn't my job to judge.'

'You do a lot of listening in your job, and little talking. You listen for inconsistencies in the patient's story, don't you? You assess constantly.'

'It's my job to identify psychological conflicts, the origins of pathology, anything clinical to best help them. Yes. Is that about control? Making me sit here, stinking and wet from my urine in this bloody chair?'

'I haven't heard you swear before. It suits you.'

'No, it doesn't.'

'A sign that you aren't in control. It isn't pleasant, is it? You know, it's hard to really know what is real to the patient, and what is real to everyone else. It seems to me you and I are alike. We share something. We both like to be in control.'

Emma-Jane averts her gaze to the grubby carpet. 'Therapists and patients must ethically maintain boundaries.' She pulls her hand away and closes her eyes, seeing tiny stars behind her eyelids.

He laughs. 'Is that a quote from a textbook?'

'I still don't understand. Why me? Therapists choose which patients they work with. If I feel I can't help someone, I refer them on.'

'What goes on in this room is confidential.'

'Doctor–patient confidentiality protects the patient except in safeguarding issues, but who is the doctor here? I thought I was the patient?'

He folds his arms and crosses his ankles. The room is tense and stiflingly hot. If only she could open a window, flood the room with air, with sounds from the outside world. A crack in the curtain allows a slice of light to fall on the carpet, showing a perfect circle from a cigarette burn.

'My wife took her own life and my son's.'

'What? You told me she—' She stops herself and keeps perfectly still for a few moments. At last, he is telling the truth. 'I'm sorry, Drew. That's a terrible thing to deal with.'

'Why would you be sorry? Defender of murderous mothers! Compassion? What compassion have you shown to the fathers who are left behind? How can you understand my feelings?'

'Then help me understand. Tell me. Why did Evie take her life and James's?'

'To punish me! Punishment. But I suppose in your next article you will use some big words and justify her actions. "Altruism"? Is that what you'll say? It was a punishment. I had affairs, several, and a business to run.'

'My article!' she exclaims. 'Is that why I'm here?'

Drew continues, deaf to her reaction. She grits her teeth. 'James didn't sleep a lot as a baby. Then Evie had a miscarriage and I suppose she was unhappy; she wanted more from me. Bulimia, depression, smashing things, but I never thought for one minute she would do what she did. Be so spiteful, so revengeful. I had no idea she hated me that much. All those years I thought she loved me. I just can't see how she could hate me that much to kill her own son. I can't see how anyone could do that to a little boy, a beautiful little boy who had all his life ahead of him.'

She shakes her head, feeling his pain. 'I'm sorry.' When Drew is vulnerable, when he is grey skies and heavy white clouds, she could almost reach for him. It's an impulse she's felt more than once, and it scares her that she might be experiencing Stockholm syndrome – when the captive falls for their abuser – rather than genuine empathy, or even something more. Love? If not love, then what? It isn't loathing. It would be simpler if it were.

'I don't pretend for a minute I was a perfect father or husband; I wasn't, and in my own way, I think I loved Evie. I would never have left her, not with James so young. It's difficult to know now, after what she did. My heart is just full of hate and fury for her and everything she once meant to me. I heard you on Shropshire Radio, you know, and I read your article, and everything seemed to fit into place then. I needed to meet you, to try and see how a doctor, a learned person, a female, could write those things. I kept meeting you and I hated you because you were real, so human, and yet what you wrote was so cold and callous. So… wrong!'

'I don't know what to say.'

He looks up at the ceiling, thinking. 'What was that line you said on the radio?' He touches his chin. '"Murder can be motivated by altruism."' Drew laughs a cold, sardonic laugh. 'A doctor, a learned woman – and yet, so horribly ignorant and misguided.'

'I—'

'I'm talking. You women. What do you know about how men feel, about our hearts, how we love our families? You know nothing.' He clears his throat. 'So, you are here, Dr Glass. It's part of your education and training. CPD,' he says with another sardonic laugh. 'Think of it as being a student, extending your knowledge of the mind. Of course, you have no option but to stay in that chair, to watch and listen, because I think if I gave you an alternative you wouldn't learn of your own free will. You wouldn't understand, but now you will see. You will see what it's like to be a victim of maternal filicide: to use your words, you will see inside my heart and mind. Now, you see this knife?'

'Yes.'

'Now you'll understand.'

'I've seen enough, Drew. I've even eaten your blood. I've sat in my own stink. Listen, just let me go. I have always expressed sympathy for the victims. The police don't know about your hate letters.'

Drew laughs. 'I have the letters, my dear.'

'Let me go and they don't need to know about this. Or, if you want, I will be your spokesperson. I will write and publish an article; I will tell your side of the story. If you want me to do that, you have to let me go.'

'When you come home after a long day's work to find your wife and child have left you and your life will never be the same again you expect some kind of debris, something which manifests the car crash in your existence. A snapped heel. A stray toy. An unmade bed. I came home to a clean, neat house. Everything was horribly in its place. Except for a note on the door of the fridge.'

'Tell me. What did it say?'

'"This dish is best served cold."'

'What made her do it, though? If she knew you had affairs. Something must have happened. A trigger.'

'If it did, I'll never know. We'll never know.'

Drew gets up and pads upstairs. She hears him rummaging around up there and then he spends ten minutes in the kitchen, filling up the sink. There's a smell of bleach. Bile comes up into her mouth.

Oh God. He's going to poison me. I'm going to drink bleach. It's going to burn my insides: a slow and painful death.

'What?' he asks when he sees her anguished face.

He has returned, holding a plate of food. A sausage roll and a cupcake. He removes the cuffs. Famished, she does not care whether there are drugs or poison in the food and wolfs it down. He passes her a bottle of water and watches her drink it in one go.

He produces a comb and a pair of scissors from his rucksack and immediately starts combing her long, black hair. At first she tenses her shoulders, but after a while she relaxes and succumbs to the intimacy of the gesture. Her hair's usual gloss is lost under grease and dirt. He combs as gently as possible, but still her head is jerked back and side to side.

'There were more people I didn't know than people I did know at the funeral of my own wife and son. Imagine that. Every chair was filled, and they kept looking at me as if to say I was to blame: I was the one who murdered James. I had Evie wear her mother's pearl earrings because she liked to wear them for best occasions, and I felt she deserved an open casket after putting on such a show of her unhappiness. I insisted they dress her in red; a colour she loathed. The dress was hers, but I can't remember her ever wearing it. She'd said it drained her of natural colour and clashed with her bleached blonde hair. It gave me some comfort to think of her in an outfit she hated for all eternity.'

'What are you doing to my hair?' Her voice sounds funny to her, like it's a long way away. She realises she's drowsy. Soon, she'll pass out. The food was doped. Sometimes it's a relief to not be conscious. Not that she has any choice in the matter.

'It surprised me how good a job they had done of concealing the ligature marks and the bulging effect in her eyes from the asphyxiation. That's what they do, I suppose, day in, day out. Conceal the horrible reality of death on a face. James deserved the dignity of a closed coffin, with the finest peach silk interior. The coffins were so dark they were almost black. His was such a small one, too.'

'Can you stop?'

He keeps combing and jerking her head with the knots. 'My wife was blonde. I used to like blondes. It's a good thing Lucy doesn't dye her hair blonde.'

'Lucy? You—'

'Obviously at first I saw her just to learn more about you, but actually, to my surprise, she is pleasant company. God knows my wife spent enough on her hair over the years. She used to say her hairdresser was a friend, a counsellor and a hairdresser all in one. I guess they have to listen to a paying customer drone on about themselves so they can justify their charges and take twice as long as they need to.'

'Wh—'

'Evie used to buy glossy magazines: the new trends sort, the fashions. She had bright plastic fingernails up to the day she left me. She scraped, rather than touched, me. I should have noticed. They were shining, often red and perfect, but the day she left to hang herself and James she wasn't wearing them. I suppose they would have gotten in the way with the noose and the knots… I see you have short nails. Practical.'

'You couldn't have known, Drew.'

'I miss stroking James's hair, and his cheek. It was as smooth as a stone from a river.'

'Ouch!' she shrieks, as he yanks through another knot and begins cutting her hair.

'One day I will start a new family. Someone young, fertile. Have a boy, of course. He'll hear stories about magic trees and forests, Hansel and Gretel, Little Red Riding Hood. No rope swings, of course. James. We'll call him James.'

'Sha—' she slurs, and then her head drops like a stone down a well.

'Sweet dreams.'

Satisfied that the shorter length is like his wife's hairstyle, he releases Emma-Jane from the chair and drags her into the kitchen, where he's placed a second kitchen chair by the sink. Drew pulls on the gloves.

When Emma-Jane comes around she sees several inches of her hair on the floor. The smell of bleach is stronger than before, and she knows what he's done. In her peripheral view, the straw-like colour catches her eye. Her glossy black hair had been her best feature. A tear rolls down her cheek and into her mouth. She tastes the salt, happy for a drop of water and a human reaction in private. If she were on an aeroplane, she'd look out of the window so no one would see. Her teardrops reassure her she is still Emma-Jane – still human, female – no matter how damp her armpits and groin, no matter the microbes festering and stinking.

To be bleached blonde couldn't be further from her natural colouring. She knows why he's done it. If she looks like Evie, whom he loathes, it will be easier for him to harm her, kill her, even. What's next, she's less sure about. Ordinarily, a hair disaster like this might make her tearful. But not now. It's only hair. She's just glad it's still growing. Perhaps he's dyed her hair to move her to some new place, so people won't recognise her.

Is anyone looking for me?

Is she even a red dot on someone's map? Perhaps her supervisor, Celia, her neighbours, have noticed her absence. Are there messages on her landline and mobile delivered in urgent, agitated tones?

As the days go by, perhaps someone will act on the vacancy of her home, her office. Maybe Derek at the dry cleaners, or Maureen at the Post Office. Maybe one of her clients has acted on a suspicion that something isn't right because she is a reliable, punctual professional. Vanessa might call the police and they'll come looking for her, like the prince with a glass slipper. Might Vanessa sound the alarm, or is Emma-Jane just a lost glove?

Chapter 22

It dumbfounds AJ when Drew picks up his phone. It's the first time in a week he's answered his phone calls; AJ usually leaves a message and waits for a call back. Even Hannah looks surprised to hear Drew's voice on the speakerphone in the van.

'Glad you called. I could do with your keys to the farmhouse. I need to hand them over.'

Surprised by the upbeat tone of Drew's voice, AJ raises his eyebrows at Hannah. 'I could drop them off at the farmhouse. We're not far from there now as it happens.'

'Perfect.'

Drew hangs up before AJ can clarify whether Drew is at the farmhouse or not, but he figures he can always leave them in the hiding place and text him.

Hannah looks nervously at AJ. 'Do you think he knows?'

'What?' he says, with a shrug, keen to hide the tension building across his shoulders and neck at the sound of his ex-boss's voice. He'll be glad to cut all ties and start afresh.

'About us sneaking in that night.'

'We didn't take anything, anyway. The mirror would have been all wrong in our place. If he knows, I'll say we were checking up on something. Don't worry: if he was angry, I'd know.'

'I'm not going inside the house. I don't mind standing in the yard with you, but that's it.'

'Suits me. Drew would have to drag me in there.'

Hannah giggles nervously.

'We'll only be there for a few minutes. I promise.' He touches her hand and she grabs his, holding it in hers.

Ten minutes later, they pull up in front of the farmhouse. 'Is that Drew's motor?' Hannah asks, wide-eyed.

AJ nods, hating that Hannah is impressed by the Range Rover, by money and swank, by the soft leather seats in a vehicle which lifts the passengers up to a height where they cannot help but look down their nose at people in regular cars and vans. Pete reckons a high-spec vehicle like that would have cost around £70,000. Drew is sat inside it, talking on the phone.

People are always impressed by money. Him too, he concedes, and then he looks at the farmhouse, inconspicuous and unchanged. Doors and windows closed and locked on secrets. The house would look respectable: money can hide dark secrets, which poverty cannot.

Opposite the farmhouse there's an old shippon built for lambing at one time and, at one end of the yard, an old barn, once home to cattle when this was a working farm. The open sheds are now home to nests of starlings in the spring, and to a family of doves, who come and go and coo. If anything, it's those outbuildings which reflect the true identity and history of the place and the previous owners. A lost way of living. A kind of history remembered. AJ almost pities the new owners who have bought the sad farmhouse. Will Evie haunt them?

All the buildings are neglected and uninhabitable in his mind; even the charming facade of an old farmhouse which pretends to be welcoming, warm, a family home. Once, it had been. If Drew hadn't changed his plans, AJ could have been working for twelve months, possibly two years on those outbuildings, earning a decent wage without tax to get himself and Hannah on the property ladder. At twenty-eight, he isn't even on the bottom rung.

As he closes the door of the van with a slam he's reminded of the antique chest in the dining room. The jealous streak in him wants Drew to go inside and for the chest to open and close, like the lid on a coffin at an open-casket service. He glances up at the house briefly, like it's watching him and his every move. He half expects the door to suddenly open and smoke to rise from its chimney, only it's Drew who opens and closes his car door with an expensive click.

'AJ!' he says cheerfully.

Hannah hops out of the van to join them, looking a little sheepish.

As always, Drew is smartly dressed in a shirt, navy slacks and brogues. It's his usual look: countrified, but businesslike. AJ looks Drew up and down, just like Drew looks at Hannah, as she smiles benignly at him.

'You must be the lovely Hannah,' Drew says, reaching for her hand, which he lightly kisses while she nervously giggles. He is the epitome of charm and agreeableness: a true snake charmer. 'Good of you to drop by. I'm here to say farewell to the place. The new owners move in next week.' He steps back with his hands in his pockets, looking at the property. 'Mixed emotions to see it go, which I didn't think I'd have.'

Hannah shuffles her feet and is about to say something when Drew continues, 'I expect the new owners will develop the outbuildings, carve it up into two dwellings. That was my original plan until… things changed.'

AJ passes him his keys to the farmhouse and says ingratiatingly, 'Are you happy with everything Pete and I have done to the inside? That's why I was calling you.'

'The place is sold. I haven't been inside, AJ. I've no intention of doing so, either,' Drew says, smiling. 'I can trust you, can't I, without having to check your work with a red pen?'

'Sure. Only you normally like to, as I would, and I left a box in the darkroom. Mainly photographs, and a few bits I wasn't sure whether or not to skip.'

Drew's phone buzzes in his pocket. 'Well, nothing important then. Thanks for dropping the keys off.'

A sound causes them to turn and look back in the farmhouse's direction: a light tapping, like a fingernail on a window. Tap-tap-tap. AJ and Hannah exchange a knowing glance while Drew looks at each window and then takes a step back.

'Must be a bird trapped inside. Rooks used to get stuck in the chimney. Damn pests. Well, thanks for the keys. Lovely to meet you, Hannah,' he says with a half wave and moves towards his vehicle, seemingly in a hurry to get away.

AJ doesn't take the hint. 'Hold up!' He likes to see strain on the man's face, to delay Drew; make him wait, like he has made AJ wait time after time on jobs he forgets to show up for as previously arranged. Once, you can forgive someone, but when it's a regular occurrence, that's just plain rude. Disrespectful. 'I haven't seen you in a while,' AJ says. 'Did you get my messages? Kat's been here a few times.'

'Sorry, yes, busy, busy. Anything urgent I need to know about?'

'I dunno. Kat left a letter for you. I have it, but it's at home.'

'Next time I see you. It can wait. I guess you'll be glued to the TV tonight with Liverpool playing Manchester City?'

Hannah rolls her eyes. 'You bet he will.'

'I won't take up any more of your time.' Drew turns to leave again, then stops in his tracks when AJ speaks again.

'Pete and I are setting up our own business.'

'Excellent! You will make a talented team. I can put you in touch with a few contacts if you like. Developers who need regular trades on hand. The chap who bought this place might be interested. Worth a try.'

'Yeah, I'd appreciate that, though I expect if he is a developer he'll have his own labourers.'

'Quite possibly. People's circumstances change all the times, though. Unexpected things happen! Stephen and his family fancy living here for a bit before selling on, and raising a few cattle, I think. Or ponies. I can't quite remember, but I will mention you and Pete to him, as you just never know, do you?'

'So, did you sell the ten acres off separately or not?'

'No, the new owner wanted it, even though I've let the land grow rough. It's worthless; nothing but nettles and thistles now.'

'A family is moving in then?' Hannah asks.

'Yes. It's a family home. I would go mad living here on my own. It pains me to sell something at this underdeveloped stage; it's got such potential. It would sell for a couple of million all done up, but I'm here to say goodbye to the place for good.'

AJ can't help but quietly gloat.

'Are you prepared to travel, to stay away, AJ? It's not ideal, I appreciate,' Drew says, looking directly at Hannah, 'but I have contacts further afield who'll have work for you, if you are.'

AJ looks Hannah in the eye, relieved when she smiles at him and not at Drew. 'If the money's right, I will. Short-term, like. Hannah's got a good job as a trainee accountant, so we want to stay put.'

'I'll text you. There's a good chap I know up near Hexham. An old friend who's doing up another barn into several catering cottages. He's gone into tourism in quite a big way. We stayed there last year for a family break one bank holiday. It's a beautiful spot, a few miles out of town, overlooking the River Tyne. We walked a section of Hadrian's Wall with James on my back in a carrier.' He pauses for a second. 'Seems like a decade ago now.' Hannah looks at her feet. 'Well, good luck.'

'Catch you again, Drew,' AJ says, heading towards the grubby van and waiting for Hannah to follow.

'Bye!' Hannah calls and waves, blushing slightly. Inside the van she says, 'I feel sorry for him. He misses her and his son. I can tell.'

‘Do you think so?’ he glances at Hannah, disliking the sympathy she is showing for his ex-boss, who has happily dropped him like a stone and driven off into the sunset.

‘I know he was unfaithful to his wife, but yeah, I do. Anyway, he’s a decent bloke really, isn’t he? Helping you out with contacts, I mean.’

‘If I cheated on you, would I still be “a decent bloke”?’

‘No, that’s different.’

‘How? They were married. We’re not, but I still wouldn’t cheat on you because I know it would hurt you.’

She reaches for his hand and squeezes it. ‘I bet he knows plenty of people with cash needing people like you. Everything is going to work out fine.’

People like me, he thinks, and accelerates out of the drive, the wheels of the grubby white van spinning and churning up gravel like a whirlpool of dirt and debris.

His toolbox slams into one side of the van in a metallic punch. They drive in silence for several minutes: his knuckles white on the steering wheel, Hannah oblivious to his frustration.

Even if the new owner of the farmhouse contacts him about labouring in the outbuildings, he has no intention of going back there, not ever. Not once. He'd sooner beg on the streets of Shrewsbury and pray Hannah didn't walk by on her lunch hour in that smart suit of hers.

Chapter 23

The cat flap rattles. Emma-Jane could open her eyes in a minute or count sheep and hope to go back to sleep. Her eyes don't need to be open for her to know what the room looks like. Its antique wallpaper and grubby, grey carpet. Her muscles ache, but she doesn't move.

If only a cat would walk in and wrap itself around her legs, purr a little to remind her of what it sounds like to be happy, contented, and bring in the cold and dew of the early morning on its fur. She remains still while Drew sleeps beside her on the mattress. The silence in the room is profound and heavy. It feels different today, like the seeds of Evie and James, watered so frequently, have taken root, and their bones move under the carpet. His memories of them float like dandelion seeds, to land and settle wherever they please.

Drew's body is in the sleeping bag, curled into a ball like a dormouse in hibernation. She doesn't move, afraid that she isn't scared of the man beside her. It isn't just gravity that is tethering her to this man, this moment, this house. If she begged, would he let her go? If she tried, could she escape?

As each day goes by, the pull on her past, the clarity of memories and the signposts she's carefully constructed to navigate days and evenings are fading, fading. More than the sight of him, it is this which frightens her the most. If he were cruel, nailed her palms to a cross, made her gaunt from lack of food or water, the suffering would occupy her mind and senses. The immorality would remind her of who and what she is.

To be civilised to one another – a new torture. The mind is her dungeon this time.

Drew's breathing is deep and slow. Then he stirs a little in his sleep and she feels the imprint of his breath on her neck. Emma-Jane licks her bottom lip. Her face appears as if it's been stung by a rogue insect. The tears start quietly, trickling. She softly turns to look at his sleeping face.

Why can't I hate you?

Ordinary things. The known and familiar. A world she understands. Street lights, the tarmac and puddles speak to her, and cars splash, and those things make sense. Even shop windows selling luminous dreams do. A dog chained to a lamp post wags its tail at her, which lifts a low mood.

As time goes on it is increasingly difficult for Emma-Jane to imagine petrol stations, supermarkets, bars and shops, office buildings opening and closing at defined times, or people moving in and out of them talking on phones, smiling at the first hints of summer in planted hanging baskets.

She closes her eyes, like a red admiral closes its wings tight when the wind is playing rough. It waits for the gust to pass before fluttering away. The impulse is to pull his wings together. Shut. She had been brave before, though. She can do it again. Her heart and head battle until she slams her heart like a door in a wind tunnel.

The fruit bowl is on the carpet, beside the mattress. He regularly adds plums and cherries to it. Only once or twice has she seen him take something from the bowl and eat it. She's watched juice from the plum squirt down his chin and found her own tongue wiping her lips. The fruit is spoiled now. Time goes on. Perhaps that's why he leaves them there, these dying reminders of supermarkets, fields, trees – alien places to her. Will she grow fur the way the plum has? Or shrink, the way a plum becomes a prune, a dried grape a sultana?

Suddenly, he moans. A dream, or perhaps a nightmare, stirs him. Should she crawl on her hands and knees to the kitchen to hunt for the key? No; he will only wake up and the trust between them will be over. Drew's grief is the only real thing she can think about right now. His life must be a constant bleed, waking up each day to the ugly ending Evie chose.

She hears his grief, like ghosts playing in an orchestra. It's snowflakes, it's an avalanche, and it's a light bulb popping. His grief is fierce, a sharp pain. Its hue is coloured by the nature of the deaths, premature: one suicide, one murder. Like a season stopped prematurely, from summer to autumn. Like a tree that has disrobed itself of leaves and colour having been in full life, full bloom, the sap rising. Rising.

Do I love him? She squeezes her eyes shut so she doesn't cry. God, I hope not.

He takes a while to come round, as though he is resisting waking up. Emma-Jane knows that, wherever he's been diving in his dreams, it was dark and frightening. This troubled man perplexes her; a man who likes to watch her, a millionaire who sleeps on a mattress in a dirty, stuffy room.

Drew suddenly sits up and looks at Emma-Jane. His eyes open like a camera clicking a long-anticipated shot. He wipes his mouth with the back of his hand and blinks several times. 'I haven't slept that deeply in a long time.

You are good therapy for me, but did something happen to you?' He swallows and rubs at his face. 'I mean, something frightening, which has scared you?'

'Why do you ask me that?' she asks, moving away.

'You have nightmares.'

'This isn't my idea of a holiday.'

They both remain looking at each other, neither wanting to give in and look the other way or decide what to say or do next.

'So, you are as damaged and deformed as I am, now. We are both used goods with trauma in our past and present. How similar we are! We each have a heart of stone; nothing but emotional leftovers to give to the opposite sex. It is sad.'

'I am not angry or bitter.'

'And I am?' Suddenly, Drew moves closer.

She stiffens. 'You won't—'

'You already know the answer to that.' His smile unnerves her. Is it genuine?

'I've been here for over a week now, Drew, and my clients need me. Some are very vulnerable. I need to contact them, please.' He doesn't respond. 'Drew?'

'That isn't possible.' He suddenly stands up and strides into the kitchen, where he takes two pasties and a bottle of water from the fridge. 'Breakfast is served!'

The plate is outstretched. She grasps it, still wearing the handcuffs. He removes a keyring from his trouser pocket and uses a small key to unlock them. 'Eat those.' He puts the bottle of water in her lap. 'Drink that. Don't even try to move from that spot.'

'You can trust me,' she says, with more conviction than she was expecting, like she is carving the words into the bark of a sycamore tree.

Drew removes a make-up bag from his rucksack. It is pink, with 'Lancôme' written on one side. 'Your fingernails are all chipped.' He dabs nail polish remover on a tissue and begins to remove the residual colour. 'Do you have a man in your life? Someone who loves you?'

'I'm single,' she states, not wanting to be drawn into talking about her private life and struggling to comprehend his strange moods and actions.

'So, who loves you, Dr Glass? Your patients might think they love you when you make them feel better. Ah, Lucy; she is fond of you. What about family?'

'Don't you already know my family tree? Somehow, I thought you did.'

'I'm flattered. No, I don't know. Enlighten me.'

The nail polish remover stings where the cuticle is raw and she flinches. 'There isn't a great deal to tell. I was an only child. My father disappeared before I was two. My mum raised me until I was eighteen, and then I left home for university on a scholarship. Mum passed away the year before I graduated. Breast cancer.'

'I see. So, who is waiting for someone heroic to rescue you?'

'You will let me go. I am sure of that, because this situation isn't what you want. It's not you. It's a reaction to a terrible event, but you aren't that terrible event; you are a separate self. A good man. Someone who was a good father.'

He laughs and puts the nail polish remover away. 'Done. You haven't suffered yourself, Emma-Jane, that's the thing. You've done well for yourself – a credit to your mother, to have a doctor as a daughter. While you might know the right answer, the right thing to say to people who are suffering, you yourself have never felt your chin go under the water… perhaps till now.'

'My role as a psychologist requires me to keep some emotional distance in order to help my clients. Sympathy isn't involved; that is personal. Empathy, however, which I do have, allows the person to talk and be understood without being judged or enticed down a certain path. I am good at my job. If you want therapy you don't have to kidnap me.'

'Defensive, aren't we? And by God, do you flatter yourself. Talk, talk, talk. Evie was the same. On the phone, text. God only knows what she found to talk about, except complaining about me.'

'You must have been very dear to her for you to be the centre of Evie's universe. Only a good, kind man could be that.'

'I left school at sixteen. Worked as an apprentice for a builder. Saved by living in my car so that, by the time I was twenty, I could put a deposit down on my first house. Between work in London and Surrey, I did it up. That's how it was for ten years or so, and then the property boom gave me a fair wind and I was away. Moneyed, married, a son. Three properties to my name before I was thirty.'

'I miss my home. I miss—'

'The Glass House. Yes, quite a statement to live inside so much glass. It did not surprise me to find you lived in a sparkling palace. Our homes are our castles, aren't they? I mean, all that glass, and a name and a job where you're meant to be squeaky clean. It's a cliché. When I dropped that letter off, saw your blinds and that fancy one-way glass, then I knew your conscience wasn't so clean.'

She frowns and wipes her sticky mouth with her sleeve. 'My conscience is clean, Drew. I have nothing to hide.'

His eyes flash. The mood change is swift. 'Of course you do! Everyone does, unless they're living in a cave on a rock off the British Isles! That's why I'm here, to help you see it's not clear. A degree and a doctorate mean nothing in this world, Dr Glass. You'd be better off getting some bloody life experience, if you want to help people and understand what drives them to do the unthinkable. An ignoramus wrote that article.'

Drew removes a handheld mirror from his rucksack. Her mouth closes and makes a soft popping sound. Judging by the dainty design, it must have been Evie's. He holds it in front of her face, his hand shaky from all the wine he drank yesterday, while peering into her face like it's a deep well. The man is a narcissist, but she's still surprised he has a mirror with him! There's a smell of body odour and something else, sour. Fear, sadness perhaps, or just the grey neglected state of the house waiting for someone to love it and refresh the walls and carpets and paint the skirting boards and the ceilings.

'Look! Take a good, long look at yourself, Dr Glass.'

The hairs on the back of her neck stand up. The bleach blonde short hair shouts at her.

'If I cut you, would your blood be blue? Do you see a female, a woman born to nurture, protect, procreate, or a supporter of child-killers? Which one are you?'

Frustrated that she can't bat the mirror away, she closes her eyes.

'Look! Are you just like Evie, like all those other women who killed themselves and their offspring to spite their husbands? Are you? Because I think you pity those monstrous women. Do you like what you see?'

'No!' she sees a warped version of herself. A painting edited to the point of deformity. Words from his hate letter return with a vengeance.

How many more are going to die before you stop meddling? One, two, ten, Dr Death?

I hope you're listening. Can you hear glass smashing? Those sharp little pieces will be your only legacy. No family. Just shards of glass.

'You are like all women!' His anger slides from him in waves. 'Oh my God, you women, mothers – how can you live with yourself? Your face gives your guilt away.'

'You don't understand,' she pleads. 'Much of what a woman experiences during pregnancy, childbirth and then into motherhood is taboo, which is why I wrote that article about Angela Lamb. Yes, in your mirror I see a woman's face – a doctor, a therapist, a friend – and I will live the rest of my life protecting the things I believe in.'

The room is still and silent. Her voice cracks. She longs to be alone, to be at home, to breathe fresh, clean air and to feel nothing. Drew's face bobs in front of her like an ugly misshaped balloon. God, she wants to pop it. Make it shrivel away and flop on the carpet.

'Oh my God! Woman, you are evil!' He thrusts the mirror closer still to her face. His eyes are red and wild with fury. 'Where is your shame for defending monsters? I see none etched on your face or in your voice.'

Her head falls. Is he right in what he's saying about women? It is a thought so misshapen it could only grow in a dark, damp place.

'You don't need to do this to me; to anyone, for that matter. What Evie did to James and what Angela did to Teddy was terrible, tragic. I never said it wasn't! And I never said I was perfect. By God, I know I'm far from it.'

'You defended those actions and lived with your own thoughts while sitting in an office with your "Dr

Glass" name on the door, comfortably telling other people how to live their lives.' He throws the mirror across the room and it smashes.

The sound makes Emma-Jane shiver. Not with surprise, but the knowledge of the foresight he'd put into those horrible hate letters. Was it all carefully planned and constructed up until this moment in time?

'Those evil, unspeakable actions: you are as rotten as them.' Drew falls onto his knees in tears and his head drops suddenly, like a broken sun.

'Yes! I am, and that's why I do my job.' She breathes more easily and closes her eyes to the horror of a broken man, until he crawls on his hands and knees to retrieve the smashed mirror. Its glass is shattered, but the wooden handle is intact. He peers at his own reflection like he hasn't seen himself before.

How she longs for an ordinary sound, like a phone ringing, a radio or the news on television at six o'clock. A knot of emotion forms in her throat; astonishingly, it is pity she feels for him. Not hate. Seeing him there lying on the carpet, as if staring into another time in a deep dark trance, she can imagine what he might see: a wreckage of James's toys, a rusty scooter, a spoiled chocolate Easter egg. The debris and ruins of his family life must keep rising, because his mood changes so starkly. He moans and rocks as if they are up to his shoulders, his mouth. She wishes she could exhale a strong wind to blow it all away. But she can only count the seconds she lives as he stares at the carpet.

'It wasn't your fault,' she says softly, and the tears fall. Her head feels heavy, so she lets it fall too.

To have talked so intensely has exhausted her completely and, like catharsis, a sense of calm and peace washes over her, almost to the point of detachment from the situation. There can be no judgement from him or her in this quicksand, in the bizarre reversal of roles from therapist to client. The paroxysm of sobbing is so intense she does not hear Drew move towards her.

'You're crying!' Drew says, his face concerned and his eyes wounded as he kneels beside her.

She sniffs to stem the flow of snot and raises a shoulder blade to wipe one side of her face, then the other. By looking away she avoids looking at him, avoids feeling exposed and vulnerable.

Drew scrutinises her face.

'How much longer must I stay here?'

Gently, he holds her chin to tilt her blotchy face towards him. First, he applies red lipstick to her lips. 'Did you know no two lip prints are the same?'

Not expecting an answer, he then inexpertly drags blue eyeshadow across her eyelids. His fingers rummage through the make-up bag, unsure of which item he needs next. He chooses a blusher, and gently sweeps the brush against each cheek.

Lastly, he removes a hairbrush from the bag. There are knots in the ends of her hair. Having been bleached, it is dry and brittle, ready to snap – just like her.

Chapter 24

The red-haired woman she had met last time had hydrated, unblemished skin and a waterfall of hair. This version has a different appearance and aura. Perhaps it's the eyeliner that hasn't been scrubbed from her face, or the yoga pants which hang off her in such a way they shout she doesn't give a damn. From the items of furniture on the lawn, and the piles of rubbish strewn around the bins, it looks like the woman is leaving any minute.

'You'll have to come in if you want to talk to me; I'm busy. What's your name?'

'Lucy. Yours?'

'It's Kat.'

Lucy reluctantly follows Kat into the kitchen. A stray sock, unopened post and a bra are on the lounge floor and the sofa has a creased look about it, like it's only just been vacated after a lot of use. A blue throw is scrunched up at one end. They move towards the sound of a washing machine whirring its way through a cycle and the smell of sausages or greasy bacon. There are enough wine bottles on the kitchen counters to open a shop, and stained glasses and a frying pan in the sink. Kat heats a mug of coffee in the microwave. It's hard not to wonder how old and stale the coffee tastes.

'What do you want this time? I ain't got another phone number for Drew, if that's what you're here for,' she says, stuffing a saucepan and a frying pan into the open cardboard box. 'The bastard wants me out tomorrow.'

'So, have you spoken to Drew Rogers? That's why I'm here.'

'No, he won't speak to me.' She sighs, and her shoulders drop. 'The solicitor or the estate communicate with me. Drew doesn't.'

'Oh, well—'

She takes a slurp of coffee and seems to soften at having someone to talk to. 'I kidded myself about that for a while, but it's not like he doesn't know where I live!' She rubs her neck until it is red. 'It's the estate agent who rings me and sends me one letter after another. It seems Drew doesn't stoop so low as to speak to me anymore. What a bloody fool I was!' She aggressively points to a plastic bag on the kitchen counter. 'That's his stuff in there. Expensive shaving stuff, mainly. Take it, will you?'

'Oh, I see.' Lucy nods, and a wall calendar depicting an enormous snake catches her eye. She takes a peek inside the bag. The Drew she knew sautéed potatoes, cooked with garlic and seasoning, took his time shopping, preparing, cooking. Seeing a bottle of aftershave and his shaving gear in the plastic bag unsettles her some more. He is less and less the man she thought he was. A man who had an affair with his tenant and then disappears. 'The telephone number you gave me, it only goes to voicemail. I mean, I've left messages, but Drew hasn't called back. Do you have any idea where he might be?' There's an open bottle of milk on the kitchen counter, which looks to have curdled. The kitchen has an air of sadness about it. Lucy can't wait to get out of there and back on the road.

'I don't know and he won't call back, unless you've got something he wants. Not that long ago he had one of his labourers round here doing the house up. I had a new shower, as the old one leaked. There was me thinking what a great guy Drew is. The bloke wanted a power shower after we—' She takes a slurp of coffee and Lucy gets a whiff of body odour from her unwashed body. 'Anyway, since then, Drew's changed his business, changed his whole bloody life probably, 'cos of grief – or running from something – and I'm not in the picture. He's made that loud and clear. Are you in the picture?' She attempts to smile, but the muscles quickly give way like it's too much effort. She tosses a cheese grater into the box and it makes a loud clatter. On its side, Lucy sees it could do with a wipe.

'No, I'm not. It's my friend who's missing. She was Drew's therapist. I'm worried about her.'

'She? I thought last time you said – Oh, never mind. Was she seeing Drew or something?' she asks sharply. 'I mean, I don't know who he is seeing anymore,' Kat says bitterly, giving away her lingering feelings for him.

Lucy looks at her shoes on the linoleum floor as she faintly flushes, remembering how attracted she had been to him. The troubled look on Kat's face suggests she still has feelings for Drew, and perhaps she has invited Lucy into her house only to investigate Drew's habits now he is on the brink of a new life. Something about the woman unnerves Lucy this time.

'Emma-Jane is a professional therapist and, with Drew being her client, they wouldn't have a relationship. She is a person of routine, and her disappearance is out of character.'

'So, like being married, only without the ceremony? Is that the kind of relationship you mean? Well, I'm sorry to disappoint you, but marriage meant nothing to Drew. I can say that, hand on heart. Why do you think your friend is with him, of all people?'

'I'm not sure she is, but I want to check. That's all. Listen, do you know the addresses of his other properties? I can see you're busy.'

'Well,' she grins, 'his farmhouse is sold. He owns another terrace like this just round the corner opposite the bus stop, but I know the couple who live there.' She scratches her chin. 'The name of his business is Amver. That might turn up something if you google it. I dunno, love. Look, I need to crack on.'

'Sure, sorry to hold you up, but it's important. Did you know Drew's wife, Evie?'

She stops reaching inside the cupboard and turns to glare at Lucy. 'Why would I?' Her voice is thick, as if she were drunk. The tilt of her head and fix of her eye holds a portentous interest.

Lucy shrugs, sensing her time is up and something irrevocable has happened. She isn't there to judge. 'I… Thanks, anyway.'

'Take this; in case you see him. I know I won't.' Lucy accepts the bag out of courtesy, happy to get away from the woman who makes her feel so on edge. 'I was gonna chuck it, but now you're here you might as well take it. See yourself out.'

Back in the car, Lucy puts her seat belt on and then rummages in the plastic bag. It feels like an invasion of Drew's privacy but, right now, that's not her priority: knowing Emma-Jane is safe and well is. Inside there's an electric toothbrush, aftershave, a shaving kit from The White Lemon and a round tin of aftershave balm scented with lemongrass. The label makes the product look expensive: 'Hand Made Natural Skincare by The White Lemon. Lemongrass Essential Blend'. The shop is on the high street in Shrewsbury. The familiar name gives her a trickle of hope. The shop is not one she goes to because the products are fancy and out of her price range. Not having a better idea, Lucy turns her car round and heads in that direction.

Chapter 25

Drew's empty wine bottles catch the lines of sunlight coming through the gap in the curtain. There are more and more of them strewn on the carpet, taunting her with the idea of a message in a bottle thrown straight through the window and onto the sea of tarmac outside. She tries to remember the song about empty bottles to divert her mind from the vain hope of being found and rescued. Those veins and arteries of his must be drunk on red wine because he is drunk night after night and sometimes during the day. Drew forever seeks obscurity, vacancy, but can't seem to find it.

The wine doesn't make him laugh or smile. Sometimes he lifts a limp, heavy hand to wave at her. He always sits opposite her: his version of the sessions in her office, only now the roles are reversed. Metal shadows spill onto the carpet. Light will nose its way inside. It's a Sunday or a Monday, she thinks, but she can't be sure. Perhaps, elsewhere, church bells ring. She keeps still and quiet, not wanting to antagonise him and see those purple veins rise in his throat, like angry snakes from a pit, when all she wants to feel is close to him. His past lingers in the doorway and the four corners of the lounge.

He's going to cut himself. She knows it because he's bare-chested and the bag where he keeps the knife is beside him.

She wishes that a rebirth of each day would heal him and that the bustling of life would banish the lethargy and staleness from this house. Not a sanctuary; a tomb, a horrible freeze-frame. If he were an ant, she'd lift whatever was in his way so he could push on to his path, moving on, letting go.

'My wife's magazines say yellow is in fashion this season,' he says, tossing a glossy magazine back into his rucksack with force, like it's Evie. He throws Emma-

Jane a look. The threads of red lines, like electricity, around the bulb of his eye make her tense.

He digs out his knife and starts cutting. It's like he goes to work, to a quarry or an abattoir, and the room is silent as he carves into himself. What is it he is trying to cut out of his flesh? The cutting seems to give him peace. Or fatigue. The undoing of his seams. Lately, he never speaks when he cuts and cuts, but she has to watch. His heads nods and his eyes move around his body as slow as an ache and, like now, he looks at her and sobs, and each sob is like a fist in her stomach. The criss-cross pattern of cuts and welts are a vivid confession of sorts. She sees pain expanding in his eyes as he makes an incision into his bicep.

Slick wet blood trickles into his clenched hand and a waft of iron permeates the room. Sweat glistens on his temple. Perhaps he hopes to be reborn when he cuts, because there is anger living under his skin. Something he wants to remove to undo himself.

'You are not bad, Drew. You are not bad. Can you hear me?'

His face is flushed from the pain, the heating. A sadness sneaks up over her shoulder and a hollowness opens in her stomach as the wound of him fills the stark room. This man is no longer a stranger to her. He flinches as a chunk of skin is lifted from where it belonged on his forearm. His chest flushes as the pain grows. The blotches form like watercolour on paper.

'Out!' His voice is full of metal and his hypnotised face is far away from her now. She cannot call him back. All she can do is keep her mind toward logic; for him, and for her.

Her throat closes up when he moans in pain. To him, his organs are black. His insides are rotten and wretched. His wounds give him relief. A shimmering sky of stars. The routine of making her watch is eating away at them both. It's a relief to see his stone eyes stare back, his face like a deserted chapel. He hates it when she turns to look the other way.

'I'm here, Drew.'

She imagines gently closing his eyes with her finger and thumb: those dark eyes that seek clemency which only he can give himself. His mouth is open, and a line of dribble works its way down his chin. Blood has run to the gutters of his nails and cuticles, where it dries. Then, his eyes open so unexpectedly it's like a doll that suddenly sees and stares at its owner. He swallows several times, lubricating his throat and mouth, never once taking his eyes off her face.

'You,' he says, his head lolling to one side.

Hours pass in what she thinks is a small 1950s build. As time goes on, someone will notice she's missing and find her here. Her clients, perhaps. Lucy, not yet but in a day or so, Lucy will realise she isn't on holiday by the missed appointments and confused clients hovering outside her door.

All the days Emma-Jane had sat idle on her sofa daydreaming about travel weigh her down. Celia used to say that she needed to find an equilibrium between work and life. The work bit came more naturally, somehow. Work was all she wanted to do, but there are so many places she hasn't seen yet. America, Canada, Europe. The Golden Gate Bridge. The Red Sea.

I'll travel. If I don't die. I'll see the sights. The Seven Wonders. Start local. Start with London. Big Ben. Madame Tussauds. Then further afield. Break the routines of work, work, work. Learn to swim.

She watches a spider slowly crawl across the ceiling and onto the lampshade, sprinkling dust like dandruff. All that ceiling, all those walls, they're like acres, countries, to a spider. Such freedom. Here she sits, trapped in a web. The spider's unhurried movement stirs the mounting hysteria building inside her.

An hour later, Drew gets to his feet and staggers into the kitchen to wash his hands and prepare something to eat. He returns with a bowl of chicken soup, which he feeds her, spoon by spoon. It is delicious; a comfort food she would choose to eat herself. It's his way to leave it a long time between meals, so she suffers with hunger and thinks about all the food she can't eat in the meantime.

'You can trust me to feed myself,' she says, between spoonfuls.

'I enjoy feeding you.'

'You don't trust me.' She wonders if he sees her as a child or a sick patient. He doesn't hurry her. As he kneels beside her, she savours his familiar scent and the shape of his long fingers. Nearness to him is a strange comfort and discomfort. The movement of that spoon reminds her of how much she needs him to stay alive. It reminds her of how far away from normality they are. She has a flash of self-consciousness about her unbrushed teeth, bad breath, body odour. It is good that she knows these things about herself, that the weird isn't acceptable. There is more of her than just a husk of her old self, and so she believes civilisation and her civilised being are still within reach.

The bowl is almost empty. 'Is there more?' she asks, hating herself for wanting him beside her, looking at her, and the sustenance filling her hollow insides.

During her training to become a psychologist she had read case studies on Stockholm syndrome, where a captive believed in a bond between them and their abductor. It's a coping mechanism, but the feelings she has for Drew, her empathy, are as real as the drawn curtains at the window.

He gets up and returns with a bowl of ice cream. He makes a show of placing a lump of vanilla on her tongue, which she lets sit there for as long as possible. It's like taking communion.

'Mmm.' Ice cream has never tasted so good. If only she could stick her fingers in the tub. Part of her wishes she could grab the tub and deposit the lot in her mouth; the other likes this slow eating.

'No one is looking for you, are they?' he says with satisfaction. 'You are more of a workaholic recluse than I thought.'

'You don't know that for sure.'

'I do. We are so alike.'

Drew disappears into the kitchen. She hears the lazy drone of a fly. Helpless to defend her skin, her nostrils, from it, she listens to its hypnotic sound. She must look like a lost soul to it, squinting like that. The fly rushes towards her – a fuzz of static and indecision making it hang in the air like a light aircraft, stalled above her – and then it lands near her left eye. The tiny insect makes her feel so horribly helpless.

Perhaps Drew is right. No one is looking for her. She violently shakes her head, sending the fly's fuselage and wings off into the air, only for it to land in almost exactly the same spot again. It's not just the tickle of its tiny legs on her face that bothers her; it's the helplessness it writes all over her face. She surrenders to its message and imagines herself as a carcass with flies crawling over her, swarming her oily, sweaty self. In the heat and odiousness of the room, she longs to be in the shade of an oak tree in a meadow on a summer's day. A gentle breeze. Fingers of sunlight stroking her hair. If only.

Suddenly, Drew reappears in the lounge, holding a half-full bottle of white wine in one hand. He takes a swig straight from it.

'Tell me, doctor, why do women kill their children? All that longing to be a mother and nurture, the goddamn awful pregnancy that they suffer through, then childbirth, the sleepless nights and the complete and utter loss of their separate self and a complete absorption on the child.' He leans against the door frame. 'How can it happen?'

'Mental illness, for one, which underlines pretty much all reasons. I mean, mothers will suffer from post-partum blues without knowing it and then it can get serious and become psychosis. A mother of a dead child receives a great deal of attention. That is desirable for some women who are mentally ill. Sometimes, it's caused by mental illness combined with something else.'

'Like what?'

'Some mothers believe their child is ill or evil, or that the world is cruel, and then it's a kind of mercy killing, born out of altruistic intentions. Others do it because the child is unwanted. Emilia Fray, for example, killed her stepchild because she just wanted to have a relationship with the father. Accidental deaths also occur, from abuse or anger.'

'Anything else?'

'Spouse revenge, perhaps, because of their infidelity or abandonment.'

Drew remains still, leaning heavily on the door frame to hold himself up, seeming to absorb the information very gradually.

'A jealous rage, for example. Or a divorce. There was a Canadian woman who drowned her two children because she feared her ex-husband would get custody of them.'

'Poor man.'

'Poor children, and poor woman. She was ill, desperate. Still is, as she serves a lengthy prison sentence. Life, probably. A human has to be ill to go to such an extreme, but not necessarily insane.'

'Don't you dare talk about pitying those female monsters!'

'I'm aware of the science and the social taboo around the act. It's not about pity.'

'Abhorrent act.' He takes a long swig. She listens and watches him drink and it's like a scream from a long way away. 'Abhorrent.'

'Did Evie take drugs or abuse alcohol?' she asks, enjoying the irony of the question in the face of his own alcohol abuse and mental instability. 'That can be a factor in a tragedy.'

'No more than the rest of us,' he says, holding up the wine bottle to toast her, smiling sarcastically. 'The woman starved herself, probably to fit in her pre-pregnancy clothes, which I'd paid through the nose for, but she wasn't mentally ill. Evie was sane when she killed James and herself. There was a thought process behind what and where. Evil. Plain evil.'

'How do you know there was a thought process and that it was not a spontaneous decision?'

He stares at the bottle for a time, as if it were a piece of unusual art. 'The house was perfect. She looked great, as usual, doing yoga, and James was always immaculate. We had a meal out at the weekend and shared a bottle of wine back at home, listening to Leonard Cohen. She was fine. Moody and needy, but that's how she was. We had sex on the sofa; first time for a while.'

'So, everything was good between you?'

'Don't put words in my mouth. You're not married. You're not a mother. She was never satisfied with me, always wanting more and more. That meal, the drunken sex, the music. She cried afterwards. I didn't understand.' He strokes the wine bottle. A finger traces its curve as if it were a woman's body.

'Did something happen? Like, I don't know, a trigger, like a loved one falling ill. Something to make her desperate, to snap?'

He looks down at the floor and speaks in barely a whisper. 'Reasons. I mean, does a reason even matter? When people kill each other, it's bad enough, but children… My boy. I'm done talking.'

He slams the front door behind him. The click is like a bite. It is the first time he has left in an angry mood, leaving her without water. What if he forgets about her? Her death would be slow, painful. The car speeds away. He's driving over the limit. What if he crashes?

She swallows down the rising panic. Urine trickles down her leg and she winces at the unpleasant smell.

Chapter 26

Drew returns around two hours later, drunker than when he'd left, and immediately falls asleep on the mattress, snoring loudly. Emma-Jane is so dehydrated she has a coughing fit, and the sound wakes him up.

'What the…' He wipes his mouth with his hand and gets up from the mattress. A deep frown etches on his forehead when he looks up at the ceiling for several minutes. He staggers a little and stops to listen once more. 'I heard footsteps upstairs, running one way, then back again.' Drew's eyes bat open and closed and then he stares directly at Emma-Jane, as if she has an answer for the footsteps.

Emma-Jane could cry. He looks insane. 'No. I don't think so, Drew.'

'And giggling. A ball bounced down the stairs: bump, bump, bumpety-bump.' Drew cocks his head, expecting to hear just that. He covers his face with his hands. 'It was so real. James was playing with a football.' Thin sadness leaks from her heart for him. 'James said I was never there when he needed me!'

Rocking an imaginary baby in his arms, he quiets down. The room is as silent and dead as an empty shell. Drew, as if cradling James, leans forward and tilts his head to one side to admire his baby, listening for a heartbeat. Then, he feels for a pulse in an imaginary neck and wrist. 'Nothing. Nothing. Nothing.'

She thinks Drew's body looks shipwrecked. The tide has come in and taken his reason away. He is a hull on the bottom of the seabed. With light fingertips, he makes to close James's imaginary eyelids and strokes his imaginary hair so gently, and with so much love, it should bring James back to life if there was any goodness left in the world.

Crying with jerking spasms, he hugs himself, still standing in the middle of the room. An actor in the warped theatre of his mind. She winces when he drops to the floor because his body is slumped at an angle and she cannot console him, touch him. One arm, like a rag doll's, remains limp underneath him.

'My baby! I'm so sorry. My baby!'

Snot is running down his face and his cheeks shine, from that and the tears. How pitiful he looks, wearing grey tracksuit bottoms and one flat brown shoe. Suddenly, he crawls into a ball and bangs his head on the carpet over and over. He is breathing hard. When he puts one hand to his brow, she finds the gesture unspeakably touching.

'Drew?' She shivers, frightened for herself, and for him. He is so horribly uncomfortable inside his own skin, his own head.

Drew uncurls his body and stands up tall, with one hand on the wall. He looks around the room like he hasn't seen it before and staggers out of the lounge. Drew has dropped the keyring with the key to her cuffs within inches of her feet. Emma-Jane stares at the carpet. She could escape. The fear, the control, would end. And so would their closeness.

She hears the interior door to the kitchen fly open and Drew's feet ascending the stairs – at surprising speed, for a drunken man. The room has never felt hotter. She hears him play a game of something upstairs, perhaps hide and seek, or snakes and ladders upstairs, only it sounds like there are too many snakes and not enough ladders.

'James! I'm coming! It's Daddy! I'm here for you!'

His torment reverberates around the house. The shouting and running beat a tuneless sound above her head. It is dark inside his head; darker than ever. She has to get away, get help, for her and him. The key is right there.

There's an unmistakable arrival of thunder in his brain this time. This time, the fear she feels is intense. It's brittle and sharp and building with every minute. Emma-Jane is sombre as she senses Drew's mood change like the weather. She is tearful because each hour it can change. A sudden brightening, then a brief storm and a rainbow hanging in the room when he sleeps. She keeps a mental report. It's something to occupy her mind, to treat it like a weathervane. Now, it's time to get away before the storm comes.

Run.

As usual, the radio is left on in the kitchen on low. He likes to untune it, leaving them to listen to loud crackles and sizzles, like she's in space and losing contact with ground control. Perhaps it echoes the sounds in his brain?

'Here I come!'

His world is spilling out upstairs, like a cracker pulled in two. Now, in his mind, white doves are covered in soot. The flute of Evie's voice or the harp of his son's is all he hears. He runs along the landing, trying to catch the words in nets, like moths and butterflies, to preserve them behind glass.

Save yourself. Save yourself, she chants, willing herself to find the strength to act, to leave.

She lifts one leg and turns her foot at a ninety-degree angle. The key is only millimetres away. She flexes her foot backwards and forwards, then makes little circles with it to loosen the muscles. The sound of Drew crying disrupts her movements and thoughts.

Focus on yourself. Remember, Drew's peace of mind flickers on and off like a light switch. The gentle, calm Drew who feeds you, pours cool water into your mouth, is invisible, and only a red outline of rage and a silhouette of grief are left.

Her foot reaches the keyring, and she drags it – slowly, slowly, catchy monkey – towards her. It is hers, but she has no way of picking it up and using the key to unlock the handcuffs unless she can fall forwards. She pushes it under one shoe.

The slightest movement brings a fresh burst of perspiration to her forehead and upper lip. Whether

Drew enjoys living in a tropical house or the radiators are broken and can't be switched off, she's not sure, but in weak moments she's let herself think about how a cool breeze on her skin feels, how it would move through her hair in waves and ruffle her clothes. He mustn't see signs of effort on her face should he return.

'I can't find you, James!' His voice cracks. 'Where are you, James? It's Daddy! I'm here now. I am.'

Drew is laughing and giggling one minute then crying hysterically the next, at the mercy of the broken synapse in his brain, of the ghost of his guilt. His nightmare is caught in a net. He won't let it go. Doors are opening and closing upstairs. Some are banged shut. Drew's anger, back again. He runs down the stairs and she braces herself. Drew is in the kitchen. He opens the front door. He is walking around the house. She imagines him out there, moving around, like a lost plastic bag in the wind. Absence owns this moment.

Moments later, the door slams, and Drew's malignant presence fills the lounge. He is ashen. It looks like he's aged ten years in less than ten minutes. He continually runs one hand through his hair, the other at his collar, which is now open and gaping. The sweat stains under his armpits are almost down to his waist. The buttons on his cuffs have come off, so they gape and flap.

'It was so real. James was here.'

Emma-Jane doesn't answer at first. Part of her wants to reach for his hand and help tether him to reality, but when she moves her hand the metal click of the cuffs makes her decide against that. She feels herself balancing on a tightrope of saving herself or pushing Drew over the edge, sticking one finger at a time through the lacework of his mind.

'It's over now.'

'No,' he wails. 'It's not. She killed poor James out of spite! How could she do that?' Saliva dribbles from his mouth as it opens and closes. 'The pain, the hunger, it never leaves me. I want to unearth his little body and hold him in my arms and stroke his hair, his poor throat.' He touches his neck where he imagines the rope and the ligature marks would have been. 'Evie knew I didn't love her. I didn't even like her. Why would I care if she starved herself? James,' he moans. 'Poor James.' His voice croaks. 'I never thought she'd do what she did.'

'Did you hurt Evie?'

'Yes, I hurt her.' He snaps. 'By screwing other women. I didn't bother hiding it. Why pretend? I…' He removes a camera from his rucksack and looks at it like a child holding a new toy in their hands, feeling its weight, absorbing its colour and shape. 'This is hers.' The black strap dangles in the air like it's looking for its owner. It's lost its muscle memory. The owner isn't alive to hold it. 'Smile,' he orders.

Emma-Jane gives the camera a smile: the one she uses for headshots at work, for websites and such like. Suddenly, he lobs the camera through the window; it takes the curtain out into the fresh air through the cracks. Was there something in her smile which had sent him over the edge? Or was it something else he'd seen through the lens?

Most of the smashed glass is outside, but some splinters on the carpet catch the light when the curtain billows. The movement of air is like a person coming back to life, like a broken bird growing new wings, fresh feathers. That movement, a fresh flutter. It's so difficult not to watch it ripple; as fresh as water, she thinks. The sound of ravishing wind comes, the rustle of fabric. Freedom.

'Fucking hell!'

He kicks her chair, picks up the porcelain fruit bowl and throws it against the wall. The bowl smashes into small pieces, like the breaking of difficult words into single letters. His gnashing eyeballs look for something else to break. A single piece of glass, shaped like a teardrop, catches her attention. Her chair wobbles slightly, so she steadies it with her planted feet.

Emma-Jane opens her mouth and closes her eyes to feel the breeze finger her face and hair. She could shout or scream and someone might hear, now that the window is broken. The world outside takes a step closer, peeks in. It comes to life, like a magic mirror inviting her into another dimension. Soon, she will step through the looking glass. She will. How merciful of his rage to take out the leg of her chair.

She waits as his anger keeps burning and his wild carnivorous eyes look for more menace. Not seeing suitable prey he flies into the kitchen, opens and slams cupboard doors, throws a saucepan, kicks the door.

'Bastard! You fuck—'

The glass from the broken window twinkles and winks on the carpet. It reminds her of the letter he'd sent to her, telling her she would shatter into tiny pieces of glass. The curtain flutters and the breeze licks her neck. She leans forwards and the broken chair topples over, winding her and squashing her face against the carpet. Plates continue to smash in the kitchen as she uses the keys to unlock the ankle cuffs. The click is painstakingly quiet and beautiful, followed by the smashing of glass as she throws the chair and then herself through the window.

The shock of being outside brings her to. Air! Sky! She quickly gets up from the ground and runs along an unadopted road lined with trees. In her wake, there are two peculiar objects: an old, broken kitchen chair and a camera – its long, black strap coiled around it like a serpent. The sky is vast and wide above, and even the trees look strange and threatening. Emma-Jane runs as fast as she can in the direction she thinks leads to a main road, where a faint hum of traffic gives her hope. She is oblivious to the bleeding cuts on her face, limbs and hands.

'Help!' she shouts breathlessly as she runs and staggers. 'Help me!'

When she sees the first vehicle, she waves wildly at it, but they accelerate away. A second car slows down and the face behind the wheel gradually comes into focus.

‘Stop! Please! Help!’ she screams, still running, now on the main road, prepared to stay in the middle of it if she has to, to make the car stop. Her patchy bleached hair and filthy clothes work better than any stop sign. ‘Help!’

The blue car comes to a halt and Lucy gets out. ‘Bloody hell!’ She opens her arms, just in time for Emma-Jane to collapse into them.

Chapter 27

'Turn back!' Emma-Jane shrieks as she stares out of the back window. Blood is dripping down onto her nose from a cut on her forehead. When it reaches her mouth, she licks it and swallows the copper taste without flinching. 'Lucy!' she shouts, almost with hatred. 'Did you hear me? Turn around! Go back to Drew's house! Now!'

Lucy speeds up as her now bleached blonde friend cries unconsolably. The woman is a wild animal, released from its cage, violent and scared.

'Now! I mean it!'

'Emma-Jane! For God's sake!' Lucy child-locks the doors.

Emma-Jane flares all the way home: a human firework, sparks flying, hitting the windows and roof.

The plastic bag Kat had given Lucy is now on the back seat, sliding from one end to the other as she negotiates bends at speed, her nerves tight as a wire.

'Calm down. You're safe now.'

'Listen. Go back!'

Something plastic drops into the footwell. Drew's shower gel, perhaps.

'No.'

The air freshener dangling from the rear-view mirror suddenly irritates Emma-Jane for some reason, and she yanks it down and tosses it onto the floor. Lucy doesn't pull over until they are outside Emma-Jane's house.

'You have to go back to help him! He's sick, Lucy. Drew! He can't be left there alone. He's not well!' she wails.

'I will get help, but first we are going inside your house.' Lucy stares at her friend in horror with wide eyes, still unable to find the right words at the vision of savagery. 'It's important you listen to me.'

Emma-Jane's head drops. The adrenaline has got her so far and now shock, pain and exhaustion are taking hold. 'I'll get the spare key and let us in.'

Inside, the house is cool and unaired and there is so much space and light around Emma-Jane that she is disorientated for a moment. Her gaze travels at speed from one wall to another, from floor to ceiling.

'You're home now.'

She collapses onto the bottom stair in the hall and wipes her face, like a child with a runny nose. Blood stains her hand and creased blouse. It has trickled down her neck and between her heaving cleavage as she sobs and gasps. Lucy puts a hand on Emma-Jane's shoulder. The weeping goes on uncontrollably until she is gasping for breath.

'It's over now.' Lucy speaks softly, in little more than a whisper, surprised by the motherly instinct she feels towards another adult, but the childlike behaviour of her dear friend demands it. Somehow, she knows that intuitively. 'I've been looking for you for days. I need to make a few phone calls so people know you are alright. I need you to stay here while I do that. I'll get you a glass of water and tissues. Please, just stay here.'

She runs into the kitchen and returns moments later, afraid her friend will disappear out of sight again. While Emma-Jane wipes her face Lucy puts the chain on the front door, making it more difficult to quickly escape. It feels like a bizarre action in her friend's home, but very little has been ordinary or predictable for some time. She's spent the last few days driving around housing estates near every Co-op in the vicinity. Thank goodness she hadn't given up. The Co-op only 400 metres from where she'd found Emma-Jane was the second to last on her list and her hope had been fading. From her pocket, Lucy removes her phone.

'Who are you ringing? I'm fine,' Emma-Jane says, wiping her eyes. 'It's Drew who needs help.'

‘Has he hurt you? Touched you?’

‘It wasn’t like that!’ Emma-Jane suddenly wails, her hands twisting her blouse. Her eyes fall on Lucy like a cold sun. ‘No! He’s not a monster, you know! Please, just send a doctor round there for him.’

‘A doctor? You have to mean the police!’

Lucy goes into the kitchen to make the phone calls to the police and doctor. She locks the back door and hides the key in her jeans, stroking its shape in disbelief that she is doing this. Emma-Jane’s home is carpeted, so it cushions footsteps like the soft pink pads on a cat’s paw. It is a sanctuary, decorated throughout in neutral tones of beige or white without stain, chosen windows wearing white wooden horizontal blinds. Sunlight peeks through the slats as if the sun is tilting its head and peering inside at the spectacle.

The sky out there is flawless, but it shouldn’t be. It should be dark and windy: the rain should deluge the streets and the wind should wreak havoc. Buildings should be uniformly covered in black and white newspaper print, reporting the crime of abduction and… What else? Lucy doesn't know, but every fibre in her body tells her there is a great deal of small print to get to.

She returns to the hall with a mug of black sweet tea and a warm full-length coat from the hall to drape over Emma-Jane. It's wool: one of the coats she wears for work. Hobbs. An expensive shop for professionals like her friend who need to look smart and stylish all at once. That professional woman is on holiday at the moment, and a vagabond has moved in. It is hard to picture Emma-Jane in the office, her laptop bag over one shoulder, composed and credible.

'He told me about what happened to his wife and child. Listening to Drew talk about Evie and James – and being with him – I started to feel differently.'

'What do you mean?' Lucy asks, sharply. 'You know she killed herself and her son, don't you?'

'I know that now! I failed him before.'

'How can you fail someone who keeps secrets? He pretended to be someone he's not, to you and me. Oh my God. Has he given you drugs?'

'No!' Emma-Jane pulls up her legs to her chest, her torso leant forward to cuddle herself. The childlike behaviour calms Lucy's frustration.

'Did something happen between you?'

'That depends on what you mean. Did he frighten me? Did he strap me to a chair and make me shit and piss myself? Did he leave me alone for hours in the stifling heat, not knowing if he was coming back or whether I was going to die of thirst or starvation? Yes, those things happened, and yet, I wanted him to touch me. I wanted to be found too, but—'

'I can't believe what I'm hearing.' The shock of this eclipses everything: all the worry, the trek in the dark, the fear. 'We need to get you to a doctor.'

'When he got angry he didn't slam his fist into me, but at the door or a wall. This isn't for the police. It's between Drew and me.'

'You have to report him. If he wasn't dangerous you wouldn't have jumped through that bloody window to escape! Have you seen your cuts? You have been through a terrible ordeal, Emma-Jane. Please, just let us take care of things.'

Emma-Jane slowly gets up from the stair and looks at her reflection in the mirror. 'Can you get me a wet cloth, or a wet wipe, something to clean this blood off?'

By the time Lucy has returned with a wet towel, her friend is wearing burgundy lipstick. With dyed blonde hair, she looks like a vampire. She has sprayed perfume on and brushed her straw-like hair.

'Let me do it,' Lucy says, taking over gently cleaning the cuts and gashes on Emma-Jane's face and hands. 'You're shaking.'

Together, they look at their reflections. Is the tautness in Emma-Jane's expression a hint at the silver barbed wire around the red muscle of her heart? Same clothes, same shoes. The elasticity of her skin seems to have gone because she stares, unblinking, blankly.

Emma-Jane applies a second layer of lipstick and smacks her lips. The action makes Lucy want to cry. Her friend's face is unchanged – and so, a lie. A stranger to herself, belying the truth, history. A face which, if it were honest, should be scarred; her body too. Emma-Jane should shout, rave, rant, but she doesn't. Lucy swallows the lump in her throat and looks away.

Chapter 28

When the door opens to Drew's room in Brayley Psychiatric Hospital he doesn't need to look up to know who it is. Reclining in the soft chair, with The Daily Telegraph in his lap, he sees red in his peripheral vision. Red hair, a red top. He knows there is a red sports car parked outside. Kat's.

'I wasn't expecting to see you here,' Drew says to her with a sideways glance. It seems like the temperature of the room rises. When her strong perfume reaches him, he eyes her with suspicion and shifts in his seat.

'You weren't expecting to see me, full stop.' Kat says with a smile, then gestures to the broadsheet newspaper. 'You didn't make it to the nationals, but you've been in the local paper, though.'

'Oh, I see. So, you've heard and tracked me down. Bravo. What brings you here, Kat? I'm assuming it's not to talk about the local economy. I'm afraid this place isn't doing a lot for my libido.'

'I missed you too. I'm twenty next week. Did it slip your mind?'

'Happy birthday,' he says sarcastically.

'Silly me. I should have brought grapes and a "get well" card for the sick man.'

'Not really. Here I am, still alive and kicking. What do you want? Money? A roof over your head?'

'There's no need to be nasty. Play nice. You kicked me out of my place to make your money but I have a new base for Stan. Thanks for asking.'

'I didn't.'

'Well, I'm glad you are alive; "alive and kicking" as you put it, with your neck fully intact at least.' She steps back from his chair, sensing his intense hostility, but perches on the side of the bed and crosses her legs, like a bird refusing to leave the bird table. One ankle boot patterned in leopard skin flicks up and down, like she's counting to a beat before moving closer still to her kill. 'Nice room,' she comments, looking around like she's in a hotel suite with a punter for a night of sex and champagne. 'Very minimalist.'

'Is interior décor a strength of yours?' Drew picks up the newspaper again. 'I hadn't thought so, somehow.'

'Look, you've made it clear you don't want to see me again, but I want to know before I head off for good if AJ gave you the letter I took the trouble to write? Best handwriting and everything. You were never at home or answering my calls. I had no choice but to give it to the bloke. That's why I'm here.'

'No, he didn't give your letter to me. I'm a bit old for love letters with kisses and love hearts.' He sniggers. 'He mentioned it, though. Why?'

'I thought as much.' Her eyes flash with intense fury. 'When AJ was round at my place fixing that new shower he told me you were completely in love with me, that I was unlike anyone you'd ever met, and that you were going to leave Evie for me – you were just waiting for the right moment. I went round to see Evie; I know, it was wrong of me, but I was fired up. Jealous, I suppose, so I went round there to the farmhouse.'

He looks at her now, like he's seeing her for the very first time. The sight of her is a siren sounding in his head. At last, he manages to say, 'You spoke to Evie?'

She nods, trying to snare him in her gaze.

A shiver works its way down his spine, all the way to his toes.

'Yeah. It surprised me that she invited me in. We stood in that lovely farmhouse kitchen of yours with that huge table and the Aga. I could see myself there, I thought. It wasn't long after lunch; she was washing up, and she'd taken her engagement and wedding rings off. Your son had thrown tomato pasta all over the floor. That's when I told her you were going to leave her for me.'

His face colours. She stares at him, saying nothing, her nostrils flared like she's smelling him. Tears prickle in the corner of his eyes. He senses her waiting, watching. The blow of her words makes him crumple a little into the chair of the mental hospital he's a captive in. Eventually, he collects himself, puts the newspaper on the floor beside him and meets her gaze, like a silent collision.

'And you're here to gloat?'

'No,' she says, putting a hand on her hip, which is jutting out at an angle. She pouts her lips, exposing a small area where red lipstick hasn't been applied. It does nothing to dissipate his anger. 'I thought you should know, that's all. We were fuck buddies for quite a while and, in my book, I thought I owed it to you.'

'When was this? When did you go round to the farmhouse, Kat?'

'The same day she…'

He puts his head in his hands. 'Oh my God.'

'It's AJ's fault! He convinced me I was something special to you, so I was just moving things along.'

'Moving things… Jesus Christ.' He stares at her, crushed, unable to find the words. He stammers. 'Within hours of your visit, Evie and my son were hanging from a tree.'

'I didn't know she'd do that! She just stood there when I told her. Her face didn't change, or anything; it was weird how she didn't react. I told her to pack her things. For ages she just stood there, and then James came running in and she came back to life. Whisked him into her arms, like I was going to steal him.' She shakes her head. 'It annoyed me. Seeing her do that, so I said that James would stay with you and me.' She looks at Drew, waiting for a reaction. 'She kicked me out then. Screamed at me. It was funny, really, after her being so calm before.'

'You are poison, Kat. As venomous as that snake of yours.'

'Stan isn't venomous, you fool.'

A coldness creeps over him as she shrugs. His anger inflates him like a giant red balloon in the predominantly white room. The trance-like state is replaced with white knuckles and a look of revulsion as she reaches for his arm and lightly squeezes it, her nails painted in that signature red he remembers her by.

'I know you well enough to think you aren't here to say sorry or to pass on your condolences. Say what you've got to say, then get the fuck away from me. For good.'

'No, I'm not here to say sorry. You can thank me for telling the truth,' she says, swishing her hair. 'Besides, I didn't know the woman, did I? I'm here because of AJ. I don't enjoy being played by a little prick like him. Do you want me to get even with him before I leave this place? He could find a snake in his van. Or are you going to see to him?' She smiles.

'Leave him to me,' he says bitterly. 'You've done plenty. I don't want you anywhere near me or him. Ever.'

'You're stuck in this place,' she says, the expression in her eyes hard. 'I'm not.'

'I won't be in here forever. I'll get even with AJ. You can be sure of that.'

'If you say so, but you'd better do a good job of it or I'll finish him off. The rat. I don't like his game.' She rolls her eyes. 'You look like a beaten dog. I almost feel sorry for you.' She opens her arms, expecting a hug.

'Get the fuck out, Kat.'

'It's your loss,' she replies, and flicks her hair in the face of his agony. 'Do you want a blanket? Only you look like you're cold. Very cold, and old.'

His voice is little more than a whisper. 'Get away from me before I do something I regret.'

Her laughter travels down the corridor long after the door is slammed. It pierces his eardrums. He imagines her animal eyes heading towards the exit, a smile on that red, dirty mouth of hers, home to a pierced tongue – the sexiest, most despicable thing he has ever seen lick and bite his dick. He puts his hands over his groin, ashamed now, and thankful she hadn't eaten him alive.

Poor Evie. Poor, poor Evie. She didn't stand a chance.

After she has gone Drew touches his head, expecting his hair to be standing on end. From under his mattress, he removes the pen knife. His hands shake. Shivering, he makes it out of the chair and into the privacy of the bathroom, where cutting for contrition is his only release, until he is a free man and AJ will have his nemesis. His only wish is that he never sees Kat again, for as long as he is lucky enough to live.

Chapter 29

Lucy must have kept the spare key to Emma-Jane's house when she had been here two days ago, because she lets herself in. It's not exactly uninvited, but it still feels a little like an invasion.

'Are you here?' Lucy calls from the bottom of the stairs, presumably because she expects Emma-Jane to be in bed, like a sick patient.

'I'm in the lounge.' She sighs, knowing Lucy is going to go on about bringing charges against Drew, which she resolutely refuses to do. Please don't ask me how I am. If one more person does, I will scream!

She feels drowsy, having only recently taken a hot bath. The routine of a long bath bookends the day. She loves it; to slap the water just to disturb the perfect surface and blink at the splashes. She likes to submerge her ears beneath the water into silence, and yank the plug out to watch with satisfaction as the dirt and grime swill away into the plughole and she emerges, sweet-smelling and cleansed.

'Hi! How are you?' Lucy asks cheerfully, plonking herself and a Tesco Bag for Life on the sofa.

'I'm fine.'

Lucy leans forward to take a better look at her. 'Your hair looks great! And you look more rested. I bought us some cakes and a few other things I thought you might need. Just milk and stuff.'

'I can walk to the shops, you know. I'm not an invalid.'

'How are the cuts healing up?'

Emma-Jane self-consciously touches her face.

'Still looks sore.'

Emma-Jane's leap through the window has left its temporary mark on her face and limbs. Nothing which won't heal soon, though.

'Have the police been back in touch?'

'No, they're satisfied I've told them everything they need to know.'

Lucy bristles. 'How did you explain throwing yourself through a window if you weren't in danger?'

'Everyone has a temper. It was a one-off argument, understandable… They've got far more serious cases to deal with.'

'So, no charges. They're not pursuing it?'

'No.' Emma-Jane looks at her friend and smiles. 'I'm fine. Everything is fine. Please, stop worrying about me. Drew is in a mental hospital, getting the care and attention he needs. I'm at home and have no immediate plans to go into the office.'

'That's something, I suppose.'

She breathes a deep sigh of relief that Lucy has stopped pushing for Drew to be convicted for abducting her and that the perpetual and well-meaning inquiries about her health, her sleeping habits, her appetite, will be truly over. In a short space of solicitude, she has consumed a lot of sweet tea with friends, colleagues and telephoned clients to reassure them that she is fine. Everything is fine. Drew is fine too, as far as the word goes – safe, at least – and in a place where he can get better. There is so much she can tell no one, and barely accepts herself. Is it in a casket, a coffin, a safe, a place dark or light, that she must lock away her feelings for her captor?

Some details of the traumatic event have changed in her memory. Not Drew's face, his quiet aura, his cool look, or the lounge in that house, or the hours she spent staring at that bloody curtained window. Not those bare bones of the skeleton which give little away about the experience she had.

Some details in the short-term memory get lost, others added, but then, trauma and memory coagulate like egg whites over a specific temperature. Memory is the wooden spoon in a mixing bowl of cake batter, choosing what it clings to and what it leaves around the rim.

If she was asked to describe Drew to a police sketch artist, the details she recalls – the curve of his lips, the shape of his eyebrows and the fan of his dark eyelashes – might betray her heart. The memory of him makes her want to hop into her car and drive at speed with the windows down. She needs air, the sound of tyres on gravel. If it is love, it's like a concussion. She feels self-conscious just thinking his name.

'Do you fancy an éclair or some kind of cupcake?'

'Mmm. Cupcake, please.'

'I'll make us a brew.'

'No, stay there. I'll do it. Make yourself at home.'

Earlier, an enormous bouquet of flowers had been delivered and the signature on the card was simply D. Beneath it, a date, which she assumes is his release date. Anticipating Lucy's arrival, she had put the beautiful flowers in her bedroom, out of sight.

Returning to the lounge with two mugs of tea, she finds Lucy has already eaten her cake and is on her second.

'Are you stress-eating?'

'No.' She gives Emma-Jane a sideways glance. 'Well, I might be. I do have something I want to tell you.'

'Okay, fire away.' Emma-Jane takes a sip of tea. A memory of Drew holding a water bottle to her lips returns. Once, he'd caressed her cheek with a finger as she drank. The memory of that touch, so rare and delicate and so pleasant, catches her unaware. She knows pieces of her have been lost. The fragments are stitched together with alcohol, hope, distraction, make-up. Drew is a thief who has stolen parts of her that haven't been returned. Will they ever be? But that doesn't make him bad, she thinks, and blushes at the guilty thoughts when her friend is in the same room.

'Listen, it's not just because of Drew, but I'm thinking about returning to Carlisle. I love it up there, and my parents are getting on.'

Emma-Jane stares at her mug of tea.

'What happened with Ross and Jennifer really shattered my confidence. I need to get more experience working for someone else before I run my own business. When you weren't there and Vanessa turned up and read her stories, I'd never felt so helpless. Even before that, I never felt in control of my work with Jennifer.'

'I'm sorry that happened. In every way. You know what happened to Ross has nothing to do with you, don't you? I can understand why it's troubling, early on in your career, but don't let it derail your plans. Besides, you helped Vanessa by listening. She's got another therapist and is doing much better. You never get over losing a child but she's moving on.'

'That's really good news.' Emma-Jane nods, smiling. 'You'll have no problem finding a compatible business to your therapy to take over the spare office. I'm telling you know now because we are friends and so that you've got plenty of time to look into finding someone. I think it's for the best.'

'How much of this is about me and Drew? Honestly?'

'Do you mean, am I jealous?'

'Yes. It's best if we clear the air.'

'Dear God, no! Just the fact you even think that about me is proof you are not thinking right, Emma-Jane. Listen to me. He's got everything to do with your head being buried in the sand, but nothing to do with my future plans. I won't waste my breath by telling you to report Drew. Your mind isn't sending the right signals to your brain. I have no idea what you've been through, but I went through a fair amount of shit myself with Ross dying, and then being stuck in the arse end of nowhere with no one to help me, and then Vanessa desperately needing you, and—'

'I don't—'

Lucy gives her a hard stare. 'Mate, you're not getting it.'

'I am. I'm listening.'

'Yeah, but you're not understanding. I was out there in the middle of fucking nowhere sitting under Sycamore Gap with a dead mobile and no food or water for hours, and no one could save me except me. The only thing which motivated me to get to my car safely was fear for your safety.'

'We've both suffered in different ways. Is this a contest?'

'Of course not. All I know is adjusting is difficult, and you have come back home a different person than you were. Just, maybe, you're affected by what happened more than you realise. I mean, have you seen your supervisor, Celia, lately?'

'We have chatted on the phone and Zoomed.'

'I mean seen her in person. Please, for me! I think Celia can help you work through a few things. You need help! You can't expect to just carry on as normal, as if nothing has happened.'

'It is still me! I am well, and I want to move on with my life. You talk like I'm sick and I have just been discharged from hospital. I don't need help and I don't appreciate being told what to do! Please, let me heal in my own way and in my own time.'

'I didn't want the conversation to go this way,' Lucy says morosely.

Emma-Jane looks at her friend sadly. The thought of not working side by side with Lucy fills her with a strange mixture of relief and disappointment. They have shared so much laughter and mutual interest, but people change.

'Me neither. You know I'm grateful for you helping me. Thank you. I mean it. I know things aren't easy between us right now, but you were there when I needed you most.'

Lucy takes a deep breath. 'So, enough gratitude. How do you feel about getting back to work?'

Glad to be on safe territory, Emma-Jane makes herself more comfortable on the sofa. 'I've been thinking about that. I'll be better as a therapist than I was before.'

Lucy raises her eyebrows.

'I used to treat clients suffering with trauma. I can hear myself use the word "trauma", like "losing a loved one so suddenly is traumatic…". It was a noun plucked from a textbook, a diagnostic term, a word from a dictionary. Not anymore. I used to say surviving trauma is to live with a violated self, but it's so much more. The trauma recycles. It's a different animal from the original beast, one which mutates, and keeps on changing and surprising.'

'Is that because of your trauma?' Lucy asks gingerly. 'Is this post-traumatic stress disorder?'

'My trauma, yes – and Drew's. The thing is that, after the trauma, there's rarely anything visible to explain the irrational behaviour.'

'What do you mean?'

'Imagine you feel fear. When you see a killer beast in the same room, the fear is explained, justified. It's "normalised". But what if the fear is there, but the killer beast isn't?'

'I see.'

'With trauma, there's nothing and no one to run away from. A door bangs. A rumble of thunder. Heavy rain tapping on a window. These ordinary things and the most intelligent, educated adult can turn into a child afraid of a monster. So, what do you think they do?'

'They take it out on somebody else. The very person who was trying to help them.'

'Exactly,' Emma-Jane says. 'But I understand why.'

'But that doesn't justify what Drew did to you.'

'No,' she says quietly.

Night-time darkness, which tells your body clock to go to bed, used to be familiar and a velvet comfort, enjoyed under a duvet. It's morphed since being with Drew into lonely hours in the groin of night. For a time, their proximity on that single mattress had been like a hand over her mouth, but then the softness and scent of him around her had eased her into sweet sleep.

Last night, Emma-Jane had slept with the light on. Despite the warmth, the light, the soft mattress, her eyes moved from left to right and up and down, her skin prickled and her thoughts were tripping over themselves. She saw everything was normal. Normal, except for her, in the bed, under the cover, trembling, and a different person to the one she was before. But Lucy can't know these things. They're between her and Drew.

As soon as Lucy has gone, Emma-Jane takes a large bite out of a peach and relishes its soft flesh and juice. Peaches were one of the many things she longed to eat during her captivity. That, and fillet steak – food eaten with a fork, not wrapped in pastry and inserted into her mouth. Her appetite is returning, flourishing, her hair is coloured and styled back to how it was, and yet, how can she love Drew? The question returns again and again, only bigger each time, like a Russian doll.

Enjoyment of food eaten off her finest china plates – she had even used her best cutlery, left to her in her mother's will, for a meal of paella for one – wine and sleeping and the luxury of an afternoon nap in front of the TV have satiated those unfulfilled needs, but the hunger pangs for something are still there.

Boiling the kettle to make herself a cup of tea when she wanted one quickly lost its novelty appeal; as did the expensive coffee from the machine. Even her double bed now seemed smaller than the single mattress they had slept on so comfortably. Yesterday, she'd driven into town and spent as much money as she could in a boutique clothes shop, not even trying the clothes on before purchasing them and bundling them into her wardrobe.

Lucy calls him a monster, but that means Emma-Jane's heart belongs to one. It is a monstrous love fed by everything, and she will not have her stomach stapled or deny herself a moment longer. She wants her fill of him. Every inch of his skin, his every word a morsel to be savoured, to make her satiated.

Chapter 30

She took pains to dress in a new silk blouse, tailored trousers and suede jacket and style her luscious black hair. The mirror in the hall greeted her favourably, it seemed, as she applied plum lipstick, of the same brand and colour she's worn for years. Lancôme. The cuts to her face and hands have healed nicely. It's nine-fifteen, and she would normally be at the office by now. At one time, knowing that her name, Dr Emma-Jane Glass, is on the door, and piles of paperwork are neatly arranged on the desk waiting for her would have given her plenty of pleasure.

It hadn't been possible to eat a decent breakfast. She had stared into a cup of tea, still stirring, stirring – even though she had forgotten to add sugar (two) – the liquid spinning, spinning, spinning. She had stirred for so long the tea went cold. A little later, a pang of hunger had hit.

She'd made a plate of toast and raspberry jam but the food was tasteless, partially eaten without awareness.

Today, she is seeing Drew. It will most likely be one of those days with no end, which means tomorrow will be dream-like, hazy and she won't remember very much. Perhaps it's a good thing to not sleep well at night, because tiredness is a version of numbness that will help her through the meeting.

She checks herself in the hall mirror again, having spent an inordinate amount of time styling her hair into soft curls to frame her thinner face. She looks healthy, almost pretty. The car keys are bunched up in the china dish, where they belong. The front door is always locked, so an opportunistic burglar couldn't barge in to take them.

Am I behaving as I should?

She checks her actions as often as her appearance, no longer sure of either. The truth of her feelings for Drew clings to her like wet clothes. How can she have feelings for her captor, for a man who is an inpatient on an acute psychiatric ward, being assessed and treated, who has been sectioned under the Mental Health Act? Other men have shown her their vulnerable side, so why is Drew different?

Once the visit to Drew is over, she will treat herself to brunch: eggs Benedict with smoked salmon. Perhaps with a glass of Prosecco as well as a decent coffee at her favourite café, Cherry's. On the way from the hospital, she will stop at a garage to purchase a newspaper and avoid feeling conspicuously alone and single, in case other customers have hogged the papers at Cherry's.

She tries not to think about Lucy as she heads out through the front door, though her shadow follows Emma-Jane around. This rift between them is something sharp and new: never before has there been an undercurrent of secrets and bitterness. Then, there are her feelings for Drew, which are growing like an ailment, a condition she has no idea what to do about. To acknowledge that she'd enjoyed living with Drew came as a cataclysm.

Is it love? Yes, yes, yes.

Neither the situation nor her thoughts make sense to her. If she were driving through this moment, her windscreen wipers would be on full. The radio would be switched on, but the music would be drowned out by the torrential rain on the roof of the car and slapping the glass. She would keep driving at a slow speed – thirty, twenty, then ten miles an hour – a little afraid of what was discernible in the headlights. Disorientated, she would pull over, park up. Sit and wait for the storm to be over.

She climbs into the Golf and immediately checks her appearance again in the rear-view mirror.

He frightened me, he made me squirm and ultimately escape, yet I felt more than compassion when he shared his story with me. Never dislike. When did my feelings for him change? They seemed to jump from a mild interest to an intense passion. When he touched my hand or curled his body around mine at night, I longed for more.

Thinking. Too much. It is time to catch hold of the thoughts and feelings so she can look them in the eye, define them. Words and phrases from the time of her captivity circulate on repeat. Her words, and his. The track is getting scratched. Repetitive.

'Ruminating' is the term, she tells herself, like she should know better, and she pulls the Golf onto the road, unable to remember driving to the hospital once she walks through the double doors and into his private room.

'You look well!' Drew says, like he's greeting her in the French Riviera and about to air kiss both her cheeks. 'Your hair – black again!'

'I am well!' she says, lost for words.

'Your perfume – is it different?'

'Yes,' she says shyly, unsure of where to sit in the pristine room: its furniture consists of a bed, chair and a desk. He pulls the stool over for her. She leans towards him, clean shaven, pale. 'Poison.'

His eyebrows move upwards. It is a faint but unmistakable gesture that his senses are working. Whatever medication they have given him, he still smells, hears, sees, perhaps feels.

'How were the flowers?'

'Oh, beautiful. Thank you.'

'I've been thinking about you. About very little else, to be honest, as weak as that sounds.'

'Weak? If it is weak, then I am too.'

He smiles at her and some of the tension in the room fades. 'All this glass… It's only what I deserve. Here I am. My lack of transparency. Locked away behind glass windows and doors. A nice twist of irony, don't you think, Dr Glass? This is all your doing.'

'My doing? No. But the glass… That did occur to me, yes.'

'Glass,' he continues wistfully. 'Glass in the morning, afternoon and evening. What chance do I have to forget you?'

Emma-Jane doesn't know how to respond to this man; now gentle, sad, someone she'd shared a cup of emotion with. A warm cup of human compassion. The starkness of the room and the situation tests her feelings.

'I've missed you,' he says, lightly touching her arm. 'I don't understand my own feelings.'

'Me too,' she says.

He smiles and shifts his tense shoulders. The austere personality of the place pales for a moment in those gestures. She flicks her shoulder-length hair over one shoulder. It is now glossy and entirely black without a hint of being bleached. 'My hair had some TLC at my regular hairdressers, and I've been shopping. A few new clothes to fit my frame. I've been trying to make the most of my free time before returning to work. I have clients who need to see me, who won't accept my referrals. The office is being painted – a facelift – so it's a natural break. Time to recharge before getting back into the chair, so to speak.'

'Like New Year's Eve,' he says bitterly. 'Starting afresh. Out with the old and—'

'In with the new,' she says with a smile. 'You know how much my work means to me.'

'I do.'

'Have you had many visitors lately, to keep you company?'

'An associate of AJ's, someone who works for me, came to see me. You may remember AJ phoning me a few times. There's some business or other to take care of.' He looks down, as if seeing a smashed object on the floor. Seeing fragments of something she doesn't understand.

'It's good to keep your mind occupied while you receive your treatment. It won't be for long if you make the progress that's expected.'

He nods, and yet his eyes flash in anger. A turn in mood: a domestic to a wildcat. It must be the frustration of being here, she thinks, as time is bleached in the hospital.

'Will I see you again when I'm out of this place?' he asks, looking straight into her eyes. 'I have hard critics, and I need to prove to them that I am safe outside, but in a month they'll let me go. Unless, of course, you change your mind and press charges.'

'I won't do that.'

'Thank you. I'm sorry—'

She puts her hand up to signal there's no need to say any more. 'You must toe the line here. Engage with the therapy. Be kind to yourself. I want you to get better. I mean that sincerely, because—'

'Because?'

'I shouldn't need to say another word, Drew, if I am right about what I think and feel.'

He lowers his head in shame, knowing what she's alluding to. She sees from the movement of his Adam's apple he is touched. The edges of his face, the pencil-drawn lines of his cheekbones, nose and forehead almost soften with her gesture.

'You're a remarkable woman, Emma-Jane.'

'Ordinary. A very ordinary woman. Someone who has avoided men for the terror of loving and being unloved. Until now.'

'You and me, I feel something, and I think you do too. My farmhouse is sold, so I will live at the house we stayed in. Perhaps you'll visit me there, by choice this time?'

An image of the chair facing the curtained window flashes before her. She recalls the longing she'd felt for him to pour water into her mouth, to feel the wetness dribbling down her chin and down her blouse. She'd liked his cool gaze on her as she drank. She wanted him. All of him. And still does.

'Yes, I will. I know your release date,' she says, smiling, remembering the card he'd sent with the bouquet of flowers. 'I'll see you soon.'

She makes a swift exit from the hospital, glad to be back in her car and with a seat belt on. The leather steering wheel is firm and secure in her hands. As she drives to Corbet Hill, the road narrows and the hedges grow tall and thick, until she finds a lay-by to pull into and parks at a spot with a wonderful view of Shropshire and into Wales.

At one time, she had never dreamt of falling for a client, let alone her captor. Her image of herself is now entirely altered. A car drives past and, as the wheels turn, Emma-Jane think she sees her friend Lucy's concerned face in the hubcaps dulled by dirt, smeared on the black rubber, turning round and round. Lucy's warnings about Drew, her pleas for Emma-Jane to seek professional help, echo in her ears. But Lucy isn't around to make her question her feelings and thoughts. She closes her eyes and blinks hard.

Having seen Drew and reaffirmed their connection, the sky is like an artist's palette of pink, orange and blue worked in vast swathes, with only the distant black outlines of trees to provide perspective. She has never seen such vivid colours in the sky; it is ablaze. The remaining hues of pink deepen to purple, and the trees and the hedgerows resemble a child's scribbles in black ink.

From the sharp rise of Corbet Hill, with the wind playing with her hair, the steeple rising below from the Shropshire landscape is shaped like two hands perched together in perfect thought or prayer. She thinks of Vanessa, now buried beside Avril, and of Evie and James. The shape of the steeple reminds her of the rhyme she used to recite at primary school.

Here's the church and there's the steeple. Open the door and see all the people.

The church bells chime. She imagines the voice of the choir inside, gently reaching inside the hearts of the congregation and squeezing, squeezing.

From her vantage point on the hill she imagines the vicar beginning a sermon with 'We are blessed', and then the congregation bowing their heads, or kneeling on prayer mats. 'We are one', they say. We are one.

Who am I now?

With the sun behind her, the woman on the hill has a lonely shadow, which is long and thin like the pine trees she stands above. Can she trust her feelings, or is she suffering with post-traumatic stress, or Stockholm syndrome? From below, she might look like a distorted person, a foolish giant. Is she? The thought sends her arms to the sides to embrace the surrounding space, clawing the energy of pure nature into her fold, like a hibernating creature foraging for feed, for sustenance and reassurance in all its forms.

She feeds on the view and that vision inside the church. Eventually, when ant-like figures file out of its mouth, she steps away back to her car. The giant with its arms wide shrinks to nothing. Only the trees see her and her secret go.

Ave Maria, farewell, we are one echoes in her ears as she pushes the accelerator to the floor and smiles at the dust in her wake and the narrowing road ahead.

Chapter 31

The hospital confirmed they had released Drew a week early. It's been almost two months since she saw him, but it is rare that he is not in her thoughts. Dressed in a winter coat and boots to keep warm on a breezy afternoon in early September, she parks her Golf at the bottom of the no-through road and walks towards the house where she and Drew had lived together. By four o'clock, the light is subdued and mellow. She thinks rain is threatening, and pulls her coat around her a little tighter, wishing she'd brought an umbrella with her.

Clouds hang low, but she is still fizzing with excitement and anticipation, with the nervous kind of energy you get before an interview for a job you really want. She wills the sun to push through the clouds and for the rain to pour on another part of the country. Her palms are sweaty as she walks in the direction of the house. To be here of her own volition makes her feel powerful – and a little afraid.

How strange it is to have lived here not knowing where the house was, to now have driven and parked at the bottom of the lane knowing it takes less than twenty minutes by car from her own house, and even less from her office. She hears a lorry thundering past and a horn beeping. A pigeon takes sudden flight from the telephone pole as the wind blows, and a strand of hair obscures her vision. Leaves scurry into the air, chasing one another.

Is she ready to see him? It will set in motion a chain of events perhaps beyond her own control. Should she see him? She had asked herself that question repeatedly, at all hours of the day and night. Lucy has made it clear what she thinks.

In the maze of time at that house, she had sat through those rambling memories of his family, like he was turning a page in a photograph album until the pictures faded from colour to sepia. When she thinks about those days here, it is one heartbeat after another: hers, Drew's,

Evie's and James's. True, some days the beating was too loud to bear, but she'd listened. She did. That's what she'd been trained to do.

Lucy thinks she is suffering with post-traumatic stress disorder and is too emotionally involved in Drew's life to know how she genuinely feels about him. For the last month, Emma-Jane had felt observed at every angle by Lucy, until she took the easy way out and avoided her company and her phone calls.

As she approaches the house, Emma-Jane remembers the drab curtains permanently drawn, the lounge almost entirely free of furniture, which gave the few objects in the room – the two chairs, the mattress – prominence in an otherwise bland space. The house was deserted, like a ship at port, its decks swept clean with no one aboard, except her, Drew, the chair, the mattress and the ghosts of Evie and James.

It is an ordinary house, and yet what went on inside was anything but. Her whole life has changed because she has changed. Not because of a wedding, a birth or even a bereavement. She tries to imagine what the house is like inside now Drew is living there, having moved his furniture and belongings inside it. Perhaps a plush sofa, antiques, a king-sized bed, decorative mirrors and tasteful artwork. The TV aerial protrudes from the roof into the slate sky.

Am I making the right choice? I don't have to see him. I could turn around and go home. He doesn't know I'm coming. It's not too late to turn back.

The sky hangs low and heavy. His Range Rover is parked outside, recently washed and polished, so there is no mistaking that he is at home, perhaps relaxing with a book. She gazes at the house and car, metres away now, standing still as the rain pours down in a maudlin moment. The cool droplets fall to the ground like an unexpected baptism. Nervously, she glances at an upstairs window, Drew's voice echoing in her ears.

She self-consciously touches her cheek, hoping her mascara won't run. Yes, she recognises herself, despite what Lucy says. Her hair clings to her head. There are curtains and blinds at the various windows which weren't there before. How will she feel when she sees him? Will they kiss? She knows things about him no one else does. A sense of his quiet stillness soothes her nerves and she moves with purpose towards the lounge window, drawn to it, having stared from the other side of the room at the curtained pane of glass for hour after hour. To be on the other side of the glass, looking out, is all she wants to do right now, before going inside.

A hollow exists in her tummy, like hunger. Will he smile when he first sees her? The ground can't be covered quick enough. Her footsteps are loud in her ears, another heartbeat, only the gravel and dirt beneath her shoes are more real to her than anything now she is inches and minutes away from seeing Drew, from looking through that window in the lounge where they'd slept and talked. It is true; she has fantasised about this moment, the reunion, relentlessly, like the rain now. Truthfully, it has been difficult to think about anything else when her heart feels heavy, her feelings for him like blisters which will not heal. Today, the healing starts any minute, any second. Ever since leaving this house she hasn't felt free. That must be love, surely?

She feels the rain like she hasn't felt it before: in sheets, dense and impatient. It douses her from head to toe, and the feeling of fear and pleasure is like blotting paper. If they do start a serious relationship she may need to give up her job, on ethical grounds. If she must, she will. No doubt there will be a discussion about her relationship, after the article she's written about maternal filicide and the twist of irony in being with a man who was a victim to it. The heart doesn't choose, she consoles herself, as she steps into a deep, brown puddle.

The decision is made. Now or never. It's a good thing to revisit places where you've experienced fear or terror. This is like therapy. I tell my clients this. Look. Look through the window.

She does a double take when she sees the curtain to the lounge window hasn't been drawn. A sound makes her stop in her tracks. She peers inside and her eyes fix onto the middle of the lounge. Her heartbeat is loud and racing in her ribcage. The light is switched on. The bulb is dressed with a lampshade this time, and directly beneath it is the very chair Emma-Jane had spent her days on. Her mouth opens. No sound comes. A throttling, choking pain overcomes her, like a gag pushed hard into her mouth. There's no chloroform this time. She opens her mouth and nothing comes out. Drew, a thief. Has he stolen her voice too?

Drew's eyes are closed but Emma-Jane can clearly see a young, naked woman writhing on top of him. The bones in her spine move as she wriggles, screwing him hard, moving one way, then the other. The hairs on his bare legs are dark and thick, so dark against the pink flush of the woman's skin. The chair and the two entwined bodies cast a shadow on the new beige carpet as this strange woman is born into Emma-Jane's universe. Ignorance ends, like a collision of planets.

This terrible shop window she has chosen to peer into seems to grow larger. Inside, that girl-doll tilts her head back with abandonment and his hands search through her hair. The familiar chair. The humiliation. Emma-Jane is a voyeur looking in, a peeping Tom. Desperate, but this isn't death row. She isn't dying.

Emma-Jane collapses onto the ground and puts her head in her hands. There is no unwinding of this moment: a tongue-tied moment she cannot untangle. Her shame feels like thrown stones are bouncing off her skin. This version of herself – who, what? She rocks herself back and forth, staining her coat with mud and rain, and puts her hands over her ears because she can hear the moaning and grinding. The pleasure grows louder as they head towards a climax. It sounds like pain. It sounds...

'Hannah!' Drew cries in an eruption of sound: a crashing of syllables. 'Hannah!'

His voice saying that strange name cuts like a knife through her skin, writing a foreign name in blood across her chest. Emma-Jane takes in air like she's been half-strangled by a lanyard with the name 'DR GLASS' written across it. Her head aches and spins, her feelings confused by subdued and conflicted impulses to turn and run or to make him aware of her presence and attack him, his eyes, his face. If only she could pull her coat a little tighter and make herself invisible.

The choice isn't hers to make as a van speeds towards the house. From the way it is being driven she senses urgency, and then, from the way the man gets out of the van and slams the door, she senses fury. He is muttering as he charges towards the house.

Emma-Jane leans closer to the wall. It isn't a figure she recognises. Whether or not he has seen her, she doesn't know. He strides into the house, leaving the front door open, and then there's a muffled sound before a sudden, scuffling movement. She rests her head against the wall, hidden out of sight under the window, sobbing quietly and shivering. When the shouting and the fighting start, she remains motionless, imagining blood, thinking she can smell that, and semen.

Hannah shrieks. 'Stop! Stop it! Off! Me!'

Emma-Jane hears voices, pulled hoarse and desperate, then something breaks; perhaps the wooden chair. The line of her pulse peaks as the rain thuds against the windowpane. The combination of that and the drenching of emotion feels like a waterboarding. The string of misplaced loyalty is balled up tightly into a weapon of self-harm, slicing through the ribs to get to her heart.

'Bastard!' the bloke shouts. 'You fucking bastard, Drew!'

She ducks at the sound of punching and air expelled from lungs, thumps and bangs. Then it stops, and the motionlessness and quietness is just as frightening.

'You fucking deserve it, AJ!' Drew pants.

The sound of fighting – of bodies falling and objects being thrown – resumes.

Emma-Jane's stare at the wall is empty, like she's looking out at an ocean without a horizon. The flatline of her existence at this terrible moment of dashed hope is all-encompassing.

Hannah is screaming. Emma-Jane remembers how he had moved over to the mattress, like a lazy wasp in September, and collapsed with tiredness as slumber gatecrashed into the room; his legs and arms could have met with a car bonnet at speed they were that splayed. In those moments, peace had fallen in the room like snowflakes. Morning was a pebble skimming the surface, breaking the water.

She swallows back the tears but, for all her effort, they pour down her cheeks, smearing the mascara and blusher. Lucy was right, she thinks.

'Revenge is a dish best served cold, you bastard,' Drew shouts between pants. 'Kat told me what you said, what you did. Making her think I would leave Evie and James for her. If you hadn't fed Kat a sack of lies, she wouldn't have had the gall to confront Evie, and my family would be together. They'd be alive, you bastard!

You're welcome to Hannah now; she's used goods to me. Now fuck off!'

'You complete and utter bastard!' Hannah spits and, from the sound of commotion, she has lunged for him. 'This was just to get back at AJ! You sick fuck!'

'Get your clothes on!' AJ shouts. 'Don't you fucking come near me or her ever again or I'll—'

'Come on!' Hannah shrieks at AJ, sounding desperate to get away from Drew and the humiliation of being used. The vowels unravel like a spool and then the front door slams.

Emma-Jane cowers against the wall at the sound of hurried footsteps, sobbing and mumbling. She glimpses a scantily clad Hannah. AJ's boots thunder on the gravel and the puddles splash as the van speeds back the way it had come. There isn't broken glass on the ground; there's nothing to show for her pain. Where are the heart-shaped shards of glass, glittering like fake diamonds?

She realises how cold it is, and how chilled she feels being wet through. Her back and knees are aching from the awkward position she is crouched in. The ache of her muscles returns her to the chair in that very room. What has brought me here? she wonders, fighting a sob. I did suffer. Is she a dog, beaten so often it is obedient to its owner's heel, not knowing anything different? Her throat is dry, and no amount of water poured into her mouth by Drew will quench it ever again.

She slowly rises to her feet, keeping her hand against the wall to steady herself. Her nose is running, and she doesn't have a tissue, but it is raining that hard she thinks it doesn't matter, anyway. She takes a tentative step around the side of the building and staggers away from the window, not looking, not trying to think, just focusing on walking, getting away, listening to the sound of her feet urgently moving on the gravel. Away.

'Emma-Jane!' Drew shouts. 'Wait! Please, don't go! I need to explain!'

Emma-Jane closes her eyes for a second, readying herself for what she must do. Resigned and resolute, she turns around and sees Drew is in the door frame, dressed in a T-shirt and boxers. He isn't far away. She can see all of him so clearly. Blood from a cut lip trickles down his chin and there are deep red and purple blotches on his face and chest from the hunger of the man's fury, or perhaps the hunger of the woman's passion. At that moment, the candle of his face melts in the glow of her heart and the dirt on her shoes says everything. The wax drips and he ceases to be that wonderful waxwork. It is a breaking, a crack, a melting down.

'Wait! Please! I can explain!' he pleads. 'I used Hannah to get back at AJ! She's just an innocent fool in all of this. AJ is jealous of me: he is jealous of my money, my house and family. I…'

She shakes her head and raindrops fly off and drip down her cheeks. Whatever they had shared, the fabric is now torn and tattered. She has never been more grateful that the flimsy curtains at the lounge window were not drawn.

'Don't go! Let me explain!'

'No, I am not listening. Not this time, or ever again.' Drew looks like a criminal to her now. He is all the men who have cheated on their wives, have avenged traitors and duped loved ones, have made others suffer because of their selfishness and ego. 'I have heard it all and no longer care.'

'You've got it all wrong! It was AJ's fault Evie took her life! Hannah was just to get even with AJ. He told Kat I was madly in love with her and that any day I was leaving Evie for her. He got Kat so fired up she went round there, to our home, and told Evie!'

'It's the past. It's over. You won't accept you are as much to blame for their deaths as AJ and Kat are. You were the one having affairs, neglecting your wife and child; so, when a strange woman comes to her house, she believed Kat. If you had been a good husband, Evie would have spoken to you, not got in a car and driven north to end it all.'

'I accept Evie knew about my affairs in the past and I wasn't around much and for that I'm sorry. But Kat is a young, stupid redhead! Poor Evie, she thought I was leaving her and taking James – I would never do that. It killed her! Stop!'

'Delusions of grandeur. That's what you said about Kat. Someone who thought more of her importance than she should. You suffer from it, too.'

'No! You and me, it's entirely different. Don't punish me. I have been punished enough!'

'Punished?' she says, stopped in her tracks, her hands balled into fists ready to smash the world she is in. 'Your voice has been in my head for so long I stopped hearing my own. I thought you were dictating a love letter to me. I listened too hard, to every pause, every nuance, and you have never been far from my mind. I have done my job and more. Whatever contract has existed between us, it ends now.'

Drew's chest heaves. She feels his tears and pain, like waves coming for her. She fears he will take her into his arms, like a rip tide, so she turns to leave.

'I love you!'

'Love?' she says quietly, stopping in her tracks. 'You aren't in love with me. You're hungry, you're hurt. You're hungry for love. You need love, not me.'

'No. I know you, and you know me better than anyone.' He gestures to the house. 'We slept side by side like two palms.'

'Goodbye, Drew,' she says, holding her palm up like a mirror to him, then letting it fall to her side.

She walks away, crying, breaking, even so a doctor, a whole. Still Dr Glass, a good woman, with her own integrity in place, like a pane of glass in a window battered by a storm. She matters to herself and to her clients, to her friends. Then, she pauses and rubs her hands through her hair, blinking at the enormity of what has just happened. Her knees are quivering.

Keep walking, she tells herself. If she stays there a moment longer Drew might come, or she might collapse onto the ground the shock is so intense. She looks up at the sky, hearing the wind and the rattle of branches, the rustle of leaves, the dismantling of twigs to the ground and their final snap in half as they finger the soil and the insects. She feels a cold, long finger of light stroking her hair and shoulders, her neck and chin like moonlight viewed by insomniacs. The sound of the wind increases, rattling branch arms, more urgent, persistent, to be heard like an incessant clicking from a camera.

There is no tenderness in love, in her job, in the days she has survived, but soon, so very soon, when she curls into a ball in her bed and sleeps through the night, she will renew, put an end to the slow death of waiting for love with Drew. There is no such thing as tenderness in her life, but one day that might change. Truth tears through her and she forces herself to walk on, not look back.

The imperfection and pain of the realisation could bend her in two, but the further away she gets from that house and Drew's heaving chest, the distance between now and history lengthens. When she turns on the ignition in her car the engine sounds like it is crying.

During the drive back to her home, the windscreen wipers keep the glass clear. It seems like the radio signal improves as the wheels turn, like the static fades and the wavelengths of sound connect with her senses and her intellect, at long last. As she drives, she gains fortitude by imagining her front door, stepping inside and then closing it. Shut. Imagination is always escape.

Epilogue

The last things for Lucy to pack away in the large cardboard box are the framed posters on the wall of her old office. They illustrate a healthy meal and a balanced diet. BE THE PERSON YOU WANT TO BE. EAT TO BE WELL. LOVE YOUR BODY.

She won't be sad to leave the chairs where Jennifer and Ross had sat side by side, holding hands. The chairs will stay put, along with the desk and office chair, for whomever moves in. Emma-Jane had been inundated with enquiries from all manner of businesses, including ones performing treatments such as acupuncture, homeopathy and massage therapy. Lucy puts the potted plant in the box, closes the flaps and then slides her laptop into a rucksack. When she hears footsteps, she opens the door to greet Emma-Jane.

'I'm almost done!'

'Coming to work won't be the same without you. I shall keep the door to your office closed.' She hugs Lucy. 'It will feel horribly lonely. Who am I going to drink tea with and moan about my day after work to?'

'I thought you'd found someone suitable to move in here.'

'It's not the same. We've known each other a long time and been through a lot. I will miss you, that's what I'm making a mess of saying. Don't be a stranger!'

'I won't. I'm only a few hours' drive away. You could have a mini break with me and walk some of Hadrian's Wall – avoiding certain sections, obviously.'

'Obviously,' she says, with raised eyebrows, not wanting to mention what happened to Evie and James at Sycamore Gap or Drew Rogers, before or since.

Escape. A portal, be it moving away or staying in the same place with a different key. That's the theme for them both, which neither of them articulates right now in the comfort of the familiar office, the solid doors and the history of that electric kettle and those washed mugs in the cupboard they've shared. Like a prisoner who has been incarcerated for a long time, they both have to navigate new worlds and learn to trust, to live a free life without the stigma of their past.

'Punishment'. That word: Emma-Jane recalls it spoken from Drew's mouth as she watches her friend make her last preparations before leaving the office and Shrewsbury for good. They are all connected in one way or another, through suffering. The lives of Ross and Vanessa, in different ways, had ended here: a good place – not a dungeon, but a business, to help people.

'If there's anything you need, or if you change your mind and want to come back, you only have to say the word.'

'I'll remember that, but let's hope you won't need rescuing again.'

'Look,' Emma-Jane says, opening the lid to a square, scarlet cake box. 'Cake! I hope you've got a good appetite. I know I have.'

After tea and cake and a last hug, Emma-Jane kisses her friend goodbye and, feeling bloated from the food, she flops onto the soft chair in her office and picks up the local paper. The story about the suicide of a local millionaire is on page two.

It had happened in an outbuilding at the farm; in the shippon where, at one time, lambs and sheep had grown stronger. Drew had tossed a rope over one beam and hanged himself. He'd left a note, the article said, confirming the suicide. There was nothing suspicious about the death.

She imagines his body there, dangling like a silenced bell from a deserted church on a midweek night in August. A kind of execution, a death row of his own making without an audience, save for the owls and the stars, and perhaps a ghost or two.

THE END

ABOUT THE AUTHOR

Louise Worthington has worked in educational publishing and as an English teacher. Her first novel, Distorted Days, was described by Kirkus Review as 'a formidable work' and her next two novels, psychological thrillers, Rachel's Garden and The Entrepreneur, were published by Bloodhound Books.

Louise lives with her family in Shropshire in the UK. For more information, see Louise's website at https://louiseworthington.co.uk or follow her on Facebook or Twitter.

ACKNOWLEDGEMENTS

I am eternally grateful for the support of my husband, Nigel, sister Sally and the guidance from Karen Holmes. Most of all, thank you to the people who read my books. I hope you continue to enjoy my stories.

DID YOU ENJOY THIS BOOK?

The support readers show by leaving reviews or interacting on social media is terrific. Help to spread the word by posting a review of Dr Glass on Amazon or Goodreads.

Extract from Willow Weeps by Louise Worthington

WOULD YOU LISTEN TO YOUR DEAD SISTER?

Prologue

When Willow's older sister, Mandy, was alive, she was a collector – nothing of monetary value. Part of the fun was seeking a cluster of objects grouped by one particular theme; it was the sets of things that mattered to her. Feathers, pebbles, obsolete coins, ribbons, gloves and pins in various shapes and sizes – safety pins and dressmaking ones, especially with coloured heads. Red was her favourite. Then green.

The features that made a set weren't always obvious to Willow. She was often busy in the garden, climbing trees and splashing in mud in wellington boots with a dinosaur pattern, a hand-me-down from the next-door neighbours, or she was at school or practising sprint starts for running races. Willow never worried about falling or getting lost because Mandy kept her safe from harm.

They had their own bedrooms but Willow often liked to sleep on the floor next to Mandy's bed during the summer holidays. Eventually, their mother set up a camp bed. At night they lay awake chatting, comforted by the sound of the television in the lounge, the clicking of the kettle during advertisements, and Dad checking the front and back doors. They liked to guess which programme their parents were watching, which wasn't difficult because they had their favourites and routines.

It was an old house with a pantry and windows that whistled when the wind tuned up. It was a house that would have been a safe place to grow up in, except for the faulty electric blanket on Mandy's bed which arrived one winter when snow dropped several inches thick from the white December sky. The Christmas wreath was on the door, a fresh one with red berries and holly tied with a red ribbon. Willow remembers the birdbath was frozen over. Only two sets of footprints made it out through the front door and across the snow-covered lawn. Their dad's size-ten shoes went back inside, only to re-emerge with Willow.

Mandy had taught Willow that seventy per cent of the human body is made from water, so it made no sense to her seven-year-old self to have a sister who had died in a house fire. Why didn't that water keep her cool?

Willow was eighteen the first time Mandy's spirit sent her a message, and it was with grains of sand in the hall. Because Willow didn't recognise the message at first, Mandy sent more sand. This time it appeared overnight in Willow's bed, under the cotton sheets, under her pillow. When Willow's boyfriend, Luke, started forcing her to do things in bed she didn't want to, Mandy's message made sense.

She broke up with him.

After that, strawberry ice cream that melted rapidly and dripped down her chin and T-shirt was a message. Rain clouds. Splashes from passing vehicles over new shoes. A popped balloon caught in the railings outside her house. A sudden gust of wind rearranging a hairstyle. Cancelled trains from Chester to Neston – that was a common one. Mandy was invisible and mute, long gone, so Willow blew soap bubbles and collected seashell nacre. She paused at the sight of butterflies' wings to marvel at the iridescence of ephemeral beauty. None of those things were really messages from Mandy. They were just Willow missing her big sis and best friend, floundering with the decisions she needed to make to stand on her own two feet in the face of the challenges and crossroads of adulthood.

The second time she spoke, Mandy sent cherry stones. Willow was just twenty when the doctor confirmed she had gallstones and needed surgery.

Willow got better at listening. Now she is always listening, expecting to hear her sister. Moss and stone, dampness, glass and steel could one day tell her something. Everything has sounded different since Mandy died – even laughter and the splashing of water on the pavement, the whistle of wind through an open window. Since Mandy's death, happy sunlit times of childhood are memories in a seashell held to her ear.

Guilt makes her listen sometimes, and loss. Sometimes she listens too hard when there is nothing to hear except grief, and the silence of being an only child with no living relatives.

Guilt. Willow carries guilt around like a black shawl for being the daughter Daddy rescued from the house fire all those long years ago, while Mandy and her collections turned to ashes. Other times she feels guilty because she can't remember how Mandy's face changed when she laughed or blushed or cried.

Willow wishes Mandy would speak to her now in beautiful butterflies and moths because she is in love with Paul and he is with her. A future together is in the making, a shared home, perhaps marriage.

Mandy has been quiet these last six years but she's on her way. Willow thinks she can feel her sister stroking the soft hairs at the nape of her neck, a touch as delicate as down. It is the silent touch of another message. Mandy only visits when trouble is around the corner.

Hush.

Listen.

Made in the USA
Monee, IL
26 May 2021

69550317R00243